TAKE ME HOME FOR CHRISTMAS

A CHANCES INLET NOVEL

TRACY SOLHEIM

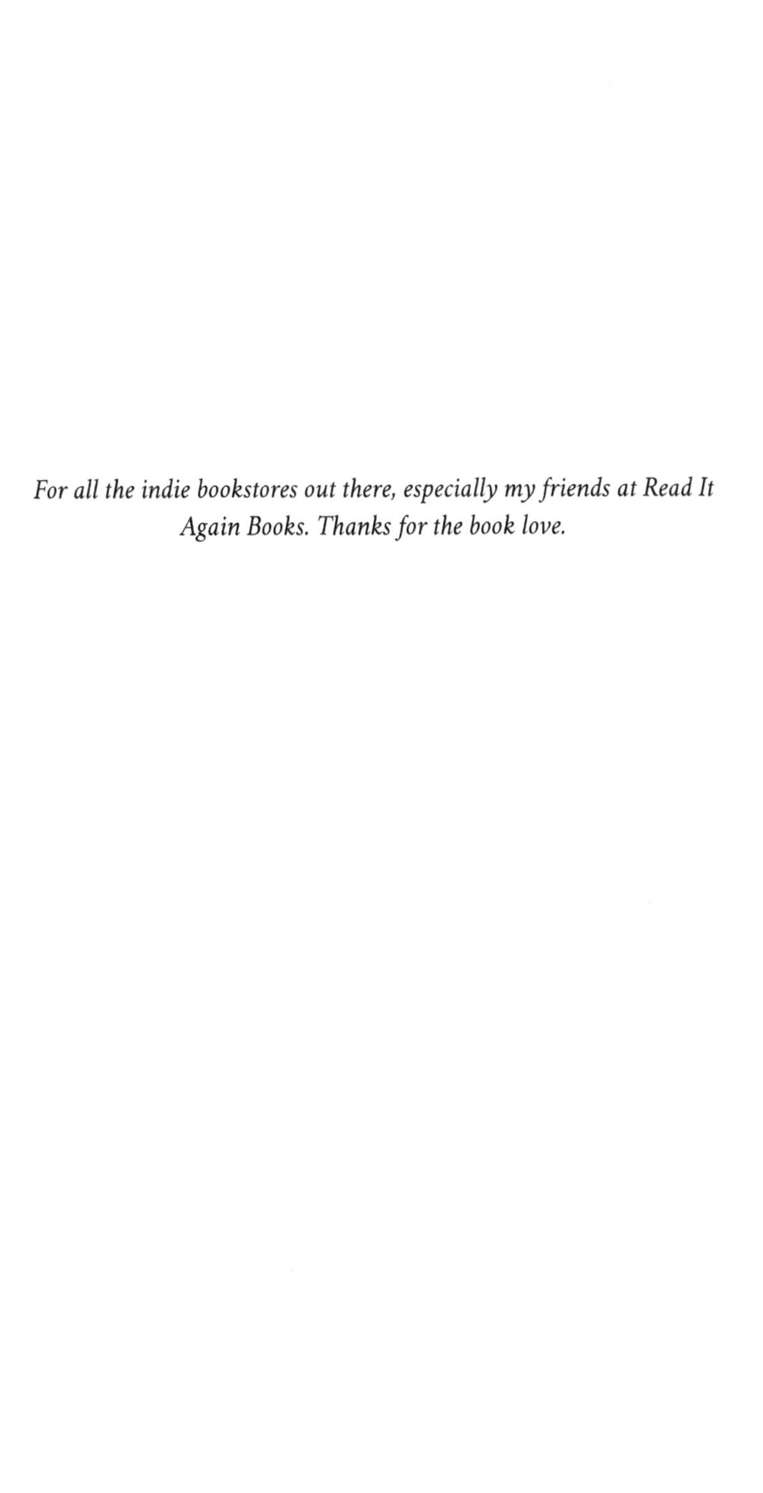

For all the indie bookstores out there, especially my friends at Read It Again Books. Thanks for the book love.

CHAPTER ONE

THE RAIN SOUNDED a lot like sleet as it tap-tap-tapped against the window. Elinor "Elle" McAlister looked up from her computer monitor, craning her neck to stare down eighteen stories to the streets of Manhattan. Umbrellas of all different colors navigated the sidewalks, bobbing and weaving around one another like the blobs on the screen of a first-generation video game.

"Ugh," her coworker Suni groaned from the other side of their shared cubicle wall. "The airport is already a zoo during Thanksgiving week. This weather will make everything ten times worse tonight."

Elle stood, stretching her back as she grinned down at her friend. "And now you know why I'm staying put in the city."

Suni leaned back in her chair. "I still think you're crazy." She shook her head. "I'd have the worst case of FOMO if I didn't get to enjoy my mom's mac and cheese for Thanksgiving dinner. Don't get me wrong, the forced family fun drives me crazy. But that's what makes it Thanksgiving, right? No way would I voluntarily miss it. Especially if I had your family."

Especially if I had your family.

If Elle had a dollar for every time she heard that line, she'd be wearing those Stella McCartney boots she'd been eyeing at Bergdorf's last month. Not that she disagreed with Suni. Family was everything. And holidays spent together at her mother's famous B & B were iconic. Elle adored each member of her big, boisterous brood. She couldn't imagine not having them in her life.

If only they weren't so . . . *impressive.*

Elle, the baby of the McAlister clan, lived in the shadows of her four older siblings. She'd dubbed them the Fab Four: a professional baseball player, a newly minted United States Congressman, a world-renowned architect, and an award-winning doctor. Even her new stepsister was living her best life as a successful bookstore owner. Not only that, but they'd all coupled up with equally fantastic partners and were busily producing beautiful nieces and nephews for Elle to dote on.

And then there is me.

At twenty-seven, she was still searching for her life's passion. At one point, she believed it might be dancing. Or the law. Except three more years of school didn't sound all that appealing, so she leaned into her writing skills. When a career as a freelance journalist didn't pan out—an editor told her she needed more real-world experience—she thought she'd find the answers serving in the Peace Corps.

Instead, she'd returned just as unfocused—and a bit more insecure—as when she left. While the Fab Four had set goals for themselves practically before they left their cribs, Elle was still trying to figure out what she wanted to be when she grew up.

Thanks to a Peace Corps connection and a few well-received freelance articles she wrote years before, she landed a job at the prestigious international magazine *Vantage.* Unfortunately, she was expected to pay her dues before she got to do any serious writing. Most days, her work consisted of mundane administrative tasks for the managing editor of the lifestyles division.

Luckily, Elle's editor was no Miranda Priestly from *The Devil*

Wears Prada. She offered Elle tons of opportunities to prove herself as a journalist. And true to her McAlister genes, she gave each assignment everything she had.

Still, after nearly eighteen months, the only "articles" she'd written were online—mostly paragraphs and teasers on social media posts used for clickbait to get readers to jump over to the actual article written by a "real" journalist. She was proud of the fact that her "teasers" scored clicks twice as high as the other editorial assistants. Yet it wasn't as if her name appeared on an actual print byline. And Elle desperately needed more cred to put her on par with her famous siblings.

Ironically, she seemed to be the only one in her family who minded that she was "underproducing." And that irked her the most. It was as if none of them expected anything more from the runt of the litter.

Well, she would show them she was just as enterprising as they were. An opening for a lifestyles columnist was coming up at the first of the year. Elle had every intention of winning it. Who said her passion couldn't be in journalism after all?

"Although, I guess it's all a matter of perspective," Suni continued. "It's not like you're headed to sunny L.A. with me. Aside from the dinner, you're stuck in a boring small town for the rest of the week. Maybe your famous family is just as annoying as mine. Under those circumstances, I'd probably skip spending Thanksgiving with them, too."

Suni had it all wrong. Chances Inlet was the only place Elle ever wanted to be for any holiday. And her family wasn't the reason she was currently avoiding her hometown. Nope. That excuse belonged to the six feet of muscled, blond-haired, blue-eyed deputy sheriff who once held the title of Elle's most trusted friend. The guy she'd made a fool of herself over. Her skin grew warm just thinking about it.

Her editor, Madelaine Harper, popped her head into the cubicle. "Got a minute, Elle?"

Anything to end this train of thought.

"Of course." Elle grabbed her tablet and followed the other woman into the hallway. But instead of heading back to Madelaine's office, she steered Elle toward the glass conference room down the hall. The very same conference room where Helen Keneally, the magazine's publisher, sat at the table idly drumming her fingers.

"Um?" Elle stopped short.

Madelaine gently pressed her hand to Elle's back. "We're meeting with her."

Elle stifled a groan. She'd been avoiding the woman for months now. Ever since Elle had dumped her boyfriend of three years—who also happened to be Helen's grandson—right before Christmas last year. It wasn't a secret that she'd gotten her position at the magazine through her connection to Jeremy. But she was good at her job, dammit. And she didn't deserve to lose it just because the woman's grandson was a philandering pig.

The older woman surprised her with a warm smile. "Elinor, dear, you're looking well." She gestured for Elle to take a seat.

She was relieved when Madelaine sat between them, providing Elle with moral support, not to mention a human buffer.

"Madelaine says you've been an extraordinary assistant, going above and beyond the duties you've been assigned," Helen said. "And it's been brought to my attention that your posts have been converting exceptionally well. You have a flair for crafting a hook that drags readers right in. Bravo, my dear."

Publisher and editor exchanged a look before Helen spoke again.

"It's also no secret from anyone who works with you that you're a team player. Someone who is kind and encouraging to her coworkers and genuinely liked and respected by the staff."

Elle had never been let go from a job before, but she was pretty sure outlining an employee's attributes and contributions before laying the hammer down was a cruel way to go about it. She gripped the arms of her chair tightly.

"We have a rather delicate assignment that just so happens to require someone with your skill set," Helen continued.

"My skill set?" Elle sat up a little taller. Perhaps she wasn't getting the ax after all. And who knew she actually had a "skill set?"

"Mm." Helen nodded.

"Do you know who Everett West is?" Madelaine asked.

Everyone with access to a television knew who Everett West was. He'd been a globe-trotting war reporter for the past thirty-five years.

"He's writing his memoir," Elle responded. "We are serializing it in the magazine. The number of readers downloading the chapters has quadrupled over the past three months."

Helen beamed at her. "Impressive. You know your stats about other aspects of the magazine besides your own."

"The serialization is meant to whet the appetite of readers in hopes of getting them to order the book when we release it in July," Madelaine explained.

"The problem we have," Helen added, "is that Everett hasn't quite finished the manuscript despite signing a contract stipulating he would complete it by the first of this month."

"Oh." Elle looked between the two women, still unsure what this had to do with her.

Helen shook her head. "Mm. Men aren't always good at keeping their promises as I'm sure you are aware, Elinor."

Whoa!

Was Helen apologizing for her worm of a grandson?

Madelaine leaned forward in her chair. "We need Everett to finish this book by the end of the year, or the magazine will run out of material to serialize."

"And we won't have any way to fulfill those preorders," Elle added.

"Exactly!" Helen slapped her palm on the table.

Elle continued to gaze at the two women, trying to divine some sort of explanation as to why they were telling her this. "That's a serious problem for the entire company."

"Everett doesn't seem to be able to focus on the manuscript here in New York." Madelaine sighed. "Too many distractions."

"Too many cronies to go out drinking with, you mean," Helen muttered.

If Madelaine agreed with her boss' sentiments, she was too professional to show it. "We need him to go someplace quiet, someplace with a lot slower pace and fewer diversions so he can buckle down and get the job done."

The man had reported from deep below the ocean inside a Polaris submarine, while rumbling along in a tank in Iraq, and even while embedded in the Afghan desert with special forces. Surely, he didn't need a convent to finish his memoir? He already knew the ending, after all.

"Do you need me to research some potential places?" Elle asked.

"No, no, dear girl." Helen waved a hand. "In fact, Jeremy gave me the most brilliant idea earlier this week when we met for dinner. He was reminiscing wistfully about the wonderful times he spent when you two visited your mother's inn in North Carolina."

Elle tried not to bristle. Why would Jeremy be "reminiscing wistfully" about the Tide Me Over Inn? He only visited there twice. Now that she thought about it, both times he found something to complain about—from the inn to Chances Inlet. He'd found the whole town to be "provincial."

"My mother's inn? You want Mr. West to go there to finish his book?"

Both women nodded.

"Um, sure. I'm happy to check with her to see what openings she has. Christmas time is usually as popular as the summer months in Chances Inlet, though. I can research some backup inns just in case."

Please, Mom, don't let your inn be full.

"No need." Helen grinned. "I've already spoken with your mother. She's arranged a suite for Everett through the end of the year."

"Oh." Elle was surprised her mom hadn't said something to her. "That's great. Do you need me to make any other arrangements for him?"

"Everything is all taken care of." Helen stood. "You'll both be flying out first thing tomorrow. Everett has less than five weeks to finish his damn book. I'm counting on you, Elinor, to see that he does. If it comes down to it, chain him to a chair. Stand over him twenty-four hours a day. Whatever it takes." She gave Elle's shoulder a gentle squeeze as she walked past. "I know you're up to the task."

The publisher was out of the room before Elle realized the impact of her words.

"Wait. What?" she whispered. "No, no, no."

Madelaine sighed. "It may not sound like it, but this is an incredible opportunity for you. And at least you'll get to spend the holidays at home. Your mother was ecstatic that you'd be home for Thanksgiving."

Elle dropped her head to the table. Five weeks in Chances Inlet. It took a lot of stealth to avoid Hayden Lovell when she was home for a couple of days. But five weeks?

"I have every confidence you can pull this off," Madelaine continued. "And when you do, the position as lifestyles columnist is all yours."

"Seriously, man? The Chipmunks?" Deputy Sheriff Hayden

Lovell complained as he toweled off his face. "Last I checked, this was a gym, not a daycare."

Xander Fisk, owner of the Ship's Iron Gym, added more weights to the bar Hayden was using for chest presses. "It's the most wonderful time of the year. What can I say? I like to keep my clients in the spirit by piping in the holiday tunes."

Beside him, Simone laughed. "More like you like to remind everyone who works out here that gym memberships make the perfect gift."

"You've uncovered my evil secret, Deputy Wills." Xander winked at her. "Nothing gets past your work-wife, does it, Lovell?"

Hayden shook his head at them both. "All I'm saying is Christmas music has been playing twenty-four seven since Halloween." He lowered himself back to the bench, wrapping his fingers around the weight bar. "It's as if Thanksgiving has been totally obliterated from the calendar."

"I haven't forgotten about Thanksgiving." Simone patted her flat belly. "Why do you think I'm in here working out for a second time today? I'm pregaming for my grandma's sweet potato pie."

"That explains it, because there's no way you're here for this guy's scintillating company." Xander gestured at Hayden. "What flew up his butt today to turn him into such a Grinch?"

"Nothing," Hayden grumbled. "Could you concentrate on spotting me here, dude?"

Simone laughed again. "If having a gorgeous woman offer you thousands for a piece of furniture you built is nothing, then"—she shrugged— "nothing."

Xander let out a whistle. "Dude, you sold the captain's desk? Way to go. I told you that you're a gifted woodworker. Mark my words, that side hustle of yours will make you rich and famous one day."

Hayden gave up the pretense of lifting weights and sat up on the bench. "Allow me to repeat myself. It's nothing. Just some decorator from New York who walked into my mom's yarn shop, saw the desk, and decided she had to have it for a client, so she bought it. End of story."

"Some decorator from New York who was interested in more than just our guy's desk, if you know what I mean." Simone gave Xander a playful shoulder check. "You should have seen his mother. The tension between Deputy Dog here and the decorator was so thick that Mama Lovell was practically naming her future grandchildren."

Hayden huffed as he stood. "You should really take up writing romance books, Simone. Your imagination is out there."

"I know what I saw." She flicked him with her towel. "You're just too closed off to recognize the opportunities right in front of your face." She nudged Xander again. "Livi—that's the hot blonde's name—is staying at the Tide Me Over Inn. Hayden is giving her a tour of his workshop this evening. Wink, wink."

"Oh, for crying out loud." Hayden shot a glare in the direction of his fellow deputy. "She has other clients who might be interested in some of my pieces, that's all."

Simone's cackle rang out through the gym. "Honey, she's the only one interested in your" —she made air quotes with her fingers— "pieces."

Xander laughed.

"That's it. I'm outta here." Hayden pulled his earbuds from his pocket and stalked off toward the treadmills. He'd drown out his ridiculous friends and the overdone Christmas music with some Eric Church while getting in a few miles of cardio before his meeting. "Let me know when the sheriff comes by. We can head downstairs together."

Hayden, Xander and several of the other veterans in town got together weekly to lend support to one another when the demons haunting them from their deployments raised their ugly heads. Theirs was a shared camaraderie that few could relate to.

Hayden counted himself lucky that, even in a town as small as Chances Inlet, he had a band of brothers when he needed them. Tonight, they were organizing the town's toy drive. He adjusted the wrap on the blade that served as his lower left leg before stepping onto the belt.

Xander followed him over to the treadmill. "The sheriff can't make it tonight. Apparently, *Livi* the Designer isn't the only important guest at the Tide Me Over Inn."

Hayden rolled his eyes at the way his friend sing-songed the designer's name. He punched up the incline on the treadmill.

"Kind of weird, though. Everett West is the last person I expected to visit a place like Chances Inlet."

That got Hayden's attention. "The war correspondent? Really? What's he doing here?"

"Rumor has it he is writing his autobiography."

"I thought he already wrote that. They're serializing it in *Vantage* magazine." He frowned. "He doesn't paint the military in a very good light."

Xander grimaced. "I know. Apparently he hasn't finished writing his tell-all. Word is he is staying at the inn through the end of the year. I really hope Elle keeps him on task. I'd rather he didn't get a chance to spread his sour grapes all over town. He's a Debbie Downer who couldn't care less about ruining everyone else's holiday."

Hayden stumbled ever so slightly. "Elle?"

The red-headed, whirling dervish with cloud-gray eyes he'd been trying to convince himself he could live without had come home for Thanksgiving after all?

"Yep. Sheriff said she's in charge of keeping him on task."

Another stumble. "Elle will be in Chances Inlet through Christmas?"

"Could be through New Year's if West doesn't finish before then." He moved off in the direction of his office. "I'll come get you in twenty."

Hayden barely heard him.

Elle McAlister is in Chances Inlet. Right now. And for weeks to come.

He let out a long-suffering groan. Simone jumped on the treadmill next to him. He didn't dare glance over at her, but he could feel her gaze boring into him. When he couldn't stand it any longer, he looked her way. Her eyes were practically dancing out of their sockets.

"Ruh roh. The plot thickens," she said before disappearing into the women's locker room, a maniacal laugh trailing behind her.

Ruh roh was right.

CHAPTER TWO

IT TURNED out that Everett West, the veteran war reporter everyone adored, was an asshole. And a cantankerous one, to boot. She'd only known the man for seven hours, and Elle was already questioning whether the lifestyles columnist job was worth it. He'd shown up at the airport five minutes before they were supposed to board, looking like he was channeling Ernest Hemingway, dressed in a khaki fishing vest, a flannel shirt, and thick-soled Timberland boots. The ridiculous boots let out a shrill squeak whenever he crossed the tigerwood floors of her mother's inn.

Any attempts by Elle at conversation were rebuffed throughout the flight. Mr. West was more concerned with keeping the ice fresh in his glass of Scotch—when he wasn't dozing off. Elle had to work to contain her pique that he didn't bother to work on his manuscript while they were en route. The first-class seats courtesy of *Vantage* certainly afforded him enough elbow room to type.

"Thank you for including me at dinner this evening," he said to Elle's mother.

It was the longest sentence she'd heard the man utter all day.

"The pleasure is all ours," her mom replied. "Tomorrow, Elle will show you around town, and you can choose from any number of restaurants for dinner. Of course, you're welcome to use the kitchen whenever you'd like. I'm sure eating out for every meal can get tedious."

Elle opened her mouth to say that Mr. West wouldn't be dining out. She fully intended to act as his personal Uber Eats for the next five weeks. Anything to keep him on track to finish his book.

Except he was a regular chatterbox now. "You'd be surprised at the meals I've had to endure while out in the field, Mrs. Hollister."

It was still weird for Elle to hear her mother called by a different last name. Donald McAlister, Elle's father, died suddenly four years ago, rocking the McAlister family—and Chances Inlet—to its core. A year later, Lamar Hollister arrived to serve as the town's new sheriff. He claimed it was love at first sight for him. Elle's mom took a bit more persuading—the man was five years younger, after all. In the end, Lamar prevailed and the two had just celebrated their first anniversary as husband and wife.

Elle's mom stood to clear the dinner plates. "Oh, please, call me Patricia. I hope you saved room for dessert. My daughter-in-law sent over a wonderful lemon cake. It's one of the most popular recipes from her new cookbook."

"I've endured a few of those MREs in my day, West," Lamar tossed out.

The hint of challenge in his voice surprised Elle. The sheriff was normally very diplomatic and careful with his words. Mr. West leaned back in his chair, resting his elbows on the arms and steepling his fingers above his chest as he seemed to size up Lamar.

Elle's eyes darted back and forth between them. It was a bit uncanny how alike they looked. Both were about the same height

—just over six feet if she had to guess—with the same well-maintained physiques. They were lucky to still have full heads of thick hair, graying attractively at the temples. Where Lamar's hazel eyes were curious and welcoming, however, Mr. West's green ones were wary and forbidding. And his nose looked as though it had seen the business end of more than one fist.

"You served." The words came out of Mr. West's mouth more as a proclamation than a question.

Lamar held up three fingers. "Three tours."

"Afghanistan?"

The sheriff nodded. A pained expression passed over Mr. West's face so quickly, Elle would have missed it if she wasn't so intent on tracking the obvious posturing between the two men. There was a subtext here that she was having trouble decoding. She knew from her many conversations with her best friend that the scars veterans brought home weren't always physical ones. Was Mr. West dealing with some sort of internal trauma left over from his time embedded with combat troops?

She'd barely had time to rush through the first four chapters of his memoir before the flight today. No way did she want to look like a groupie by having him catch her reading it on the plane. So far, the book had been about his life before becoming an international correspondent. The writing was excellent and his upbringing challenging. Elle got the nagging feeling she was missing something, though.

"A number of veterans live in Chances Inlet," Lamar continued, his words sounding like a warning to Elle's ears.

Mr. West picked up his whiskey glass and sloshed its contents around. "I'm sure there are. Small towns like yours are always proud to support their country, with many fine young men and women stepping up to serve. Thank you for doing so." He saluted Lamar with his glass. "I'm not here as a war correspondent, though," he offered as reassurance. "I've never had the pleasure of spending the holidays in a quaint town such as this.

I look forward to checking out all the cutesy activities I always see in those Christmas movies. I'm sure there has to be a gingerbread house-making contest somewhere in Chances Inlet."

Elle choked on her gasp. "Oh, we don't have any of that here," she managed to say. "Besides, you're going to be very busy finishing your book, remember?"

Both men focused their attention on her. Lamar arched an eyebrow ever so slightly. Mr. West, on the other hand, regarded her with bemused arrogance. He didn't like the idea of having a babysitter while he worked, that was for sure. Not that she could blame him. But here they were, and Elle was determined he would finish his book on time.

Her future rested on it.

"Look who I found." Patricia entered the dining room carrying a tray of neatly sliced lemon cake. She was followed by an elegant young blonde woman wearing a gorgeous smile and the Stella McCartney boots Elle had coveted online for weeks.

"Oh, wow. You're Everett West," the woman gushed as both men stood from the table. "My parents used to watch you on the network news every night."

Mr. West coughed out a laugh, but his smile seemed genuine. Not that Elle would know, because he had not deigned to toss one her way.

"In the flesh." He offered her his hand.

The other woman blushed as she held it with both of hers and pumped it up and down. "I'm sorry. That sounded ridiculous. I didn't mean any offense."

"None taken," Mr. West said. "I realize network newscasters are dinosaurs. Your generation would rather get your news in bits and pieces from social media."

Elle felt his side-eye directed her way as he spoke the words.

"This is Olivia Turner," Elle's mom explained. "Livi is heading up the restoration of the Seaward House on Bald Head Island. It's being converted into a premiere, all-inclusive destination wedding venue."

Livi held up her hands. "Just the decorating portion of the restoration. Art is my jam. Math, not so much."

"Livi, this is my daughter, Elinor. You two should have a lot in common since you both live in New York City. Elle and Mr. West will also be here throughout the holiday season. They are working on his book."

Mr. West made a noise that sounded a lot like a snort at her mom's suggestion that Elle would be working on his book. Elle ignored him.

"I love your boots," she said instead.

Livi looked down at them proudly. "Aren't they great? They're dupes. One-third the price."

"No way!"

The other woman nodded. "I can give you the link if you want."

"Oh my gosh, yes, please."

Livi returned her grin, and Elle felt herself relaxing for the first time today. The woman would be a refreshing antidote to Mr. West's surliness these next few weeks, that was for sure.

"Anybody home?"

Her eased demeanor was short-lived, however. The familiar voice had her body tensing again while waves of embarrassment crashed through her belly. She willed her cheeks not to flush as Hayden Lovell strode into the dining room. Dressed in worn denim jeans and a fisherman's sweater, he looked totally unaffected by her presence, damn him.

But then why should he be? I was the one who threw myself at him after drowning my breakup heartache in Long Island iced tea. I was the one who made a total fool of myself and wrecked the one true relationship in my life.

"Just in time for dessert," her mom was saying. "You've met Livi. Allow me to introduce Everett West."

"Sir." Hayden gave the other man a brusque nod.

"And of course you know Elle. These two were thick as thieves growing up," her mother explained for the benefit of her two guests.

"Really?" Livi said, her tone a bit incredulous.

Yes, girl. He was my best friend for twenty-three years. Until I screwed it up.

For his part, Hayden's expression was inscrutable. "Hey, Elle," he said. "Good to see you." The fact that his words lacked any real enthusiasm stung.

"What have you got there?" Lamar gestured to a piece of paper Hayden held.

"Oh." He handed it over to Livi. "They were handing these out in town. It's a schedule of all the events Chances Inlet has planned for the next few weeks. I thought Livi might be interested."

"Ooo!" Livi exclaimed. "A gingerbread house-making contest. Doesn't that sound fun?"

Elle's stomach dropped to the floor.

"You don't say?" Mr. West practically growled beside her.

"Hayden and Elle won that competition a few times, if I'm not mistaken," Lamar said.

Elle shot the troublemaker a pleading look, but he was already tucking into his piece of cake.

"Is that so?" Livi asked. She turned and aimed a dazzling smile up at Hayden. "You are very talented at building things. I'm not surprised."

Hey! Two people were creating those gingerbread houses! I contributed!

Mr. West reached for the sheet of paper. "May I?"

It was all Elle could do to keep from grabbing and ripping it up.

Of course he took his time perusing the damn thing. "A Turkey Trot 5k on Thanksgiving. Children's holiday readings at the bookstore on Friday. An ugly sweater party and holiday cocktail-making contest at Pier Pressure," he read out loud. "The annual tree lighting. A holiday flotilla and concert." He nodded at Livi. "A gingerbread house-making contest. A magnolia wreath demonstration and exhibition. A craft bazaar. A snowman-in-the-sand contest—"

"We don't have one of those!" Elle snatched the paper from Mr. West.

"Actually, we do. It's new this year," Lamar said.

To her humiliation, there it was in black and white.

"Oh, wow. I'll bet you'd be skilled at that, too, Hayden," Livi cooed. "I can offer some great advice for the aesthetics. We should enter together."

Why the heck was Elle's chest suddenly tight?

Hayden cleared his throat softly. "If I can fit it into my work schedule, then sure. That would be fun."

Livi beamed as if he'd just told her chocolate cake had no calories.

"My editor has given me an all-expenses-paid trip to a picturesque small town for the holidays. I plan on participating in all these events while I'm here," Mr. West announced.

"Your editor paid for you to get out of New York City so you can get some work done," Elle snapped as she tossed the paper onto the table. "You won't have time for any of this."

She didn't need the shocked silence in the room to tell her she'd gone too far. *Way too far.* Since when had she become so bitchy?

"Elinor," her mother chastised her, deservedly so.

Mr. West held up his hand. "My jailer has spoken. I'd better get my tail back in the chair." He inclined his head toward Livi. "Ms. Turner, it was a pleasure meeting you. You as well, Deputy. Patricia, thank you again for a delicious meal. However, it seems I didn't work hard enough to deserve my dessert this evening."

Elle sighed as she fought to keep her eyes from rolling.

"If you could point me in the direction of the study you offered that I may use?" he added.

"I'll show you," Elle said. She had no desire to face her mother right now. Or to watch Livi Turner fawn all over Hayden.

"I'll wrap up the cake and leave it in the kitchen for you in case you want it later," her mother called as Elle led him down the hall to the small study at the other side of the inn.

A banker's lamp glowed softly on the desk. Floor-to-ceiling oak shelves lined one wall of the room. Another wall featured wide, mullioned windows overlooking the inn's lawn. Two leather chairs situated in front of the desk filled the rest of the space.

Elle loved this room at this time of year because her mother filled it with mementos and decorations personal to their family. All of them held memories of early McAlister Christmases. She tried not to flinch when Mr. West made a beeline for the carved Russian Santa on the desk. It was one-of-a-kind and a stunning focal point in the room. It was also her favorite.

"My parents got that on the Alaskan cruise they took for their fifteenth wedding anniversary," she said softly.

He didn't respond, seemingly transfixed as he gently ran his fingertips over the carving.

Elle sighed. "Look, Mr. West—"

"Can we dispense with the mister?" He placed the Santa back on the desk before spinning around and glaring at her.

"Um, okay, Everett—"

"It's West to you," he barked. "And let's get a few things straight here, Gidget. I've never missed a deadline. Ever. So you can untangle your panties and take your foot off my neck. I have no idea why Helen thought I needed some nepo baby to mind me, but you work for me, not the other way around."

Nepo baby?

"I have some emails to answer, so you can go scroll on your phone somewhere else. I won't need you for the rest of the night.

Tomorrow, I'll have some emails for you to finalize and send out."

Elle opened and closed her mouth. She owed him an apology. He was right to be angry with her. She had behaved totally inappropriately back there.

Not that he made it any easier. They'd both been thrown into an awkward situation that neither wanted. Her role in all of this was to help him finish his book. She couldn't pull the words out of him no matter how much she wanted to help. They were his words. But she could make things easier for him. And she would. Starting right now.

"Yes, sir. If there's anything you need, I'll be around."

He reached for the bottle of Scotch on the sideboard. "Nope. I have everything I need right here."

Great. Just great.

As if the night couldn't get any worse, she almost plowed into Livi and Hayden at the end of the hall. He pulled the inn's front door open and was about to usher her through. Elle owed this man an apology, too. Anything that would take them back to the way they were before. She hadn't realized until tonight how painfully she missed her best friend. How much she needed him in her life. Especially if she was going to survive the next few weeks with West.

"Oh, you're headed out?" She directed the question at Livi.

The other woman practically bounced on her toes. "We are. Hayden is going to show me the nightlife in town."

Elle snorted. "That should take all of five minutes."

Livi looked at Hayden adoringly. "I hope not."

Despite her throat tightening painfully again, Elle managed to push out words. "Have fun."

She meant it, too. Livi seemed decent enough. And Hayden's happiness had always been important to her. They looked good together.

"Night." Livi practically floated out of the inn.

With a heavy sigh, Elle headed for the stairs.

"Belle?"

Her heart skipped a beat at the nickname only Hayden used for her. He'd anointed her with it during her *Beauty and the Beast* days. She forced a smile before she turned around to face him. "Hey."

"You okay?"

His eyes showed so much genuine concern that she nearly wept with joy. Maybe she hadn't damaged their relationship as badly as she imagined. Perhaps there was a chance their friendship could be resurrected.

"Yeah. Just trying to get this new work arrangement sorted out, that's all."

He stared at her for several long heartbeats. "I hope you get it all figured out soon. Night, Belle."

"Night," she whispered before hurrying up the stairs.

CHAPTER THREE

ELLE ALWAYS FORGOT how dark it was in Chances Inlet at night. And quiet. The only nocturnal sounds were the muted chime of the grandfather clock in the inn's music room and the crash of the waves where the Atlantic pounded the beach a quarter of a mile away. One would think it would be easier to fall asleep without the never-ending soundtrack of New York City at night.

Except it wasn't.

She'd managed several more chapters in West's book, but the descriptions of battle and explosives weren't exactly conducive to a peaceful night's rest. Hanging her head over the side of the bed, she double-checked that her shoes and emergency clothes were tucked neatly beneath the nightstand. Too bad her nightly safety net didn't provide its usual reassurance.

"Argh!" She kicked off the covers and grabbed the pile of clothes.

A walk always did the trick. She tugged on her leggings and pulled a sweatshirt over her sleep camisole before toeing on her sneakers. Two minutes later, she slipped out of the secret staircase smugglers and bootleggers once used to sneak in and out of the inn undetected. Her brothers had discovered the hidden passageways shortly after their father began the restoration of the centuries-old home a decade earlier.

Elle loved that she could come and go from the inn without disturbing the guests. Her family hadn't grown up there, so it felt a little awkward to share the space with strangers when she came back to visit. Her mother and Lamar lived in the carriage house behind the main house. Perhaps they were still awake, and her mom would make Elle her favorite tea. She always knew what to say and do to calm Elle's racing mind.

The carriage house was dark, however. Elle glanced at her phone.

10:40.

Breakfast came early at the B & B. No doubt her mother was fast asleep. A walk would have to do.

She sucked in a deep breath of the night air, tasting the salt from the nearby ocean. Her feet were moving before her brain registered the route. Several of the houses in town were already decorated for the holidays. Though she suspected Mr. McDaniel kept the lights in his towering pine tree up year-round and simply plugged them in after Halloween. Still, the familiarity of the gorgeous big tree with its colorful lights dancing in the night sky was comforting.

Three doors down, the lights were on in the garage-turned-workshop. One of the windows was open to the night air. Elle peeked in. Hayden stood with his back to her, meticulously brushing stain across the top of what appeared to be a table.

The image stole her breath. She was transfixed watching the muscles in his back move beneath his T-shirt as he worked. *Lord, have mercy.* When had his biceps become so pronounced? Or his shoulders so broad? Hayden had always been fit. His passion for distance running saw to that. Tonight, though, he appeared to be more ripped than usual.

"Are you going to lurk out there all night like some Peeping

Tom, Belle? Or are you coming in?" he said without turning around or missing a stroke.

She sighed a laugh. The man had always possessed a sixth sense. She crawled through the open window, where she was immediately greeted with an enthusiastic meow as a cat rubbed up against her legs.

"Nice to see you, too, Beula." She reached down to give the silver British Shorthair beauty a scratch between the ears. "It looks like life has been treating you well."

Hayden snorted. "She's a skilled con artist, this one. She managed to convince my aunt she hadn't been fed today and got herself a second dinner."

Beula swished her tail smugly. Hayden dropped the brush in a bucket and wiped his hands on a towel. Elle dragged her fingers over a cabinet that would look gorgeous in one of the Tribeca lofts her brother designed. The rest of the workshop was filled with equally beautiful furniture.

"You've been busy," she remarked.

"You didn't come crawling through my window this late at night to do inventory, Elle. What gives? Are you still having trouble sleeping? I promise you're safe here," he reassured her gently.

This was why the man was her best friend. He got her. At first, Jeremy—the guy she once thought she was going to spend the rest of her life with—made fun of her nighttime idiosyncrasies. Then he'd belittled her about them, telling her she needed to grow up.

Easy for him to say. He hadn't been woken up by a 6.9 earthquake in the middle of the night. He hadn't been stranded in Croatia for days with nothing but the camisole and shorts she'd worn to bed. No shoes. No phone. That wasn't an experience one got over quickly. Her quirk about needing to be able to grab her clothes and shoes at a moment's notice was her way of coping.

Except that wasn't what had kept her tossing and turning

tonight. It was the need for a long overdue conversation. She sucked in a breath before she turned to face him.

"Actually, I'm here because I owe you an apology. Hayden, I'm embarrassed and so sorry for the way I behaved last New Year's. It was—"

"It was nothing." He waved a hand in the air. "Don't even think about it. I don't."

He didn't?

She'd kissed him as though she had the right to and practically begged him for more. And that was just the part of the night she remembered. Yet he didn't even think about it? She wasn't sure whether to be relieved or insulted.

He must have sensed her conflict because his expression softened. "Elle, you were heartbroken after discovering Jeremy was cheating on you. You'd had a few too many drinks. It happens. I'm just glad it was with me who took you home to sleep it off and not some stranger in the bar."

Well.

When he put it that way, it made more sense.

Sort of.

"We've been friends for practically all our lives. I would never think less of you for what went down that night," he added.

Relief washed over her at his words. "You have no idea how happy I am to hear you say that. I've missed you."

The grin he gave her nearly melted her heart. "I'm still here. And still very much your friend."

Elle launched herself into the familiar embrace of his arms. "I'm so glad you don't hate me," she murmured against his chest.

"You know you could have said something sooner." He braced his hands on her shoulders and stepped back, shooting her a stern look. "You're important to me, too. Now tell me why you were so weird tonight. Maybe I can help you figure things out."

She pressed her hands to her eyes. "I was so rude. But this whole thing with West is crazy stressful."

"Come on," he said. "It's late. I'll walk you back to the inn. You can fill me in along the way."

He shrugged into a sweatshirt and motioned for her to lead the way out the door.

"He hasn't finished his book," she explained once they were on their way. "The publisher thought it would be a good idea for him to get out of New York and find someplace quiet to write. Jeremy suggested my mother's inn."

"Jeremy?" Hayden didn't bother to keep the distaste from his voice. "I didn't realize you two were back together."

"Oh, we are *not* back together. And we never will be. But his grandmother is the publisher, remember? For some reason, the subject came up, and Jeremy mentioned the Tide Me Over Inn." She shrugged. "Beats me why he'd want to throw business my mom's way."

Hayden scoffed. "West might turn out to be the guest from hell."

Elle laughed. "He can be quite contrary. And I was sensing some strong undertones from Lamar."

"His book has rankled some veterans."

"Ah. I'm just working my way through it now. Honestly, my only concern is that the man finish it. He doesn't have time to be distracted by all the Christmas activities in town."

Hayden steered them past a tree root sticking up in the path. "I thought you were a reporter. Since when is it part of your job to watch over authors who are late on their deadlines?"

"Apparently, my skill set involves helping others. Who knew?" she joked. "The truth is, if I can help West finish his book on time, there's a huge opportunity waiting for me back in New York. I've been offered the position as a lifestyles columnist at *Vantage*."

He whistled. "Wow, Elle. That's fantastic. And it's about time."

She felt herself puff up at the enthusiastic way he responded. "Mm-hmm. I'll finally be doing something tangible with my life."

Hayden let out a groan. "Not this again. You've got to stop measuring yourself up against the Fab Four. Any job you choose is tangible, as long as it fills you up and you enjoy doing it."

"Oh, this job will check all those boxes." At least she hoped so. "I've already got some fun ideas."

They were silent for a long moment as they came to the part of the path that stretched parallel to the beach. It was low tide, and the ocean was peaceful. Moonbeams bounced off the waves as they crawled toward the sand.

"And best of all, it's in New York," Hayden eventually said.

"Of course. That's where all the action is."

"I don't remember it being on your radar growing up. I wondered if you might relocate someplace else after things fell apart between you and Jeremy."

He was right. Elle had never imagined herself living somewhere as big as New York City. She'd tested the waters one summer while in college when she interned for *Cosmo*, but the city's allure eluded her back then. Elle only followed Jeremy to New York after the Peace Corps because she assumed what they had would last forever.

It hadn't.

The hustle and bustle of the city had grown on her, though, so she stayed. Given that she still hadn't decided what to do with her life and her career options were limited to her job at *Vantage*, she saw no reason to live anywhere else right now.

"It's not like I'd ever come back to Chances Inlet. Besides, it's hard to envision the future when you're a kid," she replied. "Neither of our lives turned out how we expected."

She realized how insensitive her words were as soon as they left her mouth. Between the two of them, Hayden's life was the furthest from anything either of them imagined. A stupid, thoughtless act changed the trajectory of his future in high school, sending him into the military and combat, where he'd lost not only his leg, but also a promising future as an athlete.

Elle slipped her hand into his and attempted a subject change. "Tell me about what you've been up to this past year. More importantly, how was your date with Livi tonight?"

He squeezed her hand. "It wasn't a date. She bought the captain's desk from Knotical today and wanted to see what else I have in stock."

"Seriously? I love that piece. I'm not surprised Livi liked it. She has excellent taste. I am surprised your mom agreed to part with it, though. It's the centerpiece of her store."

They meandered up the long drive, still hand in hand.

"I've long since given up trying to figure out how my mother's mind works."

"Same. But I can tell you from a woman's perspective, Livi seems very into you."

He made a rumbling sound.

It was her turn to squeeze his hand. "I'm serious. You two look very cute together. You should definitely seek out some mistletoe while she's in town."

"That's enough out of you, Belle."

"Can I help it if I want to see you settled with someone who is not only nice, but has impeccable taste in shoes?"

When they reached the inn, he tugged his hand away. "I'm perfectly happy with my life just the way it is."

It was difficult to make out his expression in the dark, but his tone seemed to hold a smidge of bitterness.

"Got it," she said, not wanting to upset the truce she'd just negotiated. "No matchmaking my best friend with anyone while I'm here for Christmas." She smiled broadly. "I'll just be happy you're still willing to have me in your life."

Hayden mumbled something as he looked at the sky. "You were the one who misread the situation," he said when he looked back at her again. "You were never out of my life. And you never will be. What happened last year didn't mean anything. Let's go on as we always have and forget about it."

"Mmm," she said, because really? Did he have to keep trivializing it by saying it didn't mean anything? Was her kiss that bad? She decided to ignore her ego and embrace the happiness she felt at repairing their relationship.

"Will you be able to sleep?" he asked.

Elle nodded. Like he said earlier, she was safe here. And she and Hayden were going to be okay.

"Good." He pressed a kiss to her forehead. "I'm glad you're home. I'll see you at the starting line of the Turkey Trot."

She opened her mouth to object. She wasn't in shape for a 5k. He put a finger to her lips.

"No excuses. It's a holiday tradition."

EVERETT TRAILED his finger along the delicately carved wreath adorning the wooden Santa's head.

"You would love this one, Keeley. He looks a lot like the Santa we picked up in Belarus that Christmas. He's carrying the same ornate staff and has similar pearls embedded in his coat."

He set the Santa back down on the desk in the dark office with a sigh. The bundle of Keeley's journals resting in his messenger bag continued to taunt him. Two years later and he still couldn't get up the nerve to read them. He reminded himself he needed to get over being chickenshit if he wanted to fulfill his contract.

Opening those journals would be like opening Pandora's box, though. As it was, he was hanging on by a thread emotionally. A sound outside pulled him from the inner debate that plagued him day and night.

Everett moved to the window. He watched from behind the drapes as a man leaned down and kissed a woman on the forehead. It was the deputy but not the woman he'd left the inn with earlier.

"Well, well, Keeley. It seems there may be more to Gidget's story than meets the eye." He chuckled to himself. "Of course, you'd adore her. Another spunky redhead who wears her heart on her sleeve. She's fierce, like you." He wrapped his fingers around the back of his neck. "Perhaps her resemblance to you is what has me so off-kilter. Helen had to know how the young woman would rankle me, damn her." He slumped down into one of the desk chairs. "I miss you, my love."

Everett sipped his drink and watched the deputy walk away from the inn. He couldn't help but notice the other man looked as lonely as he felt.

HAYDEN ENJOYED his coffee to the tune of more holiday music the following morning. This time it was Amy Grant singing "Tennessee Christmas." Next to him, Simone was practically making love to a cranberry scone.

"Mmm," the woman moaned. "Tatum, these are so good, girl. But you know I'm jonesing for your eggnog loaf. You're killing me, making me wait a whole year for a slice."

"Not until after Thanksgiving," Tatum Fisk, the owner and chef of the Queen of Hearts Bakery said. "They wouldn't be special if you could buy one every day."

"As a fan of Thanksgiving, I thank you for not rushing the season," Hayden said.

"I swear this guy is worried everyone will forget the Turkey Trot or something." Simone mocked him with a bow. "No one will take away your champion's crown, Lovell. Don't worry. It will be safe for yet another year."

Tatum chuckled. "Speaking of championships, he's gunning for the gingerbread house-making medal, as well. Rumor has it, you and Elle McAlister used to dominate that one, too."

Simone's eyebrows shot to the top of her forehead. "You are making gingerbread houses this year? With Elle?"

"No." Tatum answered before he could. "With the decorator, Livi Turner. She talked him into it last night when they stopped in here for dessert."

Hayden groaned at Simone's over-the-top reaction of feigning choking. He smacked her on the back.

"Whoa, ho." She coughed out the words. "Dessert with the decorator. And gingerbread house making. Does Elle know about this?"

A customer at the counter flagged Tatum down. "Don't answer that until I get back. I want to hear the answer."

No way was that happening. This town was already up in his business way too much. He grabbed his travel coffee mug and headed through the door linking the bakery to the Java Jolt. A quick refill, and he'd be on his way back to the office. Unfortunately, Simone was right on his heels.

"I told you Livi was interested in your pieces," she teased. "Did she get a peek at all your good stuff last night?"

Hayden handed his mug to Lois, the geriatric proprietress of the coffee shop, who filled it without question. "Seriously, Simone, can you fixate on someone else's life for once?"

The woman blinked. "Just when yours is starting to get interesting?" She shook her head. "Nah." She winked at Lois. "Our boy here is about to get tangled up in a love triangle."

"For crying out loud, Simone. I told you, there's nothing going on with me and Livi."

"Does she know that?"

Now both women were arching their damn eyebrows at him.

"And I notice you didn't rule out something going on with Elle," Simone continued.

I want to see you settled with someone nice.

The "just not me" was implied. He was good enough to make out with when her heart was broken, and that was all.

"I don't have to rule anything out. Everyone knows Elle and I are just friends."

Best friends without benefits.

Elle's future was in New York City, "where the action is." Hayden's life was here, in Chances Inlet. End of story.

Lois snorted at his terse response as Simone's walkie began to squawk.

She groaned. "It's the day before a holiday, and people are playing bumper cars in the Walmart parking lot." She pointed a finger at Hayden as she headed for the door. "This convo isn't over, big guy."

Hayden went to take his travel mug back from Lois, but the woman held it tight in her gnarled fingers. "For such a smart man, you can be so dumb." With her words of wisdom imparted, she released his mug and went to wait on another customer.

When he turned to follow Simone out of the shop, he was surprised to find Everett West seated at one of the bistro tables, staring him down over a steaming cup of coffee.

Hayden gave the guy a nod. "Good morning, Mr. West."

"Deputy."

The correspondent's snarky tone immediately had Hayden's hackles up. Why the hell was the guy lingering over a cup of coffee at the Java Jolt when he should be finishing his damn book? From what Elle told him, her promotion depended on it.

"Don't tell me they ran out of coffee at the inn?"

West's smirk seemed to grow. "No. I enjoyed my first two cups of Lois' coffee very early this morning. I thought I'd pop into town and meet the sorceress who whips up this delicious brew."

He winked at someone beyond Hayden's shoulder, presumably Lois. Hayden's annoyance grew.

"Well then, you should be well-caffeinated and ready to work."

West tapped his fingers on the laptop case on the table. "I do some of my best writing in quaint places like this one."

Hayden suppressed a growl. No wonder Elle had lost her temper with the guy yesterday. West wasn't going to goad him into something, though. That wouldn't help Elle. He adjusted the campaign hat on his head and gave the man a half-hearted salute.

"I'll let you get to it."

"Oh, I plan to, deputy. But first, I'm going to mosey next door and sign up for that gingerbread house-making contest."

"You'll need a partner, Mr. West." Lois eyed the man hopefully.

"I've already paired up with someone, my dear. But being new in town, I could use some folks in my cheering section. Can I count on you?"

The normally stoic barista nearly swooned when West launched a smile at her. The muffin Hayden had just devoured threatened to work its way back up. He needed to get away from the guy.

"Have a nice day, Mr. West," he said as he pushed open the door.

"I'll see you at the Turkey Trot tomorrow, I presume," West said. "It's a good thing I brought my running shoes."

It's on.

He didn't trust his words right now, so he simply nodded and hurried out of the coffee shop.

CHAPTER FOUR

Elle stormed into the kitchen of the inn. "Where is he?"

The three women working at various stations in the big room turned to stare at her.

"Elle! You made it home after all." Lori, her sister-in-law, wiped her flour-stained hands on a dish towel as she waddled over to hug Elle. "Pardon my baby bump," she said with a laugh. "Miles says I'm growing a humpback whale."

"It's better than the kickboxer this little girl was." Her other sister-in-law, Ginger, bent down to kiss the head of the adorable baby girl fast asleep in a bouncy seat on top of the table.

Elle did the same, inhaling her niece's perfect baby scent and feeling it calm her nerves a bit before she embraced Ginger.

"Where is who?" her mother asked coyly because there was no way she didn't know the "he" Elle was referring to.

"West," Elle bit out. "He's not in the study."

"Oh," both her sisters-in-law cooed in unison.

"He's kind of dreamy," Lori remarked, "in a rugged, tortured-soul kind of way."

"Mm-hmm," Ginger agreed. "And that voice. So smooth. I can't believe he'll be around for the holidays."

Elle coughed to cover the disgusted sound that threatened to escape. "He sent me on a wild goose chase for a specific brand of pencils." She waved her hand, holding the neatly sharpened lead. "All so he could pull a Houdini on me."

Her mother had the nerve to laugh. "I doubt it's anything that nefarious. He mentioned something about the smells from the kitchen torturing him while he worked. He decided to walk into town to find a place to write that was—how did he put it?" She snapped her fingers. "Oh yeah, *less dangerous to his senses.*"

"Not to brag, but my apple pie has won several awards," Lori said.

"And the turkey gravy your mother is making even has Hazel drooling and she doesn't eat real food yet," Ginger added.

Her mother shrugged. Elle closed her eyes and counted to ten.

"Relax. He's not going to get lost in town. Besides, we never get to see you. Why don't you hang out with us and help Ginger with the cornbread for the dressing," Lori suggested.

Ginger made a face. "I don't need help baking the cornbread. My cooking skills have improved drastically."

Lori shot Elle a pleading look because it was no secret to anyone in Chances Inlet that Ginger's cooking skills had *not* improved anywhere near drastically. As much as she'd wanted to succumb to the temptation of the delicious smells and spend time with the people she loved, her future depended on West finishing his book. She needed to keep that first and foremost in her mind.

"Ginger has got this," she said, making a mental note to forgo the cornbread dressing at Thanksgiving dinner tomorrow and have the mushroom and sausage stuffing instead. "I have to track down a wayward author."

Ignoring Ginger's smug smile, Elle snatched a slice of apple from the pile Lori was tossing together for her pies and left through the kitchen door. Her brother's goofy golden retriever, Midas, and Lori's Australian shepherd, Tessa were sunning themselves on the veranda. Both dogs insisted on being scratched behind the ears before they would allow her to pass.

"Some watchdogs you two turned out to be," she muttered. "West probably tossed you treats to get you to allow him to slip by."

The walk into town should have been pleasant. It was a sunny fall day with a warm sea breeze. It seemed like most of the residents of Chances Inlet were out and about, many offering a wave and shouting "hello" when she passed. All Elle could think about, however, was finding West. She hated that her first inclination was to check Pier Pressure, Chances Inlet's only bar.

"Elinor!"

She cringed at the familiar voice. Good manners dictated that she stop and say hello, despite wanting to locate West as soon as possible.

"Good morning, Bernice." Elle bent down to give the petite woman a hug. Bernice Thompson had been the office manager for her father's construction company all of Elle's life. She was also the nosiest person in town. If anyone knew West's whereabouts, it would be the spry busybody in front of her.

"You are a sight for sore eyes, sweet girl," Bernice said. "I'm glad you're home. And you brought a bonafide celebrity with you, too." Bernice leaned in closer. "I've had a crush on Everett West for years. And this morning, I took a selfie with him." She pulled out her phone and swiped at the screen. "See?"

Sure enough, it was West with his arm around Bernice's shoulders. And they were standing inside the Queen of Hearts Bakery.

Gotcha.

"Ahh. What a great picture. You should print it out, and I'll get him to sign it." Elle moved in the direction of the town square. "I'm going to see what he's up to now."

"Oh, he's not at the bakery any longer."

Elle's heart sank.

"I believe he went to the bookstore," Bernice continued.

"Fantastic." Elle breathed a sigh of relief. "I'll head that way."

Bernice stopped her with a hand on Elle's forearm. "I was wondering if I could pick your brain while you're in town."

"About?"

"The PR firm we've been using to handle the social media for the town dropped us. They said we are too small of an account. Can you imagine?"

She had trouble imagining what any of this had to do with her.

"It's bad enough Garth had to close down the newspaper," Bernice continued.

Wait. What?

"The newspaper shut down? When did that happen?"

Bernice made a tsking sound. "Four years ago. While you were galivanting around the globe in the Peace Corps."

Elle rolled her eyes. "I would hardly call it galivanting, but whatever." *I almost died in a flipping earthquake, for crying out loud!* "Look, I'm sorry about the PR firm and the newspaper closing and whatever else is bringing you down today. I'm just not sure what that has to do with me."

"It has everything to do with you," Bernice insisted. "You are an expert at those little bait-click posts on social media."

She fought back a groan. "It's called clickbait."

"Clickbait," Bernice repeated. "You're good at writing things in such a way that it will grab people's attention. We need to get tourists to notice Chances Inlet. Christmas is four weeks away, and we must make money while the shop bells jingle, if you know what I'm saying. Can you help us out by creating some of those clickbait posts for the town's website?"

Not only was she stuck babysitting a grump, but now it seemed she was also in demand to write catchy social media copy about her hometown. Not that Bernice's opinion of Elle's talent wasn't flattering.

"I don't know Bernice. I'm swamped helping Mr. West finish his memoir."

Provided he'd stay in one place.

"That's odd. Because when I mentioned it to Mr. West, he said you'd be available for whatever I needed."

She was going to kill the man.

Bernice donned a cat-ate-the-canary grin. "Stop by city hall when you get a chance, and we'll get started. Yoo-hoo!" She flagged down the mail truck as she marched off.

Elle felt sorry for the poor postal worker. When she stepped over the Whale of a Tale bookstore threshold a few minutes later, three elementary school hooligans nearly took her out at the knees.

"Auntie Elle," her niece, Emily, cried. "You're here!"

"Don't tell me you three are playing hooky again." Elle tweaked the little girl's cheek. The breath always caught in her lungs whenever she saw the laughing blue eyes her niece shared with her late grandfather. She missed her dad. This town was filled with so many memories of the larger-than-life man with the booming laugh and the helping hand. It hurt to be home sometimes.

"There's no school today, silly. It's the day before turkey day," said Henry, the little towheaded boy who—if her brother Ryan stepped up to the plate—would be Elle's nephew soon.

Elle brushed her hand over the head of the littlest one, Whitney, who belonged to her new stepsister, Paige, and her fiancé, Tanner. Realizing the joy she felt seeing the eager smiles on these kids' faces, she couldn't believe she'd ever wanted to skip this holiday with her family. "Well, aren't you lucky to have an entire bookstore as your playground?"

Paige emerged from the back of the store with her hands full of garland. "They've been helping me decorate."

Elle laughed. "I can only imagine how much *help* they've been."

"The man who does magic tricks is going to read at the holiday read-a-long on Friday," Emily announced.

"The man who does magic tricks?" Elle shot Paige a questioning look.

Her stepsister nodded enthusiastically. "Everett West. He pulled a quarter out of Henry's ear."

"See!" Henry held it up proudly.

Seriously? He could be a curmudgeon to her but was charming to small children? What was up with that?

Emily held up a copy of O. Henry's *The Gift of the Maji*. "He's going to read this to us on Friday."

"I can't believe *the* Everett West is doing a reading in my store. It'll be great publicity." Paige sighed. "If only the town social media wasn't such a dud. I really need to start doing some of that on my own."

"Bernice mentioned something about that," Elle said. "Hey, is West still here by any chance?"

Paige grinned and nodded. She gestured over her shoulder. "I have a little reading nook back there. He's made himself at home. Not that I mind. I mean, it's Everett West!"

The kids giggled as they each took one end of the garland and stretched it out around the front of the store. Meanwhile, Elle stalked toward her charge. West was leaning back in one of the leather armchairs, noise-canceling headphones over his ears and his eyes closed. Much to her chagrin, so was his laptop.

Elle kicked his booted foot. The annoying man opened one eye, spied her, and closed it again. She swore under her breath.

"Mr. West," she shouted.

That got his attention. He snapped open his eyes and whipped off the headphones. Music from the Foo Fighters streamed from his Beats.

"I thought we had dispensed with the mister?"

Elle drew in a deep, cleansing breath. She'd vowed last night not to push the man's buttons. Instead, she would be cheerful and helpful.

Even if it kills me.

She pulled the pencils from the pocket of her hoodie. "I just wanted to make sure you got the pencils you asked for."

He flinched ever so slightly, as if he could sense her powerful urge to stab him with them. She placed them gently on the side table at his elbow.

"Is there anything else you need to make your writing process go smoothly?" She was proud of how chipper her voice sounded. "I can run over to the deli and grab you some lunch if you'd like. Or more coffee, maybe?"

Emily chose that moment to let out one of her signature ear-piercing squeals.

West jumped from his chair and hurriedly stuffed his laptop and headphones into his backpack. "That won't be necessary. I'm still full after enjoying your mother's delicious breakfast. I think I'll wander back to the inn and work out on the veranda."

"That's a great idea." She moved to follow him.

"Alone," West said. "As I explained yesterday, I don't need you shadowing me all day. I'm a big boy who's been writing stories solo for most of my life." He pulled his wallet out of his backpack and took out several bills. "Here. It seems I'll need an ugly Christmas sweater for Saturday night. See what you can find for me, eh?" He handed her the cash.

You don't need an ugly sweater, she wanted to shout. *You need to be writing!*

Instead, she pasted a smile on her face. "Sure," she said as she took the money. "I'll get right on that." Little did he know, she was an efficient shopper. She could grab the sweater and be back at the inn in an hour.

With a single nod, he walked in the direction of the door. "Oh, and Gidget, I forgot one other thing. We'll need some supplies for the gingerbread house-making contest. I've entered us as a team.

You should know upfront that I don't like to embarrass myself. This contest may be to raise funds for charity, but we'll be giving it our best effort. I have a reputation to maintain."

A chorus of children's goodbyes followed him out the door. Elle slumped down into the chair he'd just vacated.

"Well guess what, Mr. West," she mumbled to herself. "I have a reputation to maintain, also. I'm a McAlister. And no way are you going to best me with your ridiculous requests."

EVERETT WHISTLED to himself as he left the bookstore. He stopped to admire the magnolia wreath hanging on the entrance to the knit shop next door.

"This town makes those fake towns in the Christmas movies look lame, Keeley," he murmured. "I've never seen a place with so much authentic holiday cheer."

The big window of the knit shop was taken up by skeins of green yarn stacked in the shape of a Christmas tree. Small balls of bright-colored yarn decorated its "boughs." A woman teetered on a ladder as she attempted to place a knit gold star on top. Everett raced into the store to help her.

"Here." He grabbed the sides of the ladder. "I've got you."

The woman looked down at him, her brown eyes filled with relief. They grew wide once they registered who he was. Everett grinned up at her.

"Um, thank you," she said.

The bashful way she uttered the words stirred up something inside him. Everett was immediately transfixed by the fullness of her lips and the blush on her cheeks.

She smiled shyly at him. "If you'll step back, I can get down now."

"Oh, yes." He released the ladder and moved out of the way, extending his hand so he could help guide her back to terra firm.

After a brief hesitation, she placed her palm against his. The shock waves that coursed through his body caught him off guard. He sucked in a breath as he studied the woman's face. The lines bracketing her eyes told him she was a woman of a certain age. But one who enjoyed life. And one who the years had been kind to.

Her long silver hair was caught up in a side braid with strands of fairy string woven through it. She was tall—nearly eye level with him—and slender. Her outfit consisted of well-worn jeans and a sweatshirt that featured a handprint turkey with the phrase "Gobble 'till you wobble." He also noticed her hands were free of any rings.

"Hello," she said, not bothering to pull her hand away.

"Hi."

Hi?! You're a man of words, Everett, and that's all you can come up with?

She suddenly seemed to realize her hand was still in his, quickly clasping his fingers and shaking them up and down. "You're Everett West."

He smiled. "That I am. But you have me at a disadvantage." He hiked an eyebrow in question.

Her lashes fluttered shyly as she chewed on her bottom lip. "I'm Kitty. Kitty Johansen."

Everett covered their clasped hands with his free one. "Nice to meet you, Kitty, Kitty Johansen."

Kitty dipped her chin, presumably to hide her blush.

"You have a lovely shop here, Kitty," he continued.

She jerked her eyes up. "Oh, it's not mine. It's my sister's place. Everyone assumes it's mine because Claire wouldn't know a bubble stitch from a moss stitch. Fortunately, she makes up for it with her mad business skills. I'm happy simply being the artist in residence for once."

The sound of heels tapping on the hardwood floor came from

the back of the store. Everett instantly loathed the sound because it had Kitty yanking her hand out from between his.

"Well, hello," the interloper—presumably Kitty's sister, Claire —drawled.

The two women could not have been more different. Where Kitty was more earth mother, her sister looked like she'd just stepped out of a *Southern Living* magazine spread on proper Southern hostesses. The other woman was plumper than Kitty, with brassy blond hair cut in a chic bob that curled around her chin. It was hard to decipher her exact age through the expertly applied makeup she wore. The smile she gave him was as genuine as her sister's, though.

"My stars." Kitty's sister put her hand to her chest. "I heard a rumor you were in town."

"Mr. West—" Kitty began.

"Everett," he interrupted.

"Everett," she said softly.

He relished the blush that was back on her cheeks.

"This is my sister, Claire Lovell. Knotical is her brainchild. Claire, this is Everett West."

Claire looked back and forth between the two of them. "I see." Her tone indicated she saw a lot more than he wanted her to.

Everett glanced around the colorful shop, his eyes landing on a stunning captain's desk in the center of the floor with skeins of yarn careening over its sides.

"You've done a wonderful job here, Claire. It almost makes me want to take up knitting. And you have a fantastic eye for furnishings." He wandered over to the desk. "I've always wanted one of these."

The sound of hurried footsteps had him looking up.

"Oh no you don't, Mr. West!" The blonde from the inn—Livi something or other—came charging out from the back of the store. "I saw it first, and it's already bought and paid for." She gestured at Claire. "Mrs. Lovell, put that sold sign on there so everyone knows it's spoken for."

"Oh." Claire pulled a red tag out of her dress pocket. "Of course." She taped it carefully to the side of the desk. "If you're genuinely interested, Mr. West, I'm sure my son, Hayden, could build another one."

As if her words had conjured him up, the bell above the shop's door rang as Deputy Lovell strode in. He stopped abruptly, his gaze taking in each of the room's occupants.

"What's going on?" he asked.

"Everett is admiring your desk," Kitty explained.

The deputy startled slightly at his aunt's use of his given name.

"*My* desk," Livi countered. "I bought it."

Kitty chuckled softly. Claire sidled up to Livi. "Yes, dear. And I'm so happy you did. Your clients will be thrilled with it." She looked over at her son. "Isn't it wonderful, Hayden?"

If the deputy thought it was wonderful, he didn't bother saying so. His mother gushed on.

"You're a paid artist now," she said. "Hayden's grandfather was a brilliant craftsman. He taught my son everything. Kitty's brother-in-law is a furniture maker, too. He keeps hinting he'd like Hayden to apprentice for him so he could take over the business someday. But his work isn't the same quality as Hayden's." She beamed at the decorator. "Why, I have some other fabulous pieces at our home you should see, Livi. What are you doing for Thanksgiving dinner tomorrow?"

"Mom, I'm sure she'll be spending it with her family," Hayden said.

"Not this year," Livi replied. "My parents are on a five-month cruise that doesn't end until next month. My siblings are all with their spouses' families." She shrugged. "We've never been into Thanksgiving normally. We usually go to a restaurant if we are together. It's not much of a holiday to me, to be honest."

Claire gasped. "Heavens, we can't have that. You must come to our house and see how Thanksgiving should be done. It will become your favorite holiday, I promise."

Livi shot the deputy a demur look. His stoic expression melted into a resigned smile. He nodded to her.

"I would like that very much." Livi let out a squeal only a few decibels lower than the little girl from the bookstore. She raced over to the deputy and patted him on the chest. "Pick me up at the inn?"

Lovell nodded again. With a wave to everyone, she disappeared through the door.

A customer came in looking for alpaca yarn, and Claire led her over to the other side of the store. Kitty went to the counter to answer the ringing phone. The deputy seemed to be frozen in place.

"You do nice work," Everett told him. "If I didn't live out of a suitcase, I'd be inclined to hire you to make me one."

"I guess you'd have to settle down first."

Everett looked over at where Kitty was still on the phone, taking an order.

"I lost my reason for settling down," he said quietly.

The deputy followed Everett's gaze, his mouth hardening. "I doubt you'll find one in Chances Inlet."

The uniform certainly fit the man. The guy was a protector. Everett had to admire that.

Deputy Lovell was also correct. Everett had no business chasing Kitty. Except that for a few minutes there, the loneliness constantly gnawing at his gut had eased. He'd forgotten how good it felt to be free of it.

"You might want to load up on those carbs, deputy," he challenged. "I plan on giving you a run for your money tomorrow." With a nod to Kitty—who blushed again, he was pleased to note —Everett left the store.

CHAPTER FIVE

HAYDEN WANDERED through the crowd milling around the Turkey Trot's starting line the following morning. The weather wasn't as comfortable as the day before. The sun was nowhere to be found. Not only that, but the wind had shifted, and a stiff, chilly breeze now blew in off the Atlantic. It didn't seem to dampen the spirit of the crowd, though. The donuts that Xander's sister Tatum was handing out didn't hurt either.

"You're missing out, man," Xander said around a mouthful of French cruller. "These are damn tasty."

Hayden made a face. "How can you run with all that yeast in your belly?"

"It's not the Olympics." Xander licked his fingers. "Just a 5k with a bunch of townies."

"I assume you'll be handing out free weekend passes to all the stragglers again?"

Xander slapped him on the back. "Damn straight. They don't call me the P. T. Barnum of gym owners for nothing."

A couple of the high school track kids came over to smack talk with Hayden, who helped coach the team in his free time. He loved that the kids looked up to him. He loved it even more that no one had come close to his state record in the ten thousand meters in the decade since he graduated.

Xander's low whistle had Hayden spinning around to see what his friend was jazzed up about. He followed his gaze to where it landed on Livi Turner. She was making her way toward them looking like she'd just stepped out of a Lululemon catalog—except for the headband with bobbing turkey legs she wore.

Elle walked slowly behind her wearing a similar headband and a mulish frown. The McAlister family were all athletic. Everyone except Elle. Sure, she was graceful from years of ballet, but she didn't possess the ruthlessly competitive spirit of her siblings. The joy of a good run was lost on her. This morning was no exception, judging from her expression. Hayden couldn't help it, he laughed at his best friend.

Livi mistook his grin as being for her. "Aren't they cute? Elle and I found them at the dollar store yesterday. I got one for you, too. Pick one." She held out a headband with the turkey legs and one that was a pilgrim hat.

Oh, hell nah.

Beside him, Xander cough-laughed. "You've picked the wrong guy for that, sweetheart. The deputy is the no-frills type. All he cares about is crossing the finish line before anyone else."

Livi's face fell. "Oh."

Crap. Hayden took the headband with the pilgrim hat and planted it on Xander's fat head.

"Mr. West didn't want one, either," she said.

Of course not.

Hayden watched out of the corner of his eye as West cozied up to Elle's three brothers. He wondered if West knew Miles was also a seasoned triathlete as well as a congressman. Elle's other brother, Ryan, was a professional athlete, so there was no disguising his skill. Gavin McAlister might have played college football had it not been for a knee injury. Not that it held him back now. The three men normally kept Hayden company at the front of the pack.

"Well, you two have fun. I'm going to head to the back and run with the stroller crowd," Elle announced.

"No, you're not." Livi linked her arm with Elle's and tugged her closer. "You can't give up before it has even started. You really should consider joining a running club when you get back to New York. There are lots of fun people in mine. I'll hook you up."

When you get back to New York.

Their friendship might be mended, but the physical distance would still be there. He hated how the thought made his chest ache.

"Are you ready to kick everyone's ass, Blade Runner?" Miles clapped Hayden on the back.

"Blade Runner?" West asked.

Miles pointed at Hayden's left leg. The prosthetic blade he wore when he ran was partially obscured by Xander's beefy calf. "Even as a wounded warrior, he smokes the field."

West's face paled. "You lost your leg? In Afghanistan?"

Gavin McAlister wrapped an arm over Hayden's shoulders. "He gave that leg to save two other soldiers. And don't think we let this guy win this thing every year. He kicks our asses fair and square."

The bullhorn squeaked when Bernice turned it on, causing the crowd to grimace. "Okay, we are almost ready to start," she shouted into it. "Everyone be safe and have fun."

West shot Hayden a pained look as the others jostled for position along the starting line. Hayden swore. He hated the pitying looks he got when people found out about his injury. And it especially stung coming from this man.

"Show me what you got," Hayden challenged.

A slow grin formed on the reporter's face. The horn went off, and the sea of bodies surged forward. West had the smooth stride of a man who ran for the joy of it. He easily kept pace with Hayden and Elle's brothers.

The high school runners sprinted to the front. A rookie move. They'd tire out before the halfway point.

Livi wasn't lying when she said she was in a running club. She kept an easy pace beside him without breaking a sweat. He glanced over his shoulder at Elle who was huffing and puffing several yards back. When their eyes met, she gave him a pathetic thumbs-up before waving her hand as if telling him to shoo.

At the halfway point, West had settled in with the high schoolers. The McAlister brothers peeled off—Miles for a photo-op with his constituents, and Ryan and Gavin for an iced coffee Lois was handing out. Livi lengthened her stride.

"Come on, Hayden. You don't want to let that old man beat you," she said, gesturing to West.

No way was that old man beating Hayden. Neither was anyone else, for that matter. Time to make his move. He let Livi have the front for a few strides before taking one last look back at Elle.

Just in time to see her go down in a heap.

"Ow!" Elle cried as her body hit the pavement.

Several hands were already reaching down to help her up when all she wanted to do was crawl away in embarrassment. Preferably back to the inn where her mother's famous spiced rum waited.

"This is why I don't run," she muttered to no one in particular.

"Let me through," a familiar voice demanded.

The crowd parted, and Hayden eased down beside her.

"Elle, where does it hurt?" He reached for her throbbing ankle.

She swatted his hands away. "What are you even doing right now? The race is that way, silly."

He ignored her, aiming for her leg again. "Which ankle is it?"

"It doesn't matter. My sister—the one with the medical degree—will be along in a few minutes. She'll check it out. You need to get back in the race."

"The strollers are a good fifteen minutes behind us. And judging by the way Kate was gabbing at the starting line, she'll be the last one to come by."

She let out a hiss when his fingers gingerly examined her tender ankle.

"That's what I thought." He scooped her up as though she were a sack of corn chips and not one hundred forty pounds of out-of-shape ballerina.

"Hayden, stop," she protested. "You're being ridiculous. You need to get back in the race. I can walk over to that bench and wait for my sister."

"You can walk, huh?"

He set her on her feet, only for Elle to wince when the pain shot up her leg.

"Liar."

He jerked her back into his arms and was striding to the first-aid tent before she could object again. Not that she could find the words. Hayden held her so close that it was impossible not to inhale his masculine scent. And it was doing idiotic things to her brain—like making her snuggle in closer.

"I need to commandeer one of these golf carts," he called to the EMTs without breaking his stride.

"Set her down here, Deputy." One of the paramedics indicated a gurney. "We'll check her out."

"No." Hayden gently deposited her in the front seat of a golf cart. "She needs an X-ray."

"I'll run her over to the ER," another EMT offered.

"Yes. Let him take me. You can still finish the race," Elle insisted. "This isn't anything serious. Just an old dance injury."

He jumped into the driver's seat and turned the key. The golf cart lurched into motion. "Stop worrying about the stupid race."

Elle bristled at his clipped tone. "It isn't a stupid race. Not to you, anyway. This is the one day you look forward to every year." The lump forming in her throat grew painful. "This race—or the idea of running it—kept you going when—when you were hurt. When we thought you'd never walk again. It gave you a goal to work toward. And it brought you back here to Chances Inlet."

To me.

Hayden had spent the bulk of his rehabilitation at a military hospital in Texas. Elle was in college at Elon at the time, but they'd kept in touch through email, texts, and phone calls. When Hayden deigned to talk to her, that was. He had a difficult time accepting his body was forever changed.

Running was his first love, and she'd tapped into that by dangling running the Turkey Trot together as an incentive for him to put his heart and soul into rehabbing his body and his mind. It eventually worked. For the past nine Thanksgivings, Hayden was the king of the Turkey Trot. Until today. And it was all her fault.

Hayden steered the golf cart right up to the ER doors. He jumped out and nabbed a wheelchair from the lobby, pushing it over to the cart before he tenderly transferred her into the chair. Leaning over her, he braced his hands on the arms. The blue eyes boring into hers were unfocused and wilder than she'd ever seen them.

"You listen to me, Elinor. Nothing is more important to me than the people I care most about. Not even a race. Nothing," he repeated. "You hear me?"

She nodded, his use of her given name startling her into silence.

"Well, if it isn't Handsome Hayden," a tall, dark-skinned

woman wearing a white coat said when they entered the ER. "My wife's work-husband. And who do we have here?"

"Hey, Gabby. This is Elle McAlister. She needs to have her ankle X-rayed."

Gabby quirked an eyebrow at Hayden. "Not *the* Elle McAlister?"

"Wait, Simone got married?" Elle asked, ignoring the death glare Hayden shot at the PA.

The other woman grinned. "It was one of those whirlwind romances this past summer." She pointed to a room down the hall. "Take her to room two."

"I missed a lot staying away," Elle mused.

"Mm-hmm," Hayden replied.

Gabby followed them into the room. "Is the race finished already?"

"No," Elle and Hayden said at the same time.

"Seriously?" Gabby leveled a stunned look in Hayden's direction.

"Hello?" He snapped his fingers at his friend. "She needs an X-ray."

Mumbling something about someone needing their head examined, Gabby sat on a stool and began untying Elle's sneaker before carefully pulling it off. Elle tried not to wince as the other woman probed the tender muscle with her fingers.

"I don't think it's broken. But we will appease Captain America here by taking some pictures just to be sure." Gabby stood and went to the sink to wash her hands. "A nurse will come in to take your vitals while I send for the portable X-ray machine."

"Told you it wasn't broken," Elle mumbled when the doctor left the room.

"We still don't know that," he bit out.

"Great. And now you're angry with me because you couldn't finish the race."

Before she could blink, his hands were back on the arms of the wheelchair again, bracketing her in. His lips were inches from hers. His breath washed over her cheek.

"No, Elinor. I'm angry because I goaded you into running today. Livi did, too. At least I knew you had no business running a 5k. You could have been hurt. Hell, you are hurt."

She could see the pulse throbbing frantically in his throat. An unexpected urge to place her lips to his skin there had her nearly passing out. She lifted her hand to his cheek as much to steady herself as to comfort him.

"It's really nothing. I'm going to be just fine. You're being silly."

Clearly, it was the wrong thing to say. A tremor coursed through him, and he jerked back to standing. His eyes roamed her face.

"Yeah," he eventually said.

And then he was gone.

THIRTY MINUTES LATER, her sister, Kate, strolled into the room. Gabby and another man wearing a white coat hovered in the doorway behind her.

"Nothing's broken," Kate announced.

Elle adjusted the pillow on the bed behind her. "I could have told you that. Where's Hayden?"

"That is the question on everyone's lips in town." Kate crossed her arms over her chest. "Him not crossing the finish line first—much less at all—has created quite the stir."

"Who won?" Gabby asked.

"One of the college kids in town for the weekend." Kate chuckled. "He promptly cast up his accounts on the mayor's shoes."

Elle groaned. "Thanks for the visual."

"How's the pain?" Kate had on her unscrupulous head-of-the-hospital face, so there was no point in lying.

"Five out of ten. But only when I put weight on it."

"This should help." The other doctor handed Kate an orthopedic boot.

Elle sat up and began strapping it on her swollen ankle. "I need to go find Hayden."

"Not happening, little sister. We are going straight back to the inn where you will elevate your foot and decorate it with a nice bag of frozen peas. If you're lucky, I'll prescribe some spiced rum to go with it."

"But—"

"Doctor's orders, Elle. Do as I say, and you'll be out of the boot in a few days." Kate dropped her voice to a conspiratorial whisper. "If I were you, though, I wouldn't rush it. I'd milk this so you not only get out of dishwashing duty this afternoon but also for the rest of the season. Let the guys pick up the slack."

Elle rolled her eyes at her sister. When she put her injured foot on the ground, however, the idea of being pampered by her family while enjoying a nice drink was beginning to sound better and better. She hopped into the wheelchair, instantly recalling Hayden leaning over her, his lips so close to hers.

Nothing is more important to me than the people I care most about.

What did he mean by that? And he certainly had a funny way of showing it. He deposited her in the ER, then disappeared to God knows where. She knew he cared about her. He'd told her enough times. Yet something was different about the way he'd said the words today. Her heart skipped a beat at the thought.

"Let's go enjoy Thanksgiving dinner," Kate said as she took the handles of the wheelchair.

"Yeah, about that. I'd skip the cornbread dressing if I were you. Ginger made it."

"Say no more, little sister. I'm pretty sure she forgot to put the egg in the cornbread last year. It was like eating sawdust."

HAYDEN'S BREATH sawed through his lungs, burning more with every stride he took. He ignored the SUV crawling beside him, trailing his movements. He wasn't running away. Just running to think. To try to understand why he'd made such a fool of himself today. His PTSD from his combat days was long under control. So why did the image of Elle crumpling to the ground affect him the way it did?

What if she'd been running in New York? With Livi's running club? Who would have helped her then?

Except he didn't have to worry about that. Elle's idea of cardio was dancing at a nightclub for a couple of hours. *Fuck.* Just thinking that brought on the crazy images of what could happen to her in a nightclub. And now those scenarios were going to take up residence in his head where they would no doubt haunt him forever.

"Dude," Xander said from the driver's seat of his Jeep Cherokee. "You're halfway to South Carolina. Your mom's texts are getting more and more frantic. She wants to know if you'll be back soon. Something about you needing to pick up Livi for Thanksgiving dinner."

Hayden slowed to a walk. "This is crazy," he said to himself.

"Pretty much," Xander replied. "But then women seem to drive us to Crazy Town."

Elle is fine, he told himself.

Xander stopped the vehicle so Hayden could climb in. They were quiet as Xander turned the Jeep around and drove back toward Chances Inlet.

"You haven't had something trigger you in a long time," Xander finally said. "Was it the way she fell or something?"

"I don't know." And that was the part eating at him.

He cared about Elle. Deeply. But she'd made no secret that her feelings didn't go beyond friendship. No matter how passionately she kissed him. Her life was in New York. She was not his forever. He knew that.

Didn't he?

"I can get the guys together if you want."

"Nah. It's a holiday. Besides, I'm good now."

Maybe not completely, but he'd get there. The truth was, he wanted more with Elle. He hadn't realized how much until today. The very idea had set him off.

Except it was time for him to stop harboring hope and admit it wasn't ever happening. Elle was his friend. His best friend. And that would have to be enough.

"Funny how the mention of a certain blonde pulled you right out of your funk back there."

Hayden turned to stare questioningly at his friend.

"Livi? The classy blonde you're taking to Thanksgiving dinner at your folks' house. I can see what you see in her. She ran well today. Finished in the top third. I think she was disappointed you weren't around at the end for a victory kiss, though."

"You're reading too much into it."

"Simone is right. You're too closed off for your own good. You keep Elle as a best friend to have a security blanket. That way, you don't have to let anyone else in. You've got a sure thing throwing herself at you, and you're worried about your off-limits bestie who flits in and out of your life on a whim."

That wasn't what he was doing. Was it? He flipped his friend off.

"How did West finish?" Hayden asked in an effort to change the subject.

"He didn't. The guy got a stitch in his side right after you left and dropped out."

Well, at least the day wasn't all bad.

CHAPTER SIX

THE NEXT AFTERNOON, Elle hobbled into the music room at the inn only to find Kate and her sister's best friend, Jane, already ensconced there.

"Hey. This is my hiding place," she complained.

"You have a built-in excuse to get out of decorating today," Kate pointed out. "You don't need a hiding place."

The Friday after Thanksgiving was traditionally the day Elle's mom finished decking out the inn for the Christmas holiday. The male McAlisters were assigned the outdoor duties of stringing lights and tying bows among the greenery draped along the wraparound veranda. Elle's mom, her daughters and daughters-in-law took care of the public rooms. Elle's mom and Lori were decorating the fifteen-foot tree in the grand salon. Since Jane was dating Ryan, she'd likely been conned into helping, too.

Except it was always Elle's job to unpack and arrange the dozens of nutcrackers throughout the music room. Every year, she'd blast Tchaikovsky and move the wooden soldiers as if they were dancing the ballet. She was looking forward to having the room to herself today so she could mope in peace.

Aside from a quick text last night asking how she felt, she

hadn't talked to Hayden. Not that she knew what she would say to him. She was still trying to come to terms with his over-the-top reaction yesterday.

"How's the ankle?" Kate asked.

Elle plopped down on the piano bench. "Better. The swelling is almost gone."

"Continue to take it easy today," Kate advised.

"Sure," Elle replied absently as she took in the martini glasses and bottles of liquors spread out on the side table between the two women. "Are you day drinking?"

Jane chuckled. "That would be somewhat irresponsible since I have patients this afternoon. Although it might make things a lot more enjoyable." Her brother's girlfriend was a top-notch physical therapist in Chances Inlet.

"We are trying to decide which martini to make for the cocktail-making contest tomorrow night at the ugly sweater party," Kate explained.

"The peppermint martini was a favorite at the bridal shower we had for Ginger and Lori last Christmas." Jane held up a glass filled with a frothy white liquid. Its rim was dusted with crushed candy canes.

"But it was the gingerbread martini that got our girl here tipsy enough to finally do something about her feelings for our brother Ryan." Kate wiggled her eyebrows. "We didn't see either of them for *daaayyys*. Maybe we should call it the horny-tini?"

Jane hopped to her feet. "We are not calling it that. Besides the peppermint one is easier to make. I'm sure we can win with it." She checked her watch. "I have to get back. Come by the clinic tomorrow morning, Elle. I'll work on that ankle with some heat therapy," she offered. "That will help with any residual inflammation."

"Or you could get Hayden to kiss it," Kate suggested. "That would certainly make your boo-boo all better."

Elle snatched the peppermint martini from Jane's hand.

"Don't be ridiculous," she said before taking a sip. She had to give her sister props. The drink was a winner.

Jane patted her chest right over her heart. "It wasn't ridiculous. It was romantic."

"There was nothing romantic about it. We're just friends," Elle insisted before taking another sip. Anything to get her through this conversation.

"If you say so." Jane waved as she left the room.

Kate remained quiet as she piled all the ingredients on a tray. *A silent Kate was never a good sign.* Meanwhile, Elle enjoyed the rest of the martini. *Why not?* It wasn't as if she was able to do much else.

"How are you sleeping?" her sister asked eventually.

"Fine," Elle lied. Not only was she stressed about Hayden, but her nightmares had returned to torment her. There was no point in telling her sister she'd slept in her clothes the night before.

"Hmm."

Elle grew defensive. "I'm not your patient."

"No. You aren't. But you are my little sister. And I care about you."

Kate was the family champion at dropping guilt bombs.

"I know. And I appreciate you. I really do. I'm handling it, though," Elle said.

"Did you talk to someone like I recommended?"

"I read some articles. Like I said, I'm handling it."

Elle couldn't meet her sister's eyes. She shifted her gaze to the big, mullioned windows with their view of the lawn where her brothers laughed together while they arranged the light-up deer in obscene positions.

Kate tsked, obviously following her gaze. "You'd think they were still in middle school."

"Speaking of annoying man-children, have you seen West?"

The reporter was invited to join the family for Thanksgiving dinner yesterday, but he declined. Of course, her mother delivered a tray to his suite later that evening. As far as Elle knew he was still up there. She said a little prayer that he was working on his manuscript.

"He left about an hour ago. Paige was giddy that he'd agreed to do a reading for the kids today. Of course, whatever he reads will pale compared to my husband's rendition of *The Polar Express*."

"Most certainly," Elle said, her tongue firmly in her cheek.

"For what it's worth, I don't think West is sleeping well, either."

It took Elle a moment to process her sister's left-field comment. "Why do you say that?"

Kate reached down and gently traced a finger beneath one of Elle's eyes. "You both have the same telltale battle scars." She moved her hand back to the tray she was balancing awkwardly. "But you'll be delighted to hear that Mom said West was hammering away at his keyboard in the study all morning."

Elle let out a long sigh of relief. *Finally.*

"You want to come to town to listen to my husband's melodic voice as he reads to the kids?" Kate asked.

"Nah. My doctor told me to rest my ankle today."

"Suit yourself. Enjoy your alone time with the nutcrackers."

When Kate left, she dug through the plastic bins to find her favorite. A bagpiper. She fingered the pompom on his Glengarry hat.

"Oh, Daddy," she sighed. "Why is life so complicated?"

After no epiphany was forthcoming from her father, she pulled out her phone, swiped it to her music, tapped on *The Nutcracker* ballet and reacquainted herself with her old friends.

THE BELL above the door jingled when Everett stepped inside Knotical. He wasn't sure what possessed him to visit the knit shop again. It certainly wasn't because he'd spied Kitty through the window when he'd left the bookstore. At least, that was what he told himself.

"Mr. West."

Kitty's warm smile had him smiling like a loony in return.

"Welcome back. Is there something special you're looking for today?" she asked.

You.

The thought hit him squarely in the solar plexus. The woman had occupied his mind for the past two days. When she'd waved at him as he ran by the store during yesterday's race, his steps had grown much lighter. His vision clearer.

Until the guilt set in.

Along with it came a painful stitch in his side that had him pulling up and returning to the inn to hide out and lick his wounds. He'd wrestled with his emotions until he thought he had them under control enough to return to the bookstore today.

But then he'd laid eyes on her again.

And, frankly, he was damn tired of waiting for a ghost.

"In fact, there is something special you can help me out with today." He clasped his hands behind his back and rocked back on his heels. "I was wondering if you could show me where I can find a slice of pizza in this town. I've been out of New York City for three days, and I'm starting to have withdrawal."

She curled in her lips as she seemed to ponder his question. Just when he thought he'd totally misread her friendliness, she rewarded him with another one of those breath-stealing smiles.

"You know, I was thinking that pizza sounded good for dinner myself. Claire," she called into the back room. "I'm taking my dinner break. I'll be back in time for the Christmas Bazaar meeting in an hour."

Kitty didn't wait for her sister's response before swiping her jacket off a hook by the counter and hurrying to the door where Everett stood waiting.

"It's not exactly New York pizza, but the Slice and Sip is as close as you get here in North Carolina."

Everett didn't care if the pizza tasted like cardboard. As long as he spent time with this beautiful creature who had captivated his imagination for the past forty-eight hours, his hunger would be satiated.

They strolled across the town square, the white Christmas lights of the gazebo beginning to sparkle as dusk fell. The storefronts all boasted fresh wreaths on their doors and poinsettias in the windows. The scent of a wood fire burning nearby filled the air.

"This place is remarkable. I almost feel as if I'm inside a giant holiday snow globe," Everett remarked.

Kitty laughed. "It's pretty special."

"Have you always lived here?"

"Oh gosh, no. Claire and I grew up in Virginia. When Claire's husband got out of the military, he wanted to start his dental practice in a small town. Coincidentally, a neighbor of his parents wanted someone to take over his dental office here in Chances Inlet and voilà. Tim and Claire ended up back in the town where he grew up. After all, it is the home of second chances." She gestured to the mural painted on the side of a building proclaiming as much. "She's been here thirty-five years. I visited often. Especially for holidays." She gestured. "I mean, come on?"

He nodded. "The only thing missing is snow."

She shivered. "I got plenty of that in Maine. My husband and I ran an art studio in Kennebunkport. He was a gifted painter."

"Was?" The journalist in him couldn't leave well enough alone. Thankfully, Kitty didn't seem to mind his gentle probing.

"Mm-hmm." Her smile was wistful but sad. "Yes. I lost him three years ago. Parkinson's. It was a long goodbye."

Jealousy clawed at his chest. What he would have given for a chance to say goodbye.

Kitty seemed to sense his sudden mood change and shifted a bit closer. "I confess to having googled you last night. You lost someone dear to you, too."

He swallowed the boulder in his throat. "I did. Two years ago. At Christmas, in fact."

She slipped her arm through his. "They keep telling me it's going to get easier."

"Didn't you know? Everybody lies."

THE TIDE Me Over Inn's kitchen was bumping again that evening. Elle's mother hosted breakfast with Santa every year on the Saturday after Thanksgiving. The money from the tickets went to a local youth center sponsored by one of the town's favorite sons who was a professional football player. The event had become a huge draw since being featured in a national magazine a few years earlier.

Elle tried to stay out of the way as she fixed herself a turkey sandwich for dinner.

"I hope you don't need an extra Santa tomorrow," Ryan McAlister said to his mother. "Jane and I have a few things we need to get done while Henry is occupied here."

Their brother Gavin snorted as he poured half a bag of chips onto his plate. "Uh-huh. I think we all know what things will be *getting done.*"

Tatum snickered from across the room where she prepared the dough for her cinnamon rolls. Lois joined in from the coffee bar, where she was putting together the urns for the peppermint hot cocoa the kids would enjoy at the breakfast.

"Boys, please." Their mother held up a hand as she navigated her mouse over her computer screen with her other one. "I have enough on my plate without having to hear all the details about your sex lives. None of these ads are serving. Dammit."

The three siblings looked at one another. Their mother rarely swore.

"What ads, Mom?" Elle set her plate down next to the desk where her mom sat.

"These stupid social media ads. I have no idea what I'm doing. No one is clicking on them."

"What's with everyone in this town and social media ads?" Elle asked. "Bernice and Paige both mentioned the same issue the other day."

"It's because we don't have a local paper anymore. Or a local magazine," her mom complained. "We have no place to advertise except social media. And every time I figure something out, they change it up. It's so frustrating that it's the only way to promote a business nowadays."

"Tell me about it," Tatum added. "I used to always include a coupon in my print ads. It brought a lot of visitors from the beach houses on the island during the summer. Now, I'm lucky if they find me when they come into town on a rainy day."

"Those dadgum computers are too complicated for me," Lois grumbled. "Give me a good old-fashioned cash register and a newspaper. Now it's all about those crazy tablets you have to touch all the time." She shook her head. "Is that even sanitary?"

Elle waved her mother away from the computer. "Here's your problem. You need a better image. And a stronger call to action."

"A what?" Lois asked.

"Never mind. Can I play with this? This is right in my wheel-house. I have some ideas."

"Knock yourself out. I'm sure you'll do a better job." She leaned down and kissed her daughter on the head. "I have to make ten dozen cookies tonight anyway."

"Let me know when you're ready for some quality control taste testing," Ryan offered.

"Both of you, out," their mother ordered. "If any cookies are left tomorrow you may have one."

Ryan grumbled under his breath. "Come on, Gav. Let's go get a burger at Pier Pressure."

"Sounds like a plan." Gavin tipped the bag of potato chips into his mouth.

"Seriously?" Elle said. "You've been eating nonstop for an hour now."

"I worked outside all day," her brother replied. "What can I say? Fresh air makes me hungry."

"Everything makes you hungry. You're as bad as your dog," Ryan joked as the two strolled out of the kitchen door.

"If you're looking for something to keep you busy while Mr. West is writing, Elle, I could use a little tutorial on how to get more clicks on my ads," Tatum said. "I'll pay you."

Elle uploaded a few images from her mother's photos as she quickly came up with copy for several ads. "It's really easy once you know the basics," she told Tatum. "You can pay me in those rum balls you make. It isn't Christmas without one. Or ten."

"Ooo, it sure smells good in here." Livi glided into the kitchen wearing a pair of Stuart Weitzman over-the-knee boots and a cashmere sweater dress. Its berry color highlighted the gold in her brown eyes. Her blond hair was gathered in a neat bun at the back of her head.

Not that Elle really noticed. She only had eyes for the man standing behind Livi. Hayden was dressed equally impressive in gray wool slacks and a black blazer. Beneath it was a crisp white shirt opened at the neck.

The same neck she'd wanted to taste the day before.

"Are you two going out?" her mother, Captain Obvious, asked.

Livi linked her arm through Hayden's. "I'm taking Hayden up to Wilmington. My client is in town. He's invited us to dinner before we head over to the island to inspect the site tomorrow."

He invited "us" to dinner? When had Livi and Hayden become an "us"? More particularly, an "us" who gets invited to business dinners.

You told him to go for her the other night, she admonished herself. *You told him they looked good together.*

And, damn, did they look good together. If she thought he was sexy in a work-stained T-shirt and worn blue jeans the other night, he was freaking breathtaking tonight. He looked very urbane. Very suited for a fancy dinner in a cosmopolitan setting. Like New York City, even.

She dusted the crumbs off her hands onto her worn leggings.

"How's the ankle, Elle?" he asked, his tone once again aloof.

"Good," she replied with a nod because, honestly, she didn't trust her voice not to squeak with frustration.

"Oh, you poor thing," Livi said. "Make sure you keep it elevated tonight. You don't want to miss the ugly sweater party tomorrow."

"Yeah, I'll probably pass."

Livi put her hand on her hip. "Elle, you aren't going to let that sour puss Mr. West ruin your holiday, are you? He can't make you work every hour of the day. Promise you'll come tomorrow. I'll sit with you. That way, you won't feel left out when everyone is dancing. Please?"

Elle wanted to scream. *Why did Livi have to be so flipping nice?* She avoided meeting Hayden's gaze. "I'll think about it."

"Yay!" Livi pulled away from Hayden to give Elle's neck a squeeze. "It'll be fun. You'll see."

"We should get going if we are going to make it to Wilmington on time," Hayden said.

"Night all." Livi waved.

Hayden helped her drape a gorgeous Christmas plaid wrap over her shoulders. Livi smiled up at him with a worshipful expression as they walked to the inn's foyer. The rest of the kitchen was silent until the front door closed.

"That was . . . sweet," Tatum said.

"Any sweeter and we'd have a mouth full of cavities," Lois murmured.

"Now, ladies, she's a lovely young woman," Elle's mother scolded. "And it's about time Hayden had someone interested in him. Isn't that right, Elle?"

The turkey sandwich was as dry as dust in Elle's mouth. She took a long sip of water. "Um, yeah, of course. Mom, is it okay if I take your laptop up to my room and work on this?"

"Have at it, my love."

Elle scooped up the computer and limped toward the backstairs. Tatum quickly stepped in front of her.

"You're going tomorrow night," the other woman announced, her tone brooking no argument.

Elle tossed out the only excuse she could think of. "I don't have an ugly Christmas sweater."

Tatum blinked. "No worries. I have three you can choose from."

"I have a couple she can try," Lois offered.

"No!" Elle's mom and Tatum shouted at the same time.

Elle looked from Tatum to her mother.

"Lois' sweaters are NSFW," her mother explained.

"They aren't that bad," the older woman argued.

Tatum groaned. "Really? Last year's had Santa's anatomically correct jingle balls."

"Like you've seen Santa's good parts to know if they were anatomically correct." Lois slammed a lid onto one of the urns.

Elle had to laugh. It was either that or cry. She loved these people and this town so much. One person more than everyone else. Too bad that one person only thought of her as a friend. At least, she hoped he still did.

"Bring the sweaters when you come for the breakfast tomorrow," she told Tatum. "I'll look over your social media then, too."

"Atta girl," her mother said.

CHAPTER SEVEN

A STORM SETTLED in over Chances Inlet in the early afternoon the following day. Hayden was already waterlogged after a busy shift when he climbed the steps of the inn's veranda to pick up Livi for the ugly sweater party. Their date the night before went better than he anticipated. He more than held his own with the investors Livi was designing for. In fact, it was nice to interact with people who weren't from Chances Inlet. Folks who didn't know his backstory. People who saw him as a sheriff's deputy and a promising woodworker. Not the guy who'd screwed up his life in high school and had to pivot.

Hayden wasn't proud of the idiot he'd been at seventeen. But he was proud of the way he'd overcome the obstacles put in his path. He was satisfied with the life he'd built in Chances Inlet. Yet lately he felt like he was standing still.

Of course, the feeling could be traced to his mom's constant nagging about finding a wife. In order to accomplish that, though, he needed to do what his friends suggested: forget about anything more than friendship with Elle.

It wasn't like there weren't plenty of other available women to choose from. Livi had dropped multiple hints this week, letting him know she was interested. From what he'd seen so far, she was kindhearted, hardworking, and very easy on the eyes.

Even Elle had given Livi a ringing endorsement. She seemed to think they'd be perfect together. He ought to be grateful his best friend was looking out for him. Especially since, unlike Elle, Livi made no secret of the fact that she didn't have any strong ties keeping her in New York City.

Tonight, he'd give the decorator his undivided attention. He was sure he'd feel some attraction if he focused on her. He'd just been tuning it out up until now, that was all. His plan made, he stepped into the foyer of the inn.

It was like entering a winter wonderland. Twinkling lights illuminated every corner of the two-story entryway, making it appear welcoming and magical. Handmade magnolia wreaths and garland wrapped with red tartan bows lined the grand staircase, as well as every door in view. He breathed in the scent of fresh pine and cinnamon while taking a long moment to enjoy his surroundings.

"Oh, Hayden, there you are." Elle's mom appeared, the nose on her reindeer sweater lighting up with every step she took. "I was just about to text you."

"Everything okay?"

Did Elle hurt herself again?

"This storm has knocked out the power on Bald Head Island," she said. "The ferry is running a couple of hours behind. Livi isn't sure she'll get back to the inn any time soon, if at all tonight. Lamar just went down to the ferry dock to see what can be done on our side of the channel."

He felt the tension in his shoulders relax, knowing Elle was fine. "Wow. Poor Livi. She was really looking forward to the party tonight." He waved his hand. "Don't worry about her, though. She's traveling with a good group of people. They'll keep her safe."

The silence stretched while Elle's mom took a long moment to scrutinize him.

"Mmm," she eventually responded. She patted him on the arm. "That's good to know. I'm sorry you wasted a trip out here, though."

"It's not a waste." West emerged from the study. "I could use a ride into town."

"I'm happy to give you a ride to the party," Elle's mother offered. "I've just got a few things to get set up for tomorrow's breakfast, then I'll be ready to go. Twenty minutes, tops."

"Thank you," West replied. "But I need to pick up my date. And, as she is living at the deputy's parents' home, it will be easier riding along with him than calling an Uber." The man winked at Elle's mom. "I can't get lost since the deputy presumably knows the way."

Few things ruffled Patricia McAlister-Hollister, but West's announcement caught her off guard. "Oh my. You—you have a date?" she stammered. "With Kitty?"

She wasn't the only one confused.

"You're taking my aunt to the party?"

The pompous ass had the nerve to grin. "At her request, yes."

Elle's mom recovered quickly, accepting the news with a knowing smile. "That's wonderful." She cocked her head slightly to the side. "And it makes a lot of sense. You two have many things in common." She nodded as if granting her approval to the match.

Hayden wasn't feeling that generous. He opened his mouth to tell the man to stay away from his aunt, but the innkeeper beat him to it.

"You're not getting out of going to the party, Hayden. I know Kitty would appreciate it if you gave Mr. West a ride to pick her up." She patted his arm. "He's right. You do know the way."

He bit back a groan. The woman had learned a thing or two about manipulation while raising five strong-willed children.

"Sure," he agreed reluctantly. "Let's go."

"Not without my shadow." West texted something into his phone.

A moment later, Elle descended the stairs, dressed in a gaudy sweater with tinsel garland zigzagging all over it. Her hair curled in soft waves around her shoulders. It looked like she'd taken time with her makeup, too. Hayden was happy to see her walking easily in the boot. She startled briefly when she spied him standing in the foyer.

"Hey," she murmured.

He nodded. "It seems I'm your rideshare driver tonight."

Her eyes went wide. "Where's Livi?"

"Stuck over on the island," her mom said.

Elle backed up a step. "She's not coming?"

West grabbed Elle's raincoat off the coatrack and handed it to her. "They've sent out a search party. I'm sure she'll arrive shortly. She'll be disappointed if you aren't there waiting when she arrives."

"I doubt I'm the one she wants to see waiting for her," Elle mumbled as she shoved her arms into her coat.

Hayden did a double take. Elle almost sounded jealous. Except that wasn't possible. He had to be hearing things. West was saying something about the cocktail contest to Elle's mom. Hayden was pretty sure neither one heard Elle's remark.

"What do you mean by that?" he whispered.

She donned a look of innocence. "I was stating a fact, Hayden. Livi was simply being kind to me when she insisted that I show up tonight. But we both know I'm not the one she wants to hang out with." She patted him on the arm much like her mother had done moments earlier. "In case you weren't listening to me the other day, she's into you."

He ought to be relieved knowing the woman he was thinking about dating was "into" him. Why then was he suddenly pissed off that Elle was acting so cavalier about it? He shouldn't be surprised. She'd been shoving him at Livi since she got home. If he needed any more evidence that their encounter last year hadn't meant anything to her, this was it.

What was good enough for Elle, was good enough for him, then.

"Excellent," he told her. "Because I feel the same way about her."

He charged out into the elements, not bothering to wait for West or Elle.

***

ELLE HAD NEVER WANTED *NOT* to be somewhere as much as she didn't want to be sharing a car with West and Hayden at that moment. West because he was gloating about taking Hayden's aunt out tonight—while *not* writing his damn book. Hayden because she hated the idea of him and Livi together. Added to that was the guilt she felt about being jealous that he might have found someone to share his life with. He was her best friend. Even if he couldn't be happy with her, she should want him to be happy. That was what self-actualized adults were supposed to do.

Obviously, she wasn't a self-actualized adult because a tear leaked out of the corner of her eye as they pulled up in front of Hayden's childhood home. She'd spent so many happy moments here, before everything changed.

The Lovell house was a neat little split-level that backed up onto the Intracoastal Waterway. A perfectly shaped Christmas tree was visible from the wide front window, it's lights glowing like a beacon in the evening storm. Two cars were already tucked beneath the carport decorated with icicle lights, which meant they'd have to walk in the rain to go inside.

Elle had every intention of remaining in the car. Not only because she didn't want to get soaked, but mostly because she had no desire to come face-to-face with Hayden's mother. West upended her plan, however, when he pulled her door open and offered to share one of the inn's big golf umbrellas with her.

Of all the times for him to be nice.

She hobbled to the door, grateful when Hayden's dad opened it as soon as they got to the porch.

"It's a frog drowner out there tonight," Tim Lovell joked once they'd all slipped inside.

He immediately pulled Elle in for a tight hug, not caring that he was soaking himself in the process.

"Where have you been hiding, stranger?" Tim asked.

She was grateful for the rain dampening her cheeks so that she had an excuse for swiping at the tears that threatened. Tim never held the events of Hayden's youth against her. He was fair and kind, attributes he'd passed down to his son. Elle adored him for it.

"Elle's been building a life in New York, Dad," Hayden said. "Putting Chances Inlet in her rearview mirror."

His terseness was so unlike Hayden that it stunned even Tim, judging by his expression.

"Great city," West interjected. "Ten out of ten, as the young folk say."

If Hayden was peeved by West's remark, it didn't show on his face.

Tim shot his son a confused look. "I agree. New York City has a lot going for it." He offered his hand to West. "I'm Tim. It's a pleasure to meet you. I've been a fan for eons."

"Eons sounds about right," West joked. "I'm a dinosaur in this business."

"Are Mom and Aunt Kitty ready?" Hayden asked, obviously eager to hurry this little tête à tête along.

"Oh, you know your mom. She's probably fussing over her hair and her outfit. Go tell her we think she's beautiful just the way she is. She'll listen to you."

Hayden disappeared down the hall.

"Can I ask how long you are in town for, Mr. West?"

West leaned a shoulder against the doorframe. "My stay is open-ended."

Elle bit back a gasp. *It most certainly is not!*

"Does that mean indefinitely?" Tim asked.

No!

West shrugged. Elle almost choked on her tongue.

Tim looked toward the hallway Hayden had just disappeared down. He lowered his voice. "Kitty has been through a lot these past several years."

"She told me," West said. "I'm glad she has someone like you looking out for her. She's safe with me tonight, though. Don't worry. Hayden and his girlfriend here will be chaperoning us the entire time."

What?

Elle spun her head around to glare at West.

Was he drunk?

That could be the only explanation. He knew darn well she wasn't Hayden's girlfriend. Tim's brows shot up as he looked at Elle.

"I'm not Hayden's girlfriend," she said.

"I should hope not," Claire Lovell stated emphatically when she stormed into the room, Kitty and Hayden following.

"Claire!" Tim and Kitty both cried.

Elle dropped her gaze to the floor, wishing it would open to an alternate universe.

"What did you do with Livi?" Claire demanded.

"No one did anything with Livi, Mom. She's stranded on Bald Head Island along with everyone else wanting to take the ferry back tonight."

Hayden's mom made a rumbling sound but remained blessedly silent. So did West for that matter. Elle was sure he was trying to come up with something pithy to pile on with.

"You look lovely tonight, ladies," he said after a long, tense moment had passed. "It will certainly be a pleasure to spend the evening in the company of three such beautiful women."

An arm snaked around her shoulders. Elle risked a glance through her eyelashes. Hayden and Tim were still standing in front of her.

Dear God. Is that West's arm?

"We should probably get going before the weather gets any worse," Kitty suggested.

"Good idea," Elle mumbled as she shrugged off the offending limb.

A cold deluge was better than another second of this.

CHANCES INLET'S only bar was exactly as Everett expected, kitschy and crowded. Portholes had been cut into the steel walls to serve as windows in keeping with the nautical theme. A ship's bell hung at the corner of the long, mahogany bar. In front of the bar was a slew of mismatched captain's chairs lined up beneath a cascade of twinkling green and red lights hanging above. Pink flamingos wearing Santa hats sat proudly in the center of the ferry boat tables. At the back of the long, narrow room were a couple of pool tables, a jukebox blaring "Jingle Bell Rock" and a cardboard fireplace, complete with stockings.

He'd been avoiding the place since arriving in town. Mainly because he found that most barkeeps preferred customers to order multiple drinks rather than sit like a barfly and nurse the same one all day long. However, from the looks of this place, he could get away with that if he wanted. It seemed Chances Inlet had different rules than the rest of the world. A guy could get used to that.

Jolene, the bar's owner and head bartender, gave him a friendly smile when she handed over Kitty's wine and Everett's whiskey. Kitty found a two-seater high-top in the corner, affording them a great view of the dance floor and the door at the same time.

"Is it okay if it's just us for a bit?" she asked. "Hayden and Elle don't seem interested in sitting with us. Not that I blame them."

"They don't seem interested in sitting with each other, either," Everett remarked. He glanced at Hayden at the dartboard, a group of men and women from the sheriff's office cheering him on in his game. Elle was quickly swallowed up by a crowd of younger couples comprised of her family and their friends as soon as she walked in.

"Yeah." Kitty sipped her wine. "Claire doesn't make it easy on them."

Everett spun his glass around, watching the ice cubes clink together. "What was all that about back there?"

Kitty sighed. "It's a long, sordid tale."

"Forget I asked." He waved his hand. "You don't have to share private family stories with me."

She laughed. "Don't you know? There is no privacy in a small town. Everyone knows everyone else's business, whether you want them to or not. You'll get a less biased version if you hear it from me." She traced a finger along the stem of her glass, seeming to gather her thoughts. "Elle and Hayden have been best friends since—I don't even know. Forever. They dated different people in high school, but she was the prom queen, and he was the prom king."

A server came by and placed some scorecards and a pen on the table. "For the contest later."

Kitty waited until the other woman moved on before continuing.

"It was the prom after-parties that set things in motion. Hayden was at one with his date when he heard that there might be trouble at the one Elle was at with her date. Of course, he had to go charging over there to her rescue."

"That explains the Turkey Trot," he commented. "Old habits die hard."

She nodded. "He took two of his buddies with him. The other party was crowded with kids from multiple high schools standing out on the lawn." Kitty blew out a breath. "Of course a fight broke out."

Everett's gut told him he wouldn't like where this story was headed.

Kitty leaned back in her chair with her face drawn. "One thing led to another, and a few candles got knocked over. A fire started. It destroyed half the family's home before it was extinguished."

"Shit." Everett dragged his fingers through his hair.

"Luckily, no one was injured badly. But the family who lost their house wanted someone to blame. Hayden was charged with a felony destruction of property because he threw the first punch. The arrest meant he lost a promising track scholarship to Wake Forest.

"Elle's late father, Donald, was very influential in the county. Since Hayden was a few days shy of his eighteenth birthday when the incident happened, Donald managed to arrange a plea whereby if Hayden went into the Army, his record would be expunged upon completion of his tour. Afterward, he could go to Wake and resume his life as planned."

Everett's stomach dropped. "But he lost his leg while he was in Afghanistan."

"And Claire has never stopped blaming Elle for ruining his life."

"That's not fair," he argued.

"No. It's not. But I'm not a mother. I'm told they can assume all kinds of crazy personalities when it comes to their kids."

Curiosity got the better of him. "Did you ever want them? Kids?"

Kitty shrugged. "My husband was one of those tortured

artists who wasn't very good at taking care of himself. Theo wouldn't have been much help in the child-rearing area. And, well, I already had him to take care of." She looked over at where Hayden was finishing his game of darts. "I've enjoyed watching Hayden and his sister grow up. As long as I have them in my life, it will be enough."

He reached across the table and covered her hand with his. "They are lucky to have you, too."

Gidget is lucky to have Hayden in hers, as well.

CHAPTER EIGHT

"I TOLD you that sweater would look fantastic on you." Tatum's smile was smug. "I'm gifting it to you as a thank-you for helping me with my social media ads today."

"Wait, what?" Ginger nearly spilled her espresso martini. "You're helping Tatum with her social media? Can you help me, too? The studio could use a boost. Ever since the local paper shut down, we get no coverage about our recitals, much less our class offerings. I'll be lucky if anyone but family shows up for *The Nutcracker* later this month."

"Of course," Elle replied offhandedly. She was resisting the urge to suck down her Long Island iced tea. Given how this evening had been going, she'd be justified in getting a good drunk on.

She'd be damned if she lost her head over a stupid guy again, though. Hayden's mother, well, that was another story. Except even Claire Lovell wasn't worth the pain that would follow.

Elle tracked Hayden as he moved toward one of the pool tables. Her stomach clenched as she recalled his earlier comments. What had she done to make him so angry with her about living in New York? Or was it simply that he was mad about dropping out of the Turkey Trot? Because that was his choice. She hadn't encouraged his white knight act the other day. And he was being a little childish if that was what had him acting like a jerk. Now Elle was angry because, really, she hadn't done anything to warrant his surly attitude. She might have been the catalyst for his life getting derailed ten years ago, but she was tired of shouldering the blame for everything else.

Hayden handed off his pool cue and headed to the back of the bar. Out of the corner of her eye, Elle saw Bernice winding her way purposely through the crowd, headed straight for her. Word had probably already spread about the help she was giving Tatum. Bernice likely wanted to get in on the action, too.

Elle set her drink on the table and slipped past Ginger. "I'll be right back," she said to no one in particular.

She headed away from Bernice, moving toward the restrooms at the back of the bar. It took her a hot minute to navigate through the crowd. She arrived just as Hayden was coming out of the men's room. Elle barely stopped herself before she plowed into his chest. The peeved expression he wore when he saw her was her undoing.

"We need to talk," she said as she wrapped her fingers around his arm and tugged him into the storage closet.

"What the hell is going on with you?" he demanded when she closed the door behind them.

"That's exactly what I'm wondering about you?"

There wasn't much room to maneuver in the tight space. With barely a foot between them, his scent was everywhere, soapy and fresh. And, dear God, was he wearing cologne? She couldn't quite place the fragrance, but it suited him perfectly.

"Nothing is going on with me. Except for my date could be arriving any time now while I'm back here arguing with you about who knows what."

Livi. She'd forgotten all about Livi. Was he disappointed that the evening wasn't going the way he'd planned? Or was he worried about her safety? Of course, he was. His reaction was the same the other day when she got injured. She'd been thinking his over-the-top response was for her. But he would have behaved that way for anyone who needed help. That was who Hayden was. His foul mood had nothing to do with Elle.

She mentally smacked herself. "I'm sorry. I just had the impression you were angry with me about something. It makes sense that you're stressing about Livi."

He closed his eyes and heaved a sigh. "I'm sorry about the way my mom treats you, Elle. She has no right to blame you for everything." He lifted his lids. "I'm not angry with you. For anything."

Elle heard the inflection he put on the word "you." It should have doused her fears. Only it didn't.

"But you are angry."

"I believe I just explained why I'm stressed out tonight. Making matters worse, West is sitting out there on a date with my aunt."

She studied his face. The square jaw and straight nose were so familiar. The closed-off expression in his blue eyes was not. And she didn't dare even let her gaze land on his full lips. Lips she now knew from her embarrassing episode were firm and quite intoxicating. She shook her head slightly, attempting to refocus her thoughts.

"Yeah. Weird," she said.

"Are we good here? Because . . ." He gestured with his thumb at the door.

"Sure."

He turned to leave without even giving her so much as a smile. And that seemed to detonate something inside her. Elle wasn't good. She wasn't good at all.

"Why did you disappear the other day? When you took me to the ER?"

He froze with his back to her, his hand on the doorknob. "Can you just let that go? It didn't mean anything."

"Seriously? You made a whole scene. Dropping out of the race. Rushing me to the ER as if my life depended on it. And then, boom, you ghost me. That didn't *mean* anything?"

Hayden turned back around to face her. "Yes, Elle. It didn't mean anything. Just forget it ever happened."

"Like you forgot about me kissing you?"

Oh, hell. Why was she bringing that back up again? She should be grateful he didn't want to make a big deal about the way she'd thrown herself at him that night. Why couldn't she just forget it like he asked?

Because it stings that he could just "forget it."

"I mean, was it that bad?" she babbled on, her brain clearly on a suicide mission. "I haven't had any complaints before."

He was so still that she wasn't sure he was breathing. "You don't want to have this conversation, Elle." The words were spoken so quietly, she almost didn't hear them over the noise from the party going on right outside the door.

You're right. I don't, her brain cried.

Too bad her heart was driving the crazy bus right now.

She jerked her chin up, willing it not to tremble. "Clearly, I'm doing something wrong if men forget me so easily."

"Don't you dare lump me in with that asshole, Jeremy," he growled.

"It's kind of hard not to when you both rejected me." She hated the hiccup in her voice.

"Dammit, Elle." He closed the distance between them, his body pressing hers against the wall. Her nerve endings sizzled to life at the contact. She'd known this man for decades. How had she not realized the exquisite pleasure his muscled body was capable of? He reached up and trailed a finger along her cheek. "You don't know what you're saying."

He was right. She didn't know anything right now. The only thought in her head was that he must keep touching her.

Everywhere.

"Hayden?"

Her whispered plea got his attention. "Mm-hmm."

An instant later, his lips crashed down on hers. She was pleased to discover she hadn't imagined how full and firm they were. When she'd let herself go back to the memories of that night, she'd always remembered his kiss had been the type to make her stomach drop—as though she'd just gone over the first hill of a roller coaster.

This one was no different.

Best of all, Hayden wasn't kissing her like a man repulsed. Nope. His lips were greedy and demanding as they feasted on her mouth. It was almost as though if he didn't kiss her, he might expire on the spot.

She could relate to that feeling.

He let out a satisfied groan as he threaded his fingers into her hair, angling her head for better access. Elle dug her fingers into his shoulders to keep from falling, her knees were suddenly wobbly. A sigh escaped the back of her throat, giving Hayden all the opening he needed. His tongue slipped between her parted lips, sliding against hers seductively.

Elle was nearly overcome at the rush of need that buzzed through her body. She skimmed her palms along the back of his neck, desperate to keep their mouths fused together. Even though other parts of her began to ache for his attention.

When Hayden tore his mouth away and stared down at her, he looked as confused as she felt. "Elle."

Her name sounded like a confession coming from his lips. She didn't want to hear what came next. All she wanted tonight was to feel. So she stretched up on her toes and pressed her lips to his once again.

She felt more than heard the low rumble deep in his chest. His hands left her hair to explore the curves of her hips. He eased one hand beneath the hem of her sweater. The heat of his touch had her gasping into his mouth. His other hand cupped her ass, lifting her body against the hard length of his erection. She nearly lost herself then and there.

When he broke off the kiss this time, he swore violently. Elle struggled to regulate her breathing while he took a giant step away from her. She immediately felt the cold in the unheated room. Her stomach clenched at the look of raw anguish she saw on his face.

Hayden shook his head, and her heart sank. *No!*

"We can't do this anymore, Elinor."

He was out the door without another word.

"IT LIVES," West said when Elle sneaked into the kitchen to forage through the brunch leftovers the following afternoon.

The irritating man had taken over the round kitchen table with his laptop and an assortment of notebooks spread all over it.

"My mom has a perfectly good study she designated for your use," she grumbled as she filled the tea kettle at the sink.

"I'd make a comment about you not being a morning person, but it's already afternoon," he quipped.

The kettle clanged against the gas stove's burner when she set it down. Elle would not let this man shame her for having a pity party alone in her suite last night. One that had lasted well into today, it seemed. Her emotional well was totally depleted after pretending for the rest of the party that everything was fine. That she was fine. The pretense was difficult to maintain in front of her family and a town full of people who'd known her all her life. It helped that Hayden had vanished from the bar.

Hayden kissed me.

Her hand shook as she fished through the tea tin for a bag of chamomile. He'd kissed her, and it changed *everything.* How could she go on simply being "just friends" with Hayden now that she knew what it felt like to have his tongue tangled with hers? Or his bare hands sliding along her skin? Or his hard length pressed against her?

He'd wanted her last night. There was no mistaking that. And then he'd left her.

We can't do this anymore, Elinor.

His words had been like water dousing a flame.

What did they even mean?

Had he left the party to "forget about it" just like he claimed he'd done after last New Year's?

How did someone even do that?

"A woman named Bernice was here looking for you," West announced, cutting into her thoughts.

Elle froze as she reached for a mug. "She isn't here now, is she?"

Bernice was camped outside the storage room when Elle emerged last night. It had been a good fifteen minutes after Hayden had stormed out. Fifteen minutes where Elle had been too numb to react. Luckily, she was able to stave off the waterworks until she got back to the inn.

But Bernice always saw too much. And even when she didn't see things with her own eyes, she was quick to surmise the basics of the story, which she then would spread around Chances Inlet as gospel. The little devil had coaxed a deal out of Elle last night. She'd keep her mouth shut as long as Elle helped out with the social media for the entire town.

"She left about an hour ago. But not before delivering strict instructions for you to report to the mayor's office at nine tomorrow morning. Sharp."

"Fabulous." Elle pulled the whistling kettle from the stove and poured the hot water into her mug.

"Does Helen know you're moonlighting while on assignment here?"

Elle aimed a glare at the man. "It's only moonlighting if I get paid. And the only thing Helen cares about is you finishing your book." She sat down at the table. "I'm supposed to give her a status update this week. Can I tell her you're almost done?"

"Tell her whatever you want," he replied.

She fingered one of the notebooks before West slapped his hand down on top of it. "At least you're working on it, right?" she asked.

Please say yes!

Something about West's expression made her suspicious. She reached for his laptop and turned the screen to see it.

"Oh. My. God! You're designing gingerbread houses?"

"I told you I intend to make a good showing."

Elle dropped her forehead to the table. "Do you realize that if you stopped dilly-dallying and put more effort into writing, you'd be finished by now?"

"Do you realize my dilly-dallying gets you more time in Chances Inlet with your family?"

"Maybe I don't want to spend the entire season stuck here!"

She quickly glanced around the kitchen making sure no one witnessed her outburst. The last thing she wanted was to hurt anyone's feelings. They'd never understood her need to keep up with the Fab Four.

West contemplated her over his steepled fingers. "Maybe you just want to avoid a certain deputy sheriff?"

Elle could actually feel the blood draining from her face. What did this man know about her and Hayden? More importantly, how did he know?

Damn Bernice.

It didn't matter. She was tired of West and his insolent attitude. The only thing that mattered was him meeting his deadline and her getting the career opportunity she needed to hold her head up among this family.

"Helen didn't send you here to psychoanalyze me any more than she expects you to build gingerbread houses. Or wear ugly sweaters. Or to swipe right," she told him. "You're here to finish the book you've already been paid a crap-ton of money to write. So please, do us both a favor and open that file and make the magic happen."

His patented arrogant look remained in place. "'Make the magic happen.' As in, wave my magic wand and the words will appear?"

She took a sip of her tea to keep from screaming.

"Have you written a book before, Gidget?"

Why must he call her that?

"No, I have not. But it can't be that difficult when you already know how the story goes. You lived that ending. Just write it."

Something shifted in his expression. It grew darker. His lips formed a grim line. West gathered his notebooks and shoved them into his backpack before slamming his laptop closed.

"You're exactly right. I do know how it goes." He slung the backpack over his shoulder and stood with such force that the table teetered. "In fact, I get to relive it every night. In vivid detail."

Guilt washed over her as he stormed out the back door. What was it Kate had said the other day?

You both have the same telltale battle scars.

No telling what the correspondent had experienced during his months embedded with troops. Or simply witnessing conflict. None of it could have been pretty. Was that what was keeping him from finishing the book? Trauma?

She dropped her forehead to the table again. Badgering a man who was wracked with pain wouldn't get them anywhere, especially since Elle was now consumed with guilt. West could be annoying, sure. And she would only get the job she coveted if he finished his memoir on time. But did the end justify the means? The last thing she ever wanted to do was cause anyone more discomfort when they were already hurting.

"That bad, huh?"

Lamar's voice had her snapping her head back up. She sighed.

"Why does life have to be so complicated?" she asked.

The irony wasn't lost on her that she'd asked her father the very same question the other day. Hopefully, her stepfather would be a little more forthcoming than a dead man.

"I'm guessing that if I said 'that's what makes it fun,' it wouldn't help."

Elle shot him a look. Lamar chuckled as he sat down in the chair West had vacated.

"West giving you trouble?" he asked.

"What was your first clue?"

"He was stomping down the driveway as if he were trying to make wine from the gravel. My guess is he doesn't appreciate your doggedness at keeping him on task." He reached over and patted her hand. "Don't let him get to you. And try not to take it personally. You're simply doing the job that was asked of you."

She sighed. "Except I think I might have become a little too sharp of a thorn in his side." A thought popped into her head. "Does your veteran's group take walk-ins?"

Lamar leaned back in his chair. "Hold on there, Elle. West hasn't made many friends among veterans with some of the things he's written in his book."

"Yeah. Hayden mentioned that. But I think he's hurting, too. I suspect the things he saw have affected him the same way it has you all. Maybe talking about it would help. I know I'm grasping at straws here. Anything to get him to finish the book. Except if it is trauma holding him back . . ." She shrugged.

Lamar studied her for a long moment. His smile was filled with wonder as he shook his head. "You are your mother's daughter. There's not an injured creature out there that you two don't want to rescue."

He was referring to a young teen in town her mom had fostered. Cassidy was in Scotland for the year, studying literature at St. Andrews, thanks to a generous grant from the good people of Chances Inlet. Elle's sister-in-law, Lori had also spent some time under her mom's protective wing. Until Miles stepped in to take over the job.

She toyed with her mug. "Of course, there's no guarantee West even wants any help."

"Mmm." Lamar got to his feet. "That's possible. But for you, I'll make the effort." He leaned down and kissed the top of her head. "It's not what you become in life. It's who you are at your core. And you, Elinor McAlister, are one of the all-time good ones. Don't you ever forget it."

"My dad used to say something like that," she said around the boulder in her throat.

"Your dad was a wise man."

Lamar was nearly out the door when she called after him.

"Is Hayden on duty today?"

She wasn't sure why she asked. It wasn't like she had the emotional bandwidth to face him today. *Or ever.* Except he'd disappeared again last night without a word to anyone. It was the second time he'd done that this week. She couldn't help but worry about him.

"Nope. He came by earlier to pick up some of Livi's things. The ferry is back up, and they are spending the day on Bald Head."

Well.

Elle tried to ignore the sinking feeling in her belly. Was that what Hayden meant? They couldn't "do this anymore" because he was with Livi? She groaned softly as she buried her face in her hands. Was he kissing Livi with the same ruthless passion he'd shown her last night? Her stomach seemed to close in on itself at the very idea.

She had no one to blame but herself. The heartache she was feeling was all her fault. After all, she'd pushed him toward Livi, believing they would be a good match. Only she wasn't feeling so magnanimous now. And it sucked.

CHAPTER NINE

THE WHALE of a Tale bookstore was blessedly quiet several mornings later. The shop's owner, Paige, didn't seem to mind her lack of customers. She offered Everett a wide smile from where she sat at the counter writing Christmas cards. He nodded his greeting as he made his way to the back of the store.

He pulled up short when he saw Kitty sitting in his usual chair. A couple of to-go cups from the Java Jolt sat on the table in front of her. Guilt licked at his gut. He'd been ignoring the woman since the party the other night. It wasn't because he hadn't enjoyed their date immensely. He had. And he was pretty sure she did, too. But his argument with Gidget had dredged up the memories of the last days of his late wife's life. It was insane, but he felt unfaithful to Keeley when even looking at Kitty.

Except looking at Kitty made him feel lighter. More in the moment. *Whole.*

"I brought you a coffee. Lois claimed she fixed it just the way you like it," she said.

No interrogation about why he hadn't contacted her. No tantrum. No artifice at all. The woman was a gem. Not only that but, she'd also brought coffee.

He let his messenger bag slide down his arm before placing it on an empty chair. Then he walked over to where she sat and stood over her. Kitty had to crane her neck to look at him. Without bothering to ask permission, he leaned down and gently pressed his lips to hers.

"What was that for?" she murmured.

"For the coffee." He kissed her again. "For being kind." His lips touched hers once more. "Most of all, for being patient with me."

"You haven't even tried the coffee." Her joke came out sounding a little breathless.

Everett liked that he'd flustered her. He also liked the taste of her lips. He liked that a lot.

"I'm sure it's perfect." *Just like you.*

Her shy grin was glorious. And it touched parts of him that hadn't been awake for a long time.

"Do you have plans for today?" he asked impulsively. His desire to spend the day with her made him sound a tad desperate.

Kitty shook her head. "It's my day off. I don't have much planned other than laundry."

"What do you say we play hooky together? We can go explore the turtle sanctuary. Walk along the beach. Climb to the top of the lighthouse."

She laughed. "Well, I do want to pick up some lighthouse ornaments at the gift shop."

He bit back the cry of jubilation that made its way up into his throat. "Perfect," he said instead.

Everett reached down and took her hand. He gently tugged her up until they were nearly nose to nose.

"I can't think of a better way to spend the day than with you," she whispered before kissing him softly.

His belly did a flip flop. "Me neither."

He grabbed his messenger bag and one of the coffees while she picked up the other. They were almost to the front of the shop when the sheriff walked in.

"Morning, beautiful," Lamar called as he swiped off his hat.

"Hi, Dad." Paige embraced her father. "What's up?"

The sheriff pulled a leaflet from an envelope he was carrying. "I was wondering if you could display this in your window."

"Of course I will." Paige took the piece of paper from her father, grabbed a roll of tape and immediately hung it beside the door. "Tanner and I already bought a pile of toys to donate."

"So did I," Kitty added. "Hayden mentioned you might want some stockings this year, too."

"That would be wonderful," the sheriff replied. "Thank you."

"The town is having a toy drive?" Everett asked.

"It's sponsored by our veteran's group, actually," the sheriff explained. "We are small but mighty. Xander Fisk over at the gym organizes our meetings. You should stop by. We welcome anyone who's been touched by combat."

Something ugly shot through Everett at the sheriff's invitation. A cocktail crafted from guilt, anger and fear. Dammit, he'd been trying to outrun the memories ever since his confrontation with Gidget the other day. Now, his heart was racing again, and beads of sweat began to break out on the back of his neck.

Kitty, God bless her, seemed to sense his unease. She threaded her fingers with his and gave his hand a gentle squeeze. The gesture grounded him immediately, and his breath came more easily once again.

"We'll pick up some toys today. Do they need to be wrapped?" he asked.

"We host a big party at Knotical where we wrap the gifts," Kitty explained.

He beamed at her. "That sounds like fun. Count me in." He turned back to the sheriff and his daughter. "Looks like we're off to do some Christmas shopping," he said, leaving the sheriff's offer to get chummy with the town's veterans unanswered.

"Yes, Madelaine, West is pounding away at the keyboard," Elle lied to her boss for the second time this week. "He hasn't given me an end date, but I'm sure it will be well before the end of the year."

Her skin began to tingle where the hives were no doubt about to break out. She hadn't lied this much since middle school when she would do and say anything to get out of gym class.

"That's wonderful," Madelaine replied, sounding as if Elle had just told her Santa Claus was real. "We knew you could do it. Now everyone will be able to relax and enjoy the holiday season."

Everyone but me.

She had no idea if West would write another word in his book. The two had been avoiding one another for the past week. According to Paige, he spent a lot of time working at the bookstore. Although what the man was "working" on was a mystery. He had less than four weeks to finish.

If he didn't, Elle could kiss her promotion goodbye. She'd be lucky to even have a job to go back to. And wouldn't that just be a big lump of coal in her stocking? Not only would she be the most *unsuccessful* McAlister, but she'd also be unemployed. No job and no best friend to speak of.

She glanced through the blinds of the mayor's office. The sheriff's department was catty-corner across the town square. She'd spent countless hours pretending to work—*West wasn't the only one who got to goof off*—while watching for any sign of Hayden. Apparently, the man had engineered some sort of invisible cloaking device because he was nowhere to be found.

Livi was gone, too. She was in Atlanta for a few days to sample upholstery. Had Hayden gone with her? The misery that came with that thought made her chest ache.

"And thank you for keeping up with the online teasers." Madelaine interrupted her spiraling thoughts, thankfully. "Your enterprising attitude is an asset to the magazine."

As if she had a choice. Still, she was glad to have something to occupy her time this week. Besides the clickbait social media pieces for *Vantage*, she'd been busy helping Bernice with Chances Inlet's social media. Once word got out that Elle was giving away free advice, every small business in town had formed a line out of the door of city hall seeking her help.

"You're right. This town does need a newspaper," she said once she finished several posts for the Bed and Biscuit kennel and groomers.

Bernice scoffed. "They say newspapers are dead. Folks want to hold the headlines in their hand."

Elle grinned. "You should have gone into advertising. That's a killer slogan."

The older woman harumphed. "We need to do something. We had a great crowd over the holidays last year. But even your mom is complaining that occupancy is down."

There had been fewer guests at the inn this week, she'd noticed. Elle was grateful for the privacy. But now she worried how this economic downturn might affect her mother's business.

"The mayor says there is no money in the budget for a new website," Bernice continued. "And none of those advertising magazines want to set up shop here. We are not 'densely populated enough.'"

Elle scrolled through the town's website. It wasn't flashy, but it did the trick. All it needed was some updated photos. And a killer story to pull people in.

A knock on the window startled her. She looked up to see her brother, Ryan with his nose pressed against the glass, wearing a goofy smile on his face. Except Elle was more captivated by the other nose pressed up to the glass. The answer to Bernice's prayers was in her brother's arms, wagging his tail.

"Bernice, do you still have that elf costume?"

HAYDEN YANKED open the door to his workshop, not bothering to hide his annoyance. As usual, Simone wasn't picking up the vibes he was putting down.

"Ooo, Lawd! You look like you've been through the wringer." She plowed past him inside.

Xander followed her. "What she said."

Simone tossed Hayden his T-shirt. "Your body is glistening like the cover of one of my grammy's old romance books." She fanned herself. "We are getting calls down at the station of women getting whiplash as they walk by."

Hayden rolled his eyes. He was covered in sawdust. Not to mention sticky from the machines in the tiny room that ran hot no matter what the temperature was outside. He pulled on the shirt anyway.

"There. Happy now?" He walked back over to the table legs he was carving with the wood lathe.

"You're right, Simone. The situation is worse than we thought," Xander fake whispered.

"For crying out loud. Can't you both see I have work to do?" Hayden snapped.

A tense silence settled over the workshop, making the hum of the lathe sound like a jumbo jet. Hayden dragged his fingers through his hair. He had no right speaking to his friends that way. It wasn't their fault his life was effed up.

"Sorry. That was uncalled for." He blew out a breath.

"Are you okay?" Simone asked, her tone more subdued now. "You never miss work."

"I had some PTO I needed to take, or I'd lose it."

Xander nodded. "I haven't seen you at the gym all week, though. And you missed a meeting."

Hayden gestured to the parts of the table he was building. "I took the PTO to finish a project."

It was a lie. And judging by the looks on his friends' faces, they knew it, too.

Simone pulled a wrapped sandwich from the Fog Horn Deli bag she was carrying. "We thought you might want lunch." She glanced around the room for a spot to put it that wasn't covered with sawdust.

"Here." Xander indicated a stool near the window where he set a drink down. "We'll let you get back to it," he said. "You know where to find us if you need us."

Hayden suddenly felt like the biggest dick alive. These two people had helped him through some of his darkest days, the trio bonding over their shared horrors of combat. Slogging through the healing process together. And now, when they were only trying to be kind, he was treating them like crap.

"I kissed Elle," he blurted out when Simone and Xander got near the door.

Xander whistled as he spun around, his brows hiked to his hairline. Simone turned more slowly. Her eyes were wide as saucers. She opened and closed her lips several times without emitting any sound. It cost her to keep her comments to herself, but she managed it. His friends stared at him wordlessly until Hayden picked up his drink and took a long pull from the straw.

"*Annnd?*" Simone demanded when he finished.

Hayden shrugged.

"Oh, no." Evidently, she couldn't keep her opinions in check for more than thirty seconds. To be fair, it was thirty seconds longer than Hayden expected of her.

She charged across the room. "You don't get to spring something like that on us without elaborating further. I need context. I need details. I need *all. Of. It.*"

Xander made a beeline for the small mini fridge in the corner. "Hell, I probably need a beer for this."

Sighing heavily, Hayden dropped onto one of the chairs he'd built yesterday. Simone found a rag and swept off the sawdust from the small table Elle had ogled the week before. Xander moved to put his beer down on top of it. Hayden let out a hiss. His friend jerked the can back.

"Have a care, man." Hayden slapped a piece of cardboard onto the table. He motioned for Xander to put his beer on top of it.

Simone dug the rest of the sandwiches from the bag and handed one to Xander. She grabbed Hayden's just as he reached for it.

"No eating until you spill the tea," she ordered. "One of us has to work today, and I only have twenty-eight minutes before I clock back in."

"I don't know what else you want me to say." Probably because he was as stunned and confused by the situation as his friends. He was supposed to be opening himself up to new possibilities. Instead, he'd kissed Elle. And it had been just as arousing as he remembered.

"You finally kissed your best friend since kindergarten. How about starting with how it came about," Xander suggested.

"It wasn't the first time we kissed," he admitted.

Simone choked on her sandwich. Xander patted her on the back until she recovered.

"Are you kidding me?" she wheezed. "And you are just telling us this *now*?"

"Seriously, dude. That would explain a few things," Xander added.

Simone shot the gym owner a bug-eyed look.

"What?" Xander said. "Am I the only one who's noticed they haven't been text buddies for the past year? Or that the few times she's come back to town, they've been awkward around each other?"

Simone slowly pivoted her gaze back to Hayden, her eyes narrowed to slits. "Now that you mention it . . ."

Hayden took another drink. "It was last New Year's. Everyone was in town because her brothers Miles and Gavin were marrying their brides in a double wedding. The week before, Elle caught her boyfriend cheating on her."

"Whoa," Xander said.

"Yeah. She didn't take it well. Even worse, she didn't want her family to know. Something about it spoiling the big day."

"Mmm," Simone said. "That sounds like Elle."

"Yeah, well not her best plan. The wedding festivities and all the associated hoopla was like rubbing salt in an open wound. She decided to self-medicate with booze."

"As one does in that situation," Xander interjected.

Hayden shot him a look. "I was on duty that night so the sheriff could enjoy the party with his new family. When I stopped by the reception to check on her, she took one look at me and started crying."

"As one does in that situation," Simone echoed.

"She begged me to get her out of there so her family wouldn't see her," Hayden continued. "I took her to my place in hopes of sobering her up before she went back to the inn."

Not his best idea.

"She was talking nonsense about not being good enough. About not being desirable. I simply meant to comfort her when I hugged her." He groaned. "She got the wrong idea and started kissing me."

For as long as he'd known Elle, he'd never looked at her in a romantic way. At least not consciously. Once her lips landed on his, however, he was a goner. Elle was no longer his "buddy" of twenty-something years, the person who knew all his secrets. She was a living breathing sensual woman who had the power to drive his body wild.

"Holy moly. And you kissed her back." Xander sounded disap-pointed.

"Are you kidding? She was drunk. No way was I going to take advantage of her like that."

He was a liar.

Given the situation, Hayden might have lingered a bit longer than was appropriate. He blamed the shock of the kiss for his hesitance to end it. His friends didn't need to know that, though.

Simone breathed a sigh that sounded like relief. "On behalf of women everywhere, thank you."

"But you liked the kiss, right?" Xander demanded.

Hell, yeah!

"That has no bearing on the situation," he replied instead.

Simone snorted. "It does if you felt something for her. She's your best friend, Hayden. And who knows? She might be more than that. Yet instead of resolving whatever this is between you guys, you avoided discussing it when she was sober. Dude, you dodged the subject for an entire *year.*"

"You said it yourself," he argued. "She's my best friend. I didn't want to jeopardize that."

"I call bull. You are too chickenshit to talk with her about your feelings is more like it," Simone muttered. "What happened after the kiss?"

"She cried herself to sleep at my place."

He got up and walked over to the window. Seeming to detect his uneasiness, Beula jumped up on the sill and nudged her head beneath his hands. Hayden absently stroked the cat's soft fur as the memories flooded back.

His months in rehab weren't as torturous as that night had been. Getting her away from the reception so she wouldn't embarrass herself in front of her family was his singular thought at the time. Taking her to his place was only natural. They hung out there whenever she was in town.

As soon as they arrived, he'd headed to the kitchen to get her some water and a packet of liquid IV. When he returned to the living room, Elle was shimmying out of her velvet bridesmaid dress, leaving her wearing only a push-up bra and thong panties. Simply recalling the vision of her miles and miles of flawless skin begging to be touched had him semi-aroused again.

Somehow, he managed to grab a T-shirt from his gym bag he'd left by the door and tossed it to her. She struggled to get it over her elaborate updo. Of course, she giggled before nearly toppling over. He reluctantly reached in to help her. They both froze when skin met skin.

Then the waterworks started again. Hayden had never wanted to physically hurt someone as badly as he wanted to punish Jeremy Keneally. The bastard made Elle feel less than, and Hayden hated him for it. Wrapping his arms around her to offer her comfort had been automatic. Brotherly almost.

That was until her lips found his.

Nothing was tentative or shy about the way she kissed him, either. She was demanding and needy, as if her life depended on their bodies being melded together. And Hayden, being a red-blooded male, was all in for it.

Her floral scent wafted over him, wrapping him in a sensuous fog. He allowed himself to savor her sweet taste. As ashamed as he was by his body's immediate and intense reaction to her, he conceded that he'd be a fool not to spend a minute sampling what she was offering.

Until his conscience began to bellow at him. When he finally dug up the strength of will to tear his lips from hers, he forced himself to take a giant step back. And then another one.

Shit, he'd whispered.

It was the wrong thing to say. Her face contorted into a mask of pain. Then, she hightailed it into his bedroom and slammed the door.

He didn't want to leave things like that. His body screamed at him to go beg her to forgive him. Only he knew where they'd end up if he did. Lucky for him, gallantry, steel will and common sense won out. He retreated to the lumpy sofa in his workshop, staring at the ceiling as he tried to sleep.

"The next day, she jetted back to New York without a word.

As Xander has so astutely pointed out, we've barely spoken since."

Simone shook her head. "Mm, mm, mm."

Xander held his hands up. "That explains the yearlong tiff. But how do you explain kissing her now?"

Hayden dragged his hands through his hair again. "Elle called me out. She reacted exactly as Simone predicted she would."

No surprise, Simone donned a smug smile. "You don't say."

"She essentially baited me into kissing her." Not that it took much coaxing. A stronger man would have made tracks out of that storage room before he made a fool of himself.

"Annnd?"

"And it was fucking amazing, okay? Are you satisfied?" He shouted so loudly the windows rattled.

His friends looked at him like he was certifiable.

Simone blinked a few times before speaking. "Okaaay, and you're holing yourself up in your workshop because . . .?"

Because Elle is my person. And I can't risk losing her if this doesn't work out.

And it wasn't going to work out. Elle's ultimate goal was to be worthy of the McAlister name. And he was fairly certain that meant pursuing what *Vantage* offered her.

He decided right then and there that he was done holding it against her. Despite her mixed signals the other night, he knew her better than anyone else. And that meant he knew what she would choose: friendship over something more. Hayden would have to be satisfied with that.

"Because that kiss won't lead to anything," he explained.

Simone looked over at Xander, who wore an equally bewildered look. "What am I missing here?"

"My guess is because Elle's life is in New York," Xander surmised.

Hayden touched his finger to his nose.

"So? Change her mind." Simone made it sound so easy.

He chuckled to himself. "Elle is a McAlister. McAlisters do big things. She doesn't want to be left out of that legacy. That will always be more important than her and me. We are better off as friends."

"Says you!" Simone shouted. "That is the dumbest thing I've ever heard."

Hayden sighed. "Just because there's a spark doesn't mean there will be a happily ever after, Simone. Chances Inlet is my home. Elle is set on making New York—or anywhere else—hers. End of story."

The room was quiet once again. None of them bothered to bring up the option of him following Elle. They all knew that wouldn't happen.

"So, what happens now?" Xander asked.

"I eat the sandwich my partner is holding captive, and I finish making this table," Hayden said with more confidence than he'd felt in the past few days. "Tomorrow, I go back to work." He reached down and squeezed Simone's shoulder. "Elle will be back chasing her dream in New York soon. As she should. She deserves it." He sighed. "If we pursue whatever this is, it will only mess up our friendship. And that's too important to me to blow up."

"Really?" Her eyes were wary. "That's your plan?"

He nodded. "I'm finally listening to you both. I'm keeping Elle in the friend zone where she belongs. And I'm making myself available for other relationships."

"Promise?" Simone asked.

Hayden gave her shoulder a gentle squeeze as his answer. Xander toasted him with his beer. Simone placed her hand over Hayden's. He was grateful for these friends in his life. His and Elle's paths may keep them apart, but he wouldn't be alone.

CHAPTER TEN

"You are a genius, Elinor McAlister." Bernice slid her arm through Elle's as they strolled down Water Street toward the city pier the following evening. "Who says lightning doesn't strike twice? That little dog, Kringle, brought the national spotlight to our town last year. And he did it again tonight."

"Give credit where credit is due, Bernice," Paige chimed in from Elle's other side. "Elle wrote the article. You have a gift, Elle. Who knew an interview with Santa's dog would bring in so many people for the tree lighting tonight."

"Just imagine what the turnout would be if the weather had cooperated. Brrr." Bernice shivered.

Paige laughed. "This is spring in Chicago."

Elle barely noticed the cold. She was basking in the glory of a job well done. Her "interview" with a dog might not be the weighty journalism she hoped to write in the future, but it did the trick of driving traffic to Chances Inlet's website. The businesses in town were happy. And that made Elle happy.

She doubted tonight's crowd was a direct result—the vlog had only appeared online two days ago. Still, the inn received three last minute reservations this afternoon, all for the upcoming weekend. That had to mean something.

"I was in Chicago last year when the story about Ryan rescuing Kringle hit. The video of that sweet pup jumping onto Santa's lap during the parade is so precious. And then Santa gave him to Henry for Christmas." Paige placed her gloved hand to her chest. "I don't know how someone hasn't made it into a movie."

"Hmm," Bernice mumbled.

Elle groaned. "Do *not* give this woman any more ideas, Paige."

"You're forgetting we don't have any way of promoting the businesses in this town. We need to pursue every avenue we can find." Bernice pulled her arm free. "Speaking of which, I see the perfect person to write Kringle's biography."

Bernice marched toward the table Elle's mother had set up. It was ladened with hot toddies, popcorn balls and Lori's famous cupcakes. West stood beside the buffet, chatting with Hayden's aunt.

"Don't hold your breath, Bernice," Elle murmured. "The man can't even finish his own autobiography."

Paige shot her a funny look.

"You didn't hear that."

"I hope not," Paige said. "Because I've already ordered a case of his books. I'm hoping he'll come back and do a signing when it gets released."

"It's the least he should do since he's writing it in your store."

"Um, I don't know about that. He has barely been in the shop all week."

Elle closed her eyes. She would have stomped her foot, but she'd just regained full use of her ankle. "Of course he hasn't."

Tanner Gillette, Paige's fiancé, chose that moment to join them.

"Evening, ladies."

The pro golfer's Australian accent never failed to make Elle's stomach flutter. He handed them each a hot toddy. Paige snuggled beneath his arm while Elle took a hearty sip of the drink.

"You look a little frazzled, Elle. Anythin' we can do to help?" Tanner asked.

She sighed. "Not unless you have an opening for a caddy. I have a sneaking suspicion I'll be out of a job soon."

"Don't say that." Paige squeezed Elle's hand. "You're so talented. Look at the impact your piece on Kringle has had. *Vantage* is lucky to have you. And if they don't want you, well, I'll take up a collection among the businesses in town, and we'll hire you." She glanced behind Elle. "Speaking of which, here is the dog of the hour now."

The rest of Elle's family descended, and suddenly, barking dogs, strollers and kids chasing one another filled the area around the table. Paige and Tanner wandered off to get a better spot closer to the tree. West and Kitty had disappeared. Hiding from Bernice, no doubt. The high school chorus was just beginning its rendition of "God Rest Ye Merry Gentlemen" when a hand landed on Elle's shoulder.

"There you are." Livi arrived in a swirl of cashmere and another pair of amazing boots. "We were looking for you."

Elle didn't have to look too far to see who the other half of Livi's "we" was. Hayden stood on Livi's other side, scrolling through his phone.

"Isn't this sweet," Livi gushed. "It's so folksy and intimate. You don't get this vibe in New York City."

Elle was about to agree when Livi began to cough. Not a polite cough, either. Violent spasms wracked her whole body. Elle grabbed the other woman's elbow to keep her from tumbling over.

Hayden handed her a bottle of water. "Are you sure you're okay?"

Livi waved her hand. "Just allergies. I always seem to trigger them when I'm on a plane."

"Should you be out in this cold?" he asked, his concern palpable.

"I've been looking forward to this all week," she managed to say before she was overcome with another coughing fit.

By now, a crowd had formed around them, including Hayden's partner and her wife, the PA Elle met in the ER last week. Gabby put a hand to Livi's forehead.

"You're burning up," she said. "You need to be in bed."

"But I don't want to miss this." There wasn't much bite to Livi's protest, however. Especially when she could barely stay on her feet.

"We do this every Christmas. You can come back next year," Hayden reassured her.

His words brought a rapturous smile to Livi's face.

And a jealous squeeze to the pit of Elle's stomach.

"Come on. I'll take you back to the inn." He tucked Livi against his side.

Elle's stomach clenched tighter.

"Our car is only a block away." Gabby took hold of Livi's arm. "We'll take her back to the inn, and I can check her out."

"Then I'll ride with you," Hayden insisted.

Livi wasn't having it. "No. Absolutely not. You stay here, Hayden. I'll be fine. I just need to take some antihistamines and sleep it off. I'll be as good as new for the gingerbread house-making contest tomorrow."

"I'll go," Elle offered. Livi wasn't the enemy. In fact, she was freaking adorable. Even sick. It was the least Elle could do.

"We've got this." Gabby's tone didn't allow for arguing.

Livi smiled at Elle. "You are too sweet. But I'd rather you keep Hayden company tonight. He is your best friend, after all."

A strange sound emerged from the back of Simone's throat. Gabby and Hayden both glared at her. Hayden and Elle were watching them go when the crowd surged forward. The mayor stepped up to the podium.

"Holy crap. Is that your brother Ryan?" Hayden asked.

"I can't see." Elle stood on her tiptoes, trying to peer over the crowd. A second later, Hayden's hands were on her waist. He lifted her six inches in the air.

It was her brother on the stage. He was dressed in the old Santa suit their father used to wear every Christmas Eve. Ryan was saying something about the suit being magic and how it helped him find his destiny. Elle was only catching bits and pieces. She was too focused on the heat of Hayden's touch.

"Oh my God! He's proposing," Ginger cried from somewhere beside them.

Jane, Henry, and Kringle ran forward. The crowd cheered. Elle slowly slid back down Hayden's body.

"Wow," she whispered.

He held her against his chest, his arms loosely draped around her waist.

"Yeah," he murmured, his breath fanning her ear.

Seconds later the crowd let out a loud "aah" as the tree at the end of the pier was lit up in a kaleidoscope of colored lights against the night sky. Everyone around them seemed to be moving except Hayden and Elle.

"It's snowing!" someone shouted, eliciting more cheers from the crowd.

Elle pressed her head back against Hayden's shoulder as she gazed up at the flurries falling from the night sky. Her cheek accidentally brushed his. They both froze for a long minute before he dropped his arms and jerked away. Elle spun around, but he was already deep into the crowd. She moved to chase him when a hand tapped her shoulder.

Xander Fisk was standing beside her wearing an impish smile. "I hear you're the girl I need to talk to about getting some social media advertising help."

THE LINE at the Java Jolt was longer than usual the following morning.

"Great. More tourists in town means more idiots doing things they shouldn't," Simone grumbled. "It's going to be a long weekend."

"More tourists mean more money in my pocket," Lois replied as she set four mugs of coffee on the table. "We have Elle to thank for that."

"The Christmas flotilla always attracts a big crowd." Xander glanced around the coffee shop. "If I had to guess though, there are more folks here than in previous years, even with this cold snap."

"Yup." Lois stared down at Hayden. "We need to find a reason to keep Elinor McAlister in town."

Hayden groaned. "Don't you have customers to serve?"

Lois mumbled something under her breath as she returned to the counter. Hayden shook his head.

"I guess now is not the time to ask why you had your hands all over Elle last night?" Xander—Hayden's now former friend— asked.

Both Simone and Gabby's heads snapped around to gawk at Hayden.

"It wasn't like that," Hayden argued.

Except it was. For all his blustering about keeping Elle firmly in the friend zone and moving on, he was having a heck of a time keeping his hands off her. It was second nature to lift her so she could see over the crowd last night. He'd been doing it for years. Except touching her felt different now. Hell, just being near her stoked a fire inside him that made him want to throw the woman over his shoulder and carry her off to the nearest bed.

"If you say so," Xander said into his coffee cup.

Simone gave Hayden the stink eye. "You said you were going to give Livi a chance."

"I am. It's not my fault the gods keep spoiling our dates. We'll get some one-on-one time today at the gingerbread house contest. Afterward, I have dinner plans for us at the marina. And a private viewing spot for the flotilla." He arched an eyebrow at his partner. "Even you have to agree I'm putting myself out there."

Gabby shook her head. "Livi has the flu, Hayden. As *Bachelor* worthy as your day sounds, you'll be flying solo."

"Are you kidding?" He dragged his fingers through his hair. "She said it was allergies."

Simone tsked. "Even a TV doctor would know allergies are not what took that poor woman down. We'll take your reservations at the marina, though. We've been meaning to go there for months now."

"We have." Gabby nodded.

"Fine. But you're taking our spot in the gingerbread house-making contest, too. I've already paid the entry fee. And it's for a good cause."

"No!" Aunt Kitty cried. She stopped by their table, juggling two to-go cups of coffee. "I'll take Livi's place. Please, Hayden. I'm an accomplished artist. We'll win for sure." She fluttered her eyelids.

He grinned in surprise at his aunt. She *was* an amazing textiles artist. One who hadn't really practiced her craft since losing her husband. In fact, Hayden couldn't recall seeing her this animated about anything since his uncle's death. He glanced at the coffee cups in her hands.

"You sure that isn't the caffeine talking?"

She rolled her eyes. "It's for a friend."

Damn, was she blushing?

"Come on, Hay," she pleaded. "West thinks he's got the contest locked up. I know you and I can beat him."

West.

"Spicing up your relationship with a little healthy competition. I like it." Simone gave her two thumbs-up. "Show your man who's boss."

"West isn't her man," Hayden argued.

The expressions on the three women's faces said otherwise.

Hayden swore under his breath.

"Please," his aunt pleaded. "You'll be my favorite nephew."

"I'm your only nephew," he muttered. "Fine."

Aunt Kitty actually squealed before she bent down to kiss his cheek. The pleasure he felt at giving her a morsel of joy after years of sorrow made his chest tight.

"I need to grab some supplies," she called as she dashed out of the coffee shop. "I'll see you this afternoon."

"Well, this just got interesting," Xander mused.

"Going head-to-head with West over gingerbread?" Hayden scoffed. "Puh-leaze."

"I meant that Elle is coming this way. And it doesn't look like she has coffee on her mind."

Hayden glanced out the window. Sure enough, Elle was marching across the town square with fierce determination in every step. She hadn't bothered to pull her hair back and the ocean breeze was having a field day. It was almost comical how much she looked like a cartoon princess storming into battle. Once she grew closer, however, Hayden could see the dark shadows beneath her eyes. There was nothing funny about them.

She's not sleeping.

Something was up. He shot up from his seat and strode toward the door.

"There he goes again," Xander declared.

Hayden ignored him as he hustled outside. He intercepted her near the town's Civil War cannon. Someone had put a wreath around its muzzle. Not that he noticed. His only concern was for the woman standing in front of him, battling the strands of her hair as the wind blew them onto her face.

"What's wrong?" he demanded.

She huffed out a breath. "You're not answering your phone."

He patted his pockets down. "Shit. It's still in my gym bag. I'm sorry."

"Apologize to Livi. She's the one who needed to speak with you. She wanted you to know she's too sick to make the contest."

"I heard."

Elle slapped her hands against her thighs. "Great. My job here is done." She spun on her heel and headed back the way she came.

Hayden should have let her go. He should have returned to the warmth of the Java Jolt and the camaraderie of his friends. His cappuccino was calling his name. And for the life of him, he couldn't figure out why he didn't.

"Belle, wait."

CHAPTER ELEVEN

"Belle, wait."

That was the last thing she wanted to do. It had taken every ounce of pride she had to come into town to find Hayden. And it wasn't like she had a lot of pride on tap after he'd run away from her not once, not twice, but *three. Freaking. Times.*

If Livi hadn't been so despondent—and Elle's mom so insistent—Elle would have stayed in the safety of her suite, licking her wounds. There was only so much rejection one woman could take, after all. Especially from the person she never thought would hurt her.

Except Livi was a bit of a force of nature even when she was feverish. She'd insisted Elle make the trip to locate Hayden and deliver the message in person. "He's going to be so disappointed," she'd moaned.

It pained her how much that was likely true. Still, she didn't have the heart to let the other woman down. Livi-of-the-awesome-shoes hadn't done anything wrong. Except, perhaps, capturing Hayden's attention. And maybe making him fall for her.

Elle sped up, trudging quickly down one of the side streets.

"Dammit, Elle."

Of course he caught up to her. Even wearing his carbon fiber leg, the man was faster than most. He wrapped his fingers around her upper arm, pulling her to a stop. She wanted to shake his hand off, but even through the fleece she wore beneath her down vest, she could feel the sizzle of his touch.

He must have felt it also because when she glanced up at his face, his blue eyes were as dark as the sea during a storm. She panted out a breath. His nostrils flared.

A car drove by, startling them both. Hayden glanced around before gripping her arm tighter and tugging her in the direction of his place. They were both breathing hard when he unlocked the side door and guided her inside the sunny kitchen.

Hayden's paternal grandparents owned the weathered two-bedroom bungalow for more than fifty years before moving to an assisted-living community further inland. They'd deeded the little home, its extensive workshop, and their cat to their only grandson when he returned from active duty.

Beula was sunning herself on the bench in front of the boxed bay window. A single swish of her tail was the only tell the cat was aware of their presence. A miniature Christmas tree sat front and center on the round kitchen table. It was decorated with photos of holidays from years past. Many of them were of Elle and Hayden sitting on Santa's lap. Hayden's grandfather, the town's postmaster, had played the part of Santa for a quarter of a century.

Elle pulled her arm free to get a closer look. She fingered the photos, many of them worn with age.

"I've never seen these," she whispered.

He made a rough sound with his throat. "My grandmother kept them."

"Such precious photos."

Tears suddenly stung the back of her eyes. The man behind

her had played a role in so many of her memories—good and bad. It hurt to think that part of her life could be over.

"How did we get so messed up?" she asked, not bothering to turn around.

He was silent behind her for so long, she thought he'd left her again. But when she worked up the courage to face him, it was to see him looking as wrecked as she felt. It pained her to take a breath.

"I don't want to lose you, Hayden."

With a slight shake of his head, he stalked across the room to her. They stood facing each other, less than an inch separating them for what felt like hours until . . . She wasn't sure who kissed who first, but it didn't matter. Teeth and tongues clashed as they tried to get as close to one another as possible.

Hayden's hands were suddenly everywhere. In her hair. Along her back. Burning a path along her skin beneath her fleece. When his mouth moved to explore the curve of her neck, she tilted her head to give him better access.

Elle wasn't going to let the opportunity to explore the body she'd been fantasizing about all week go to waste. She tugged his Henley free of his jeans and slipped her fingers beneath it. He nipped at her jaw when her fingers made contact with his ridiculously flat abs. His thumb brushed over one of her nipples, already sensitive and aroused, and her knees almost buckled. He groaned when her fingers tangled up in the happy trail of hair leading below the waistline of his jeans.

"Either tell me to stop, or tell me you want this, Elle." His teeth grazed her ear. "But you have to decide. Now."

She'd never heard him sound so desperate.

It will change everything.

Elle ignored the warning voice in her head, instead turning her chin so his lips met hers again. It was answer enough for Hayden. The sound of the zipper on her vest was loud in the room as he worked it down. Multitasking, he sucked on her tongue while shoving the bulky garment down her arms. She gripped the hem of his sweater and the Henley beneath and rolled them up his torso. When her palms stopped to explore the expanse of muscles lining his body, he broke off their kiss to finish shedding his sweater and shirt.

Eyes wild, he backed her toward the hallway leading to his bedroom. Elle shimmied her fleece over her head, only to manage getting one of her arms caught. He chuckled.

"Don't laugh at me," she said through the wad of fabric covering her mouth.

He took pity on her, untangling the fleece and pulling it free. It went flying down the hall. Elle suddenly wished she'd given more thought to her lingerie choice this morning. She was pretty sure her dingy sports bra wasn't doing her any favors right now.

Lucky for her, Hayden seemed preoccupied with her collarbone. He stared at the blush spreading over her skin as if he'd never seen such a thing before. Then he traced it with his finger. Clearly, Elle lacked a lot of sexual experience because it felt oddly erotic.

"Hayden."

Her moan refocused his attention. He made quick work of her bra, letting it fall to their feet. His hands cupped her breasts, and he made a guttural sound as he pressed her back against the wall.

"I've dreamed of these," he murmured, surprising the heck out of her, before he leaned down to take the tip of one between his lips.

You did? She might have asked if he hadn't just obliterated all her brain cells. Her head hit the wall with such force, a picture frame fell from the wall. The shattering glass yanked them out of their sensual haze. They were both panting when they looked down at the broken frame. It was a photo of Hayden and his older sister when they were very young.

"I always hated that picture," he said.

Elle gasped out a laugh before his mouth returned to her

other breast. She scraped her fingers over his scalp when he moved lower. He dragged a low stool with his foot, positioning it behind him. Crouching down, he let his tongue wander over her stomach until it dipped into her belly button. His hands moved from gripping her waist to the top of her leggings. He began to roll them and her panties down her legs. She squirmed against him when his lips traveled lower.

"Don't move," he ordered with a growl.

Swearing, he struggled to get the leggings over her sneakers. She toed them both off and stepped out of the last bit of her clothing. Elle was naked in front of him, her body pressed against the wall. The position made her feel awkward and exposed, like one of the butterflies Miles used to collect and pin to a board.

"We should find a bed," she pleaded.

"Not yet." His eyes wandered over her body reverently. "You are so damn gorgeous. It takes my breath away."

His words only added to her self-doubt about being so exposed to him. But then his mouth was on her, and she forgot all about any insecurities she had, reveling in the immense pleasure of his tongue instead. When he spread her thighs farther apart with his hands, she began to slide down. She slapped her palms to the wall, attempting to anchor herself. He hitched one of her knees over his shoulder. The change in position brought her even greater pleasure.

Elle arched her hips into him. His response was a groan of encouragement. He cupped her ass as he feasted with more urgency. Her breath was coming in hurried pants now. She could feel her orgasm cresting. As much as she wanted it, Elle didn't want it to end. A sob broke from her throat when the feeling of profound bliss rocked through her.

She slid down the wall onto his lap. He cradled her head against his shoulder, rubbing her back as she returned to the living. Elle shifted against him. A sharp hiss brushed against her neck. She lifted her eyelids. His lips were in a tight line. She tortured him with another shimmy.

"Elinor," he bit out.

She nipped at his shoulder. "Can we move this to the bed now?"

He stilled beneath her. His mouth might have been tight, but a look of trepidation shadowed his eyes.

"You sure?" he whispered.

Seriously?

It was too late to turn back now. Not that Elle wanted to. She wanted this man like she'd never wanted anything in her entire life.

"Absolutely," she whispered against his lips. Her hand reached between them and she stroked his hard length over his jeans.

She'd forever marvel at Hayden's athleticism. With a feral growl, he stood with her in his arms and strode into one of the bedrooms. He laid her on the bed and stepped back, his eyes roaming her flushed body once again. Her skin grew even warmer under his gaze.

"Do you need some help with your jeans, Deputy?" she mocked him.

One side of his mouth kicked up in a sly smile. "Don't sass me, Elinor. You'll be sorry."

She pressed up on the back of her elbows. "Or what? You'll put me in handcuffs?"

Her taunt had the desired effect. Hayden shucked his jeans and underwear in five seconds flat. She chewed on her lip, watching the muscles in his ass move as he strolled over to the dresser, where he pulled out an unopened box of condoms.

An ugly thought hit her. Had he bought those in anticipation of being in this bed with Livi? Something on her face must have tipped him off because he swore when he put the box on the bedside table.

"Whatever you're thinking, don't. I will get out the handcuffs if you don't stop letting your imagination go places it shouldn't."

She couldn't help but smile with relief. This man got her. It was as if their minds were connected somehow.

Hayden sat on the edge of the bed and unwrapped the strap securing his prosthetic to what remained of his leg. She'd seen his stump before—she'd even insisted on touching it when he first came home. It sat just below his knee. Not losing his knee joint gave him more range of motion with his leg. It also allowed him to run with greater precision.

He placed the artificial leg on the floor beside the bed where a single crutch lay and reached for a condom. She rubbed his back while he rolled it on.

"We still good?" he asked her, forever the gentleman.

She glanced down at his erection. "You'll do," she teased.

He covered her body in one smooth move. Elle sucked in a breath at the contact.

"I warned you about sassing me." He nipped at her lip.

She dragged her hands up his torso. All the snark left her when their eyes collided. The adoration and awe she saw in his had her heart feeling like it was swelling. He did want her. She bucked her hips into his.

"Keep doing that, and I won't be able to take care of you," he groaned.

A giddy laugh escaped Elle's throat. She'd never had a lover worry whether she came more than once. Of course Hayden would be that guy.

Elle wrapped her legs around his waist. He didn't have to be invited twice. Hayden let out a sigh as he eased himself inside her.

"Mmm." She adjusted her hips so that he filled her completely. "It's perfect."

He took her lips in a searing kiss. Then he began to move. Elle quickly picked up his rhythm. When she dug her nails into his shoulders, he increased the pace.

"So. Much. Better. Than. I. Dreamed," he panted each word as he drove into her.

She might have latched onto the nugget that he'd been dreaming of her had her release not been building in its intensity. It suddenly washed over, taking her over the edge with it. She cried out Hayden's name. He stilled above her. Elle could feel him staring at her again. She forced her eyelids open.

"You are so beautiful," he whispered. "So, so beautiful."

And then he was moving again, driving into her three more times before she felt his body grow tense beneath her fingers.

"Yes!" he shouted when she clenched her muscles around him. "God, yes."

Minutes later, they were a tangle of sweaty limbs, both still breathing fast. Hayden adjusted the pillow beneath her head before he slipped out of the bed. He used his crutch to hobble to the bathroom down the hall.

Elle would have peeked at his perfectly imperfect body again, but she couldn't seem to keep her eyes open. She felt the mattress sag when he crawled back into bed. He drew a flannel blanket over their bodies.

"I have to meet West for the contest later." She tried to make her body move, but it was no use.

"Sleep." He kissed the tip of her nose. "I won't let you miss it."

"I wouldn't mind if we did," she murmured as her eyes drifted shut.

"Mm." He feathered kisses along her jaw. "There would be talk if neither of us showed up."

A ripple of unease ran down her spine. Her sated body quickly extinguished it, however. As she dozed off, she promised to think about the implications of their rash behavior later.

CHAPTER TWELVE

Everett sorted through the various bags of candies and tubes of icing he'd tasked Gidget with gathering. The other eleven teams were doing the same at their workstations. Between the contestants and the onlookers, The Queen of Hearts Bakery was jam-packed.

"Remember, you only have ninety minutes to complete your house." At each spot, Tatum placed a tray containing the four sides and two pieces of roof made of gingerbread. There were also two baggies of frosting to be used as the "glue" for their structure. "Everything on your house must be edible. The only tools you can use are decorator tips and a paring knife to cut your candies, if needed."

Gidget absently picked up a gumdrop and popped it into her mouth.

"Hey!" Everett scolded her. "We may need that."

They wouldn't. His ever-efficient babysitter had over bought. Everett had enough materials to decorate a neighborhood of gingerbread houses. But that wasn't the point.

"Sorry," she said, sounding like she meant it. "I didn't get lunch."

He looked at the woman beside him, really looked at her. The ever-present dark circles under her eyes seemed less pronounced today. There was also a glow to her skin that could be attributed to the temperature of a bakery filled with bodies although he suspected something else. He followed her gaze across the room to the workstation where Kitty and the deputy set up their ingredients. The deputy sent a lazy grin Gidget's way.

"Oh, for crying out loud," Everett said. "Will you be able to concentrate with your boyfriend sitting so far away?"

That got her attention. She narrowed her eyes at him. "Why do you keep insisting he's my boyfriend?"

Everett stared at her in exasperation. "Are you going to sit there and tell me he isn't?"

"We're . . . we're just friends."

He grunted. "Men do not look at women who are 'just friends' the way that man always looks at you."

Her face went a shade pinker. She pulled the pretzel rods from the plastic container and measured them against the sides of the gingerbread house. "We'll need a cup of water to soften the edges of these. That way, they won't crack when we cut them." She wandered off to the beverage station.

"The judges today will be Mrs. Dana Martin, our high school's art teacher," Tatum was saying. "Joining her are award-winning architect Gavin McAlister and cookbook author and chef Lori McAlister."

"Great, we have a leg up with the judges already," he said when Gidget returned.

She snorted. "Don't count on it. There is no free ride in the McAlister family. You have to earn your accolades and victories."

The terse way she spoke the words had him scrutinizing her yet again. Before he could question her, however, Tatum clanged a metal spoon against a cookie sheet.

"Your time starts . . . NOW!" she shouted.

It turned out Gidget was a decent partner. Her attention to

detail was extraordinary. And, as with everything else she did, she was competent.

"The log cabin has been done a time or two before. Never with a chimney made from Rice Krispie treats, though," she said as she molded the rice cereal bars into the shape of a chimney, wide at the bottom and narrow at the top. "And the moose head made of chocolate is a nice touch over the door. The pretzel antlers are perfect. I'm impressed you thought of it."

"Wow, a compliment. You are losing your edge, Gidget."

While he waited for her to finish the chimney, Everett took a moment to glance at the other workstations. No surprise, his eyes gravitated toward Kitty. The tip of her tongue was caught between her lips while she focused intently on using her frosting bag to design something ornate on one side of her house. From what he could see, she and the deputy were assembling a Swiss chalet, complete with sticks of taffy for skis. She must have felt the weight of his stare because she chose that moment to look over at him. The guileless smile she aimed his way was nearly his undoing.

There was a lot to like about the down-to-earth artist. She was forthright and unassuming. Her beauty was uncommon, like a piece of sea glass the ocean had thrown about for years until it emerged scarred but with its own unique loveliness. Smooth yet hard enough to endure the trials life had thrown at her. Kitty was enchanting in her simplicity. And Everett felt himself falling under her spell every time he encountered her.

He tore his eyes away and refocused his attention on Gidget. She'd finished assembling the chimney and was now decorating ice cream cones with green frosting.

"What the hell are those supposed to be?" he demanded.

"Trees. This is a hunting lodge, is it not?" She shook her head. "We are being judged on the landscaping too, West. Why is it that men never think about that?"

He hadn't thought of it.

"Thirty minutes, people!" Tatum called out. "You have half an hour left."

Everett picked up some of the leftover pretzels. "I'll make a woodpile beside the back door."

She nodded. They worked in companionable silence until Tatum yelled, "Hands down!"

The onlookers applauded. They surged forward to get an up-close look at the gingerbread houses. Everett leaned back in his chair and stretched his shoulders. Gidget was already up and taking photos of all the entries.

"Can you tag the bakery in those?" Tatum asked her.

"Yep. I'll share the photos with you so you can use them on your socials, too."

"She's a dynamo, that one," Bernice, the town crier, remarked as she inspected their log cabin. "*Vantage* is wasting her talents. Did you know she's published in multiple magazines?"

Everett didn't know that. He'd assumed she was like the other Gen Zs working at *Vantage*, one who used her family name and connections to get her job rather than having any real talent. Over the past decade, he'd encountered so many of their type in his business dealings. Perhaps he was wrong about Gidget.

"Her father kept all her articles on file in his office at the torpedo factory. Miles uses the place as his congressional office now, but the articles are still in a file cabinet there. You should stop by and read them sometime."

Her challenge issued, Bernice moved on. Everett shook off the feeling that Keeley was trying to tell him something. He didn't have time to figure it out, though, because suddenly there was a commotion at the door.

"Midas, no!" a woman yelled right before all hell broke loose in the bakery.

"FOILED BY A GOLDEN RETRIEVER," Everett complained later that evening.

He and Kitty were camped near the city pier with blankets covering their legs and Irish coffee in their thermal mugs. The night sky was clearer than it had been for the tree lighting the other day. The temperature was more forgiving, too. Everett was amazed by the number of teenage boys wearing shorts in December.

Families gathered along the pier, staking out the best viewing spots for the flotilla. Others were bobbing up and down in boats just yards from the shoreline. The brightly colored tree at the end of the pier served as their beacon.

Kitty wiped the tears from her eyes as she chuckled. The chaos in the bakery would kill it on social media had someone thought to video it. Even Gidget was too busy trying to catch the dog to film for her vlog.

"You have to admit Midas has good taste, though," she said. "He went right for the Slice and Sip's gingerbread house. A breadstick cabin with pepperoni shingles. And the boughs of basil decorating the door and windows?" She acted out a chef's kiss. "It was on brand and, I'm sure, delicious."

He grunted. The dog had escaped the leash being held by Gavin's wife and immediately vaulted onto one of the tables. In the process of devouring the pizza parlor's gingerbread house, his exuberant tail swiped Everett's cabin to the floor, demolishing the moose head and the chimney Gidget had painstakingly put together before the judges even got to see it. Worse still, Kitty's beautiful chalet was flattened when a spectator knocked into her table, trying to corral the dog.

He reached over and took her hand. "Your chalet was magnificent. It would have won if that damn dog hadn't mutilated it." He brought her fingers to his lips. "He didn't bother touching the ridiculous doghouse decorated with biscuits."

"I'm glad that one survived. It wasn't ridiculous, either. You have to agree the doghouse was on brand. Addison owns the Bed and Biscuit. She's very creative."

"Hmm. I smell a rat," he said. "She and the dog were probably in on it."

They both laughed out loud until she was wiping her eyes again. Everett didn't remember ever laughing this hard or this often in forever. In fact, he was secretly glad for the dog's antics. It filled an empty spot where a memory he should have had with Keeley was supposed to have been.

A boat horn sounded in the distance.

"Here they come!" someone shouted from the pier.

Kitty slid her chair closer. "Keep your eyes on the horizon. This is one of Chances Inlet's unique holiday traditions. And my favorite. It's guaranteed to brighten your mood."

His mood was already brighter having her so close. Christmas music began to fill the air as the lead boat approached. Behind it was a line of sailboats, all of them with string lights decorating their tall masts. The brightly colored lights created a stunning image against the dark purple sky.

The spectators "oohed" and "aahed" watching the early boats float by. They grew more subdued over the next half hour as they enjoyed the spectacle playing out on the ocean. Kitty dropped her head to his shoulder with a sigh. Everett was surprised by the sudden peace he felt. He'd lost hope that his memories would ever allow him such tranquility again.

It's this place, he told himself. The noise of his past wasn't so loud here. The woman beside him had a lot to do with that. He brought her hand to his lips again.

Minutes later, the blaring of sirens and sounds of spraying water quickly vanquished Everett's sense of peacefulness. The frenetic sounds had his limbs growing stiff while his heart raced.

Kitty lifted her head. "Are you okay?"

He dropped her hand after realizing he'd begun to squeeze it more tightly than necessary. The Coast Guard's fire ship moved into view. Its red and white lights flashed furiously against the night sky, while its cannons sprayed seawater high into the air. The murmur of anticipation rose among the crowd.

"Everett?"

Kitty's voice sounded far away. His pulse began to race as soon as he spied the barge floating behind the Coast Guard ship. He knew what was coming next. And he knew there was no way he could keep from embarrassing himself.

A cheer went up along the pier as the first burst of light crackled through the air. A loud whistle followed the second explosion as sparks rained from the sky. The smell of sulfur wafted over the beach.

Everett's breath left his body in a rush. His palms were already clammy. The fireworks continued to explode into the night sky. He worked to regain a normal breathing pattern, but it was no use. The booming and whizzing continued for several minutes until rapid fire explosions erupted at the end of the pier. He instantly felt the world fade away.

"West!" a voice shouted in his ear.

He ignored it, intent on keeping Keeley safe from the firefight. "Stop struggling, Keeley. I need to keep you covered up." The thought of a stray bullet striking her had his gut clenching.

A hand palmed his cheek. "Everett. It's me, Kitty. It's alright. I'm safe. *We're* safe."

Fingers tugged on his flak vest. He struggled against them, the need to keep Keeley safe giving him the strength to hold his ground.

"West! This is Master Sergeant Hollister. On your feet. Now. That's an order."

Fuck.

Several long seconds later, sanity began to kick in. Everett pushed himself up onto his palms. The woman beneath him was not Keeley. It was Kitty. Beautiful, sensible, kind Kitty. Her hand was still on his cheek.

"Shh," she soothed him. "It's okay. You're okay."

No, he wasn't. He fucking wasn't. Everett looked away so he wouldn't have to see the pity that would surely be arriving in her eyes soon. A hand wrapped around his arm. He shook it off before jumping to his feet. The gym owner reached down to help Kitty up. Of course, the sheriff would have to be standing beside him. The look he leveled at Everett was filled with steely compassion.

And that was the last thing he wanted.

Shaking his head at the sheriff, he stalked through the ring of bystanders surrounding them.

"Everett West, don't you dare walk away from me!" Kitty called after him, adding to his humiliation.

He hesitated for a moment, shocked that she would want anything to do with him ever again. Hell, he'd practically assaulted her in front of an audience. She, and everyone present, had seen the side of him he worked so hard to keep concealed. The part he couldn't eviscerate no matter how hard he tried.

Two men deliberately blocked his way, making it easier for Kitty to catch him. She immediately slid her arm through his. He held himself rigid while Kitty nodded a thank you to the two guards. They immediately moved, letting them pass. The sheriff fell into step on Everett's other side.

"You should get as far away from me as you can," Everett grumbled to Kitty.

The look on her face was incredulous. "That's the last thing I want to do."

Somehow, they'd already made it as far as the sheriff's Bronco. Hollister opened the back door and gestured for Everett to get in.

"You're arresting me?" Everett demanded to know. Not that he was surprised. Kitty had every right to press charges.

The sheriff stared at him long and hard. "From the looks of it, you are punishing yourself enough."

Kitty maintained her death grip on Everett's arm as she climbed into the backseat, dragging him inside with her. "You need to be someplace quiet," she told him. "He's taking us back to the inn."

He forced himself to meet her gaze. There was no pity there. Only steady determination.

"You don't have to come." He hated his cruel tone. Except he couldn't bear to hurt this woman any more than he already had. To burden her with the ghosts that haunted him.

"No. I don't have to." She slid her hand down his arm, then interlocked their fingers. "I want to."

The gym owner took the passenger seat while the sheriff got behind the wheel. The sea of pedestrians strolling Chances Inlet's waterfront parted to allow the SUV through. Five minutes later, they arrived back at the inn. Patricia met them at the front door, a baby on her hip.

"Everything okay?" she asked her husband.

The sheriff leaned down to kiss the baby on the forehead before brushing a kiss on his wife's lips. "Nothing that a good cup of your tea won't cure."

Some sort of silent communication transpired between the two before Patricia nodded.

"I was just about to put the kettle on. Would you join me in the kitchen, Kitty? Hazel and I are making popcorn balls." She grinned widely at the baby. "She's really not much help, though. I could use an extra set of hands."

Kitty seemed reluctant to release his hand. Everett wasn't sure he wanted to be alone with the two men in the foyer. It was cowardly to use her as a human shield, though. And he was confident he could brazen it out. After all, he'd been doing it for years.

With a nod, he unwound his fingers from hers. Kitty surprised the crap out of him when she leaned in and kissed him gently on the lips. "I'm not leaving until we talk," she whispered before following Patricia in the direction of the kitchen.

The sheriff cleared his throat. "The study should be unoccupied this time of night."

"So not an arrest, but an intervention," Everett quipped as he sauntered down the hall.

The gym owner made a growling noise. Sheriff Hollister ignored him as he closed them inside the small room. The sheriff dug into the bar cabinet and pulled out a single glass.

"Funny," he said as he filled it with a finger of whiskey. "This bottle was full when you arrived, West."

Everett let the comment lie.

"To hear Elle tell it, you always have a glass in your hand," the sheriff continued. "Yet the bottle is still nearly full."

The man was observant—Everett had to give him that. If he was in the habit of allowing people in his life, he'd choose a man like Lamar Hollister for a friend. Only his brokenness forced him to keep people at a distance. He thought he had a shot at something normal with Kitty. Except he'd blown that this evening. She was simply being kind by sticking around.

"People see what they want to see," he told the sheriff. "When they see a drunk, they usually leave 'em alone."

Hollister nodded appreciatively as he handed Everett the whiskey. "That's a tactic I haven't heard of before."

Everett shrugged as he sipped his drink.

"I mentioned our veteran's support group to you once before." The sheriff jutted his chin in the direction of the gym owner. "Xander hosts it at the Ship's Iron Gym. Our regulars include a former Navy SEAL, a few medics, artillery, Rangers and even some Coast Guard. We've all been where you were tonight. Some of us still fight those demons. I'm telling you this so you know you're not alone. And you have nothing to be ashamed of."

Says you!

"It helps to have a place where you can go and shoot the shit, knowing everyone there will understand. No one will judge," he continued. "You're always welcome to join us."

Everett swallowed roughly. Hell would freeze over before he bared his soul to a room full of strangers.

"Seeing as I'm not a veteran, I don't see how your little group applies to me," he said.

"Wow. You are one tough nut to crack," Xander said, his tone curt.

"Who says I want to be cracked?" Everett clapped back.

Lamar chuckled. "I remember when I was like that. Me against the world. I also remember how freaking lonely it was living with only my demons as friends."

A knock sounded at the door. Xander opened it to reveal Kitty standing there.

The sheriff smiled slyly. "If you're lucky, you'll find something —or someone—special to make you want to do the work to drive them away," he said quietly, before moving toward the door. Pausing beside Everett's chair, he placed a hand on Everett's shoulder. "I hope you're not egotistical enough to ignore the luck that comes your way."

Everett didn't bother to respond. The door closed again, and he wasn't surprised when Kitty sat in the chair beside him. She was silent for several heartbeats. Sighing, she took his glass from his hands and downed its contents in one gulp.

"I'm sorry." He kept his eyes focused on the wooden Santa he'd admired his first night at the inn.

"Me, too," she replied.

He whipped his head around to face her, thinking she was mocking him. Only to find her expression was one of genuine sorrow.

"What are you sorry for?" he demanded.

"I'm sorry you went through something that still haunts you so deeply."

He closed his eyes and tilted his head back. She was too good for him. He didn't deserve someone so compassionate. Especially when he would continue to hurt her with his ugly moods and overreactions like today. She'd end up hating him. He didn't think he could live with himself when it came to that.

"Tonight . . . tonight wasn't the first time something like that has happened," he whispered.

"Mm. Hayden had many nights like tonight when he first came home, according to my sister."

He hated how angry her empathy made him feel. "It's not the same. He lost a leg, sure. But I lost . . ."

The air in the room seemed to disappear. Everett tugged at the collar of his sweatshirt. Kitty reached over to the desk and poured more whiskey into his glass. She handed it to him. He took a generous swig.

"Tell me about her," she urged.

He shook his head.

Kitty took his free hand between both of hers. "You're not being fair to either of us. I've told you about my husband. His life. His death. Everything. If *you* truly loved her, she must have been wonderful. By keeping her locked inside you, you're not really honoring her memory. Or letting her go."

He didn't want to let her go, dammit. At least he hadn't until he met this woman. Writing the last few chapters of his memoir was torturous. It meant reliving their short life together. It meant facing up to the fact that the dreams they had made for their future would never come true.

It meant admitting that Keeley chose someone else over me.

His throat burned when he threw back the rest of the drink. It didn't sting as much as the decision Keeley made that took her away from him. He cleared his throat.

"Keeley was a damn good reporter," he began. "Her instincts were always spot-on. And she could get anyone to talk. To tell her how things really were. I was in awe watching her work." He squeezed Kitty's hand. "She was beautiful. Her mother was a model for British *Vogue*. Her father was a member of Parliament. Keeley got both of their best attributes.

"It was nearing Christmas, and we'd been back in the States for several months. She was getting twitchy for an assignment with some meat in it. I did everything I could to try to combat that restlessness. I rented a lovely house in a small town in Vermont for the month. We were going to do all the Christmassy things we always missed out on because we'd spent decades living as globe-trotting reporters."

His chest grew tight thinking about what came next. As if she sensed what was coming, Kitty reached for the glass in his hand and took a fortifying sip before handing it back.

"She got word that an interpreter who had worked for her was denied a visa to come to the States. And that really made her anxious. She was worried he or his family might be harmed if it was found out that he had aided the Western media. Keeley came up with a plan to get him out of Afghanistan. Of course, it couldn't wait until after the holidays. The man's life was in danger."

He switched out the glass for the Santa from the desk.

"It was only supposed to take three days. They would get in and get out and be back home before Christmas Eve. That's what she promised me. Then we'd have the Christmas I planned for us. The one I thought we were both dreaming of."

Kitty wrapped an arm around his shoulders. Everett relaxed at her touch.

"It was a setup. She and the group of veterans turned mercenaries were ambushed. Except every one of those guys managed to get out alive. Only Keeley and her interpreter didn't make it. They were supposed to protect her, to bring her back to me. They didn't."

"That explains a lot," she told him. "Thank you for telling me."

His laugh lacked any humor. "Now you know why I'm such a pathetic mess."

Kitty took the Santa from his trembling hands and returned it to the desk.

"You are neither of those things, Everett West. The story you just told me explains why you hold a bit of a grudge against veterans, though. It also hints at the reason why you are so hell-bent on experiencing every Christmas contest and tradition this town offers. As for what happened tonight . . ." She waved a hand through the air dismissively. "You're a man who has suffered a great loss, and witnessed the world's cruelness firsthand. But you survived it, Everett. And I, for one, am so glad you did."

He risked a peek over at her. Those brown eyes he'd fallen for the moment they met were smiling at him.

"I don't want you to pity me," he whispered.

She shook her head. "What I feel for you is nothing close to pity."

Her admission should have scared the hell out of him. It didn't, though. His heart was racing again. This time with hope. He cupped the back of her neck with his hand and pulled her closer for a kiss.

Kitty tasted like whiskey.

And salvation.

CHAPTER THIRTEEN

HAYDEN WAS sure he would expire right here in the big sleigh bed in Elle's suite at her mother's inn. But what a way to go. He peered through his lashes at the erotic image she made, her naked skin dewy and pink as she rode him with reckless abandon.

"Yes," she cried when he dragged his fingers down her sweat-slicked torso to grip her hips more securely.

She was close to the edge. Hayden could feel her muscles begin to clench around him. He could sense her breaths becoming more fractured. Truth be told, he was holding on by a thread himself. His own breath sawed through his lungs painfully.

Elle was gasping now, her movements becoming more frantic. He decided to take pity on her, grazing his thumb against her sweet spot once, then twice, until she came in a rush. Hayden couldn't make out the words she was crying out because his ears were roaring. The pleasure he felt when her muscles closed in around him was nearly too much to bear. He thrust his hips into her with such force, it was a wonder she didn't go flying when he came.

Hayden gathered her up in his arms. Her wild hair formed a

curtain around them. He could feel her heart racing beneath his palm pressed to her spine. She drew lazy circles on his abdomen. Neither of them seemed to have the strength to speak.

It was a good thing because he had no idea what to say. Today had been eye-opening. And not just because sex with his best friend was everything that he never let himself imagine it could be. But because it had been more than simply mind-blowing. It had touched his soul.

He brushed her hair off their faces so he could press a kiss to her forehead.

"Mmm," she murmured.

When she looked up and her eyes met his, his chest grew painfully tight. Her expression was equal parts awe, passion and confusion. They were easy for him to identify because he was feeling them, too.

"Hayden?" she whispered.

He quickly shushed her by reversing their position and taking her lips in a possessive kiss. She moaned into his mouth while scraping her nails down his back. He tore his lips away and pressed them to each of her eyelids.

"I don't want to ruin this by analyzing it to death," he murmured against her skin. "Let's not think about it too deeply. That way, we can enjoy whatever this is for right now. Please, Elle."

She hesitated only briefly before agreeing with a nod. Her eyes fluttered closed. He rolled over onto his back and drew her into the curve of his arm before kissing the tip of her nose.

"Sleep now," he told her. "I'll be here to keep you safe."

"But I don't want to miss a moment with you."

Her words made his throat tight.

Neither do I.

The realization shouldn't have surprised him. If he were being honest with himself, he would admit he'd loved this woman for years now. He'd come clean that he never wanted to be apart from her. He would tell her she was his person.

Except doing that would likely send her scurrying back to New York long before the holidays were over. He couldn't take that chance. Now that he knew all of her. Now that his body would forever crave hers. He needed to keep this light until he could figure out a way to persuade Elle that all she ever wanted was right here in Chances Inlet.

He waited until she was breathing evenly and deeply. Carefully, he slid his arm out from under her neck and replaced it with a pillow. She didn't move when he sat up to attach his leg.

When he returned from the bathroom a few minutes later, dressed and ready to sneak out, Hayden almost changed his mind. Elle had worked a leg free and goose bumps were forming on her skin in the chilly night air. But rather than crawl in beside her to warm her up, he covered her with one of the bright Christmas throw blankets her mom had strewn about the suite. He took a minute to fold Elle's clothes and place them beneath the nightstand along with her shoes just in case she suddenly woke from one of her nightmares.

"You're safe, Elle," he mouthed. "Get some rest."

He forced his feet to move away from his sleeping beauty. Using the light on his cell phone, he crept down the stairs in the bootlegger's passageway, nearly colliding with someone at the bottom. He aimed his light at the other person.

"Aunt Kitty?" he hissed.

"Hayden?" his aunt whispered.

His aunt looked as rumpled as the woman he'd just left upstairs. And was that a damn love bite on her neck? He was going to kill West.

Hayden must have said that last part out loud because his aunt reached out and grabbed his arm.

"You'll do no such thing," she said with a quiet forcefulness that stunned him.

"How long have you been sneaking in and out of the inn?" he demanded. "And how do you even know about these passageways?" Hayden had discovered them alongside Elle's brothers a decade ago.

She dipped her chin. "Patricia might have mentioned them earlier this evening. And aren't you the pot calling the kettle black?"

A sound upstairs had them both jumping. Aunt Kitty tugged on his arm until they reached the panel that led out of the inn. The ocean breeze was bracing this time of night. His aunt wrapped her arms around her midsection. They walked a few paces before they turned and looked at each other.

"Do not tell your mother," his aunt commanded.

"Don't tell Mom," he said at the same time.

She chuckled as she began striding down the long driveway. "I'd like to go on the record as saying I'm all in with Team Elle and Hayden."

If only there were a "Team Elle and Hayden."

"What makes you think I was with Elle?"

She shot him a look that clearly said *come on*. "Livi was coughing up a storm when I passed by her room. From what Patricia mentioned, she's still pretty sick."

Guilt licked at his belly. He and Livi had barely shared a kiss on the cheek since they met, though. Hayden owed her nothing. Still, he made a mental note to let her down gently once her flu subsided.

"I appreciate the support," he told her. And he did. "But we are keeping things on the down low."

"For now, you mean?"

Could be forever.

He hated how much it hurt to think Elle might still choose her career over him. When he didn't answer, Aunt Kitty threaded her arm through his.

"The heart knows what it wants. You are her North Star,

Hayden. You always have been. Elle will always find her way back to you."

While he appreciated his aunt's optimism, he wasn't convinced Elle wanted to find her way back to Chances Inlet. "All the same, I would prefer not to let my mom in on any potential Team Elle and Hayden talk just yet."

"You leave your mother to me. When the time is right, I'll find a way to convince her to see reason."

Hayden chuckled as they passed Mr. McDaniel's brightly colored pine tree. "I don't think I want to know how you'll accomplish that."

They were both wrapped in their own thoughts as they strolled down the quiet side streets in town.

"So, West, huh?" he eventually asked.

"He's not the man you think he is."

"I'll have to take your word for it. Although he's not scoring any points with me by making you walk home alone this late at night."

"Oh, he'll be madder than a wet hen when he finds out," she replied. "He was deeply asleep when I left. I didn't have the heart to wake him. I don't think he sleeps very well."

Hmm. West and Elle had a lot more in common than either one of them knew. Although the man was likely behind much of Elle's insomnia.

"Has he finished his book yet?"

Aunt Kitty shrugged.

Hayden swore. "Does he even realize Elle's job depends on it?"

His aunt's steps faltered. "What are you talking about?"

"If Elle can get him to turn the completed manuscript in on time, she'll be promoted to lifestyle columnist. It's her dream job."

Although not for reasons anyone else desired a dream job. She'd be good at it, sure. But she was mainly after the cache it would give her among her siblings. Hayden understood her goal. He just didn't agree with her logic.

"If Everett is aware of that, I'm sure he won't let Elle down on purpose," she told him. "Like I said, he's not the man he appears to be."

Hayden grunted. "Let's hope not."

"FOR CRYING OUT LOUD, Elle. Because of your video blog, our phone is ringing off the hook with media types wanting to *interview* my damn dog," Ryan bellowed as he stormed into the inn's breakfast room several days later.

Elle looked up from the French toast casserole she was drowning in maple syrup. She had to admit that one advantage to her assignment babysitting West was her mother's fabulous breakfasts, especially since her appetite seemed to be gnawing at her constantly these past few days. Ryan lowered himself into the chair beside her and proceeded to help himself to a slice of her bacon.

"Hey! That's mine!" She tried to slap his hand, but her brother was quicker. "I'm telling Mom."

"Go 'head. She likes me better anyway. And it's the least you can do after thrusting Kringle into the spotlight again. You are going to have to coordinate all these interview requests, little sister." He jabbed the piece of bacon at her. "Besides, I thought breakfast was only for the paying guests."

She looked around the room, grateful to find it empty. It was already after ten. Hayden had kept her up well past two in the morning the past few nights. For the first time since the earthquake, sleep came easily. Whereas before she was up with the birds, she was now logging a solid seven to eight hours of quality sleep each night. She'd become a pampered princess.

It wasn't like she had much else to do anyway. West had locked himself in the study all week without bothering her with any of his ridiculous requests. She hoped that meant he was writing.

Not only that, but the town's social media was chugging along, bringing in more tourists for the holidays than the previous Christmas. Soon, Elle would have to resort to washing dishes to keep herself busy. Anything to distract her from thoughts of Hayden.

Hayden.

Elle smiled to herself. The attraction she'd felt during her drunken kiss last year wasn't a one-off. And when they'd both finally let go . . . *wow.* Jeremy had certainly never lit up her body the way her best friend did. Being with Hayden had an added level of intimacy to it because they both knew each other so well. What they shared felt like more than just sex. And it was crazy good.

Or just plain crazy.

They'd crossed a line. Going back to what they were before was impossible now. Not that she wanted to. Ever. But she didn't want to lose him either. Just the mere thought had her stomach seizing.

Hayden insisted they ignore the elephant in the room—the pesky fact that she lived ten hours away. That her career was in New York City and his was here in Chances Inlet. She'd been so caught up in the moment that she'd agreed. Why not enjoy the here and now, he'd reasoned. Except the "here and now" had an expiration date. As much as everyone wished for the holiday season to last forever, it didn't.

Ryan reached for another slice of bacon, except this time Elle was quicker. She jammed the whole piece into her mouth to keep her brother from snatching it.

"I'm allowed to eat the leftovers," she said around the food in her mouth.

"Are you this much of a bohemian when you're on a date? No wonder you are still single."

Elle had never been so relieved to see Bernice appear. The woman practically floated into the room with Kringle in her arms. She handed Elle a piece of paper.

"Read all about it, girlie. The travel network is sending a team to shoot a report about our town. They saw your video blogs on social media, Elinor. This is exactly the publicity we had hoped for. Heck, we don't need to hire a PR firm. Not when we've got you." She leaned down and kissed Elinor on the head.

Kringle squirmed beneath Bernice's hold. Ryan reached over and rescued his dog. "I think Elle intends to make a name for herself in a bigger way." He snuck a piece of bacon to the dog. "Chances Inlet is in her rearview window. She's on track to do the McAlisters proud by becoming a big-time journalist in New York."

Bernice harrumphed. "What's wrong with being a journalist here in the town that raised her? If we can't even get one of our own to help us, this place is doomed."

"Don't tell me this charming hamlet has run off all the reporters?" West asked as he sauntered into the room and headed straight for the coffee urn.

"It seems we are not worthy of a newspaper, an advertising magazine or even a PR firm to see to our measly social media needs," Bernice fumed.

West tsked while he filled his mug. "A town without a newspaper is a town without excitement."

"That's exactly what I've been trying to tell everyone," Bernice practically shouted.

"Oh my. It sounds as though I'm interrupting an interesting discussion." Livi hesitated in the doorway. Elle's mom was by her side.

Ryan stood and walked over to hold out a chair for her. "Nah. Just Bernice being Bernice."

The older woman made an unintelligible sound before disappearing in the direction of the kitchen.

"How are you feeling?" Elle asked. She felt guilty that she hadn't checked on Livi. But things were awkward enough before she'd slept with Hayden.

"I feel a lot more human now that I've showered," Livi responded.

Elle's mom set a cup of tea and some toast in front of her guest. "You sit here and recover while I go change the sheets and freshen up your suite."

"Did I overhear Bernice correctly?" Livi tore at a piece of the toast. "The Travel Channel is coming to Chances Inlet?"

"It would seem so. It says here that they are including us in their 'Top small towns to visit at Christmastime' segment." Elle handed her the sheet of paper Bernice had left.

"That's quite a coup. For your next trick, you should get Hayden's furniture some notice. He's a talented artist, and social media would eat up his stuff," Livi said. "Who knows? He could probably turn his side hustle into a full-time gig."

Elle ignored the hint of pride in the other woman's voice as she championed Hayden. Mainly because Livi's idea had merit. Hayden was a talented woodworker. And why shouldn't his business get some social media love? He'd hate it, but he didn't have to know. And if his business grew, he could potentially afford to work from anywhere.

Like New York City, perhaps.

"By the way, has anyone seen Hayden around?" Livi asked.

West was quick to answer her. "Not today, but I'm sure Elle can get him over here in a hot minute."

"I'm sure I'll be too busy sharpening your pencils," she snapped.

The man had the nerve to laugh as he wandered out of the room and back toward the study.

Good riddance!

Livi looked at her expectantly. Ryan's expression was more curious. Elle was saved by the buzzing of her cell phone. She froze for a moment, hoping it wasn't Hayden calling. Thankfully, it was her editor, Madelaine.

"It's my boss," she explained before hurrying out of the breakfast room and closeting herself in the music room.

"Good morning, Madelaine," Elle said.

"I'm very disappointed with you, Elinor."

She sank onto the piano bench, trying to catch her stomach before it hit the floor. What could she possibly have done wrong? Had West told the team at *Vantage* that he couldn't meet his deadline? Her palms were suddenly damp.

"I can't believe you haven't secured an interview with Santa's dog. Kringle belongs to your brother, does he not? *Vantage* should have the scoop over everyone else. Are they asking for a fee? Because we will pay it."

Technically, Kringle belonged to Jane's son, Henry. But Elle didn't care about that. She was relieved she wasn't losing her promotion before she even got it.

"Of course *Vantage* is getting the scoop," she told her editor, hoping that her confident tone would make the other woman believe Elle had thought of it long before this phone call. "In fact, I was just negotiating with my brother about this."

"Excellent. I knew I could count on you. And this type of interview will be a good piece to dip your toe into the lifestyles section. Well done. Let me know when you have it completed, and we will get it off to the digital side of the house."

After Madelaine ended the call, Elle jumped up and did a little victory dance among the nutcrackers in the room.

"I'm 'dipping my toe' into feature writing! And she didn't even ask about West," she told the wooden soldiers before pulling open the door and racing to find her brother and his dog.

CHAPTER FOURTEEN

HAYDEN YAWNED as he scrolled through the forms on his computer monitor. Who would guess that the relatively minor offenses that occurred in Chances Inlet required so much documentation?

"Late night again?" Simone asked from the opposite desk.

"Mm," he replied.

"Lots of woodworking to be done this time of year, I guess."

The way his partner said "woodworking" had him glancing over to look at her. As usual, Simone was the picture of innocence. Which meant she wasn't innocent at all. He decided it was best not to spar with her today, though.

"Something like that." He averted his eyes back to his monitor.

He was surprised she remained quiet for as long as she did. It was all of forty-one seconds until she slapped her palm to the desk.

"Do you expect me to believe that? Gabby saw you sneaking into the inn last night. And since she was there to check on Livi and you weren't hiding beneath her sheets, there is only one other place you could have been." She shot him a smug look. "Working your wood beneath Elle's sheets."

For fuck's sake.

He glanced around the station, frantically assessing who was within earshot. Luckily, the sheriff was in court today. Deputy Pettyjohn had the day off. Maureen, the receptionist, was preoccupied with watching *Elf* on her iPad.

"Do you ever mind your own business?" he hissed at Simone.

She had the nerve to laugh. "Hayden Lovell, you saved my ass in combat. Don't you know what that means? According to an ancient Chinese proverb, your business is my business forever."

"I'm pretty sure that's only true in Disney movies," he grumbled. "But had I known, I might not have risked my own life to rescue you."

Simone wheeled her chair across the floor so she was next to Hayden at his desk.

"Tell me everything," she demanded.

He gestured to the wide-open office. "Does this look like the ladies' room to you?"

She narrowed her eyes at him. "Hey, don't shut me out now. You are doing the boss' daughter. Have you considered that you might need some backup when he finds out?"

"There is no reason he should ever find out." He leveled a pointed glare at his friend. "Besides, Elle is the sheriff's *step*daughter. Not the same thing."

Except that didn't make him feel any better. He owed a great deal to Donald McAlister, Elle's late father. How would the man Hayden admired beyond measure feel about him "doing" his daughter? Still, Mr. Mac had been a doting dad to Elle. He'd also made no secret that he was fond of Hayden. The guy wouldn't have gone to bat for him if he wasn't. Still, Hayden had to wonder if he would have approved of their relationship.

Not all of it, he thought as he remembered the things he'd done to the man's daughter last night.

As for the sheriff, sweat broke out on the back of Hayden's neck, just imagining how his mentor would react first and ask questions later. The man had been a beast when a hit-and-run driver struck his now wife and left her badly injured by the side of the road. He was like a second father to Hayden. There was no doubt he wouldn't be in the shape he was physically or mentally had it not been for Lamar Hollister.

He swore savagely.

Simone chuckled. "Ah, so you do remember who our boss is."

Hayden picked up a pen and began clicking it. The sound was loud in the empty office.

"Have you told her you love her?"

"For crying out loud, Simone. Why don't you announce it over the intercom so Maureen can hear you," he whispered angrily.

Maureen's sigh was loud and dramatic. "She doesn't need an intercom. Everyone in this town knows you are in love with that girl, Hayden Lovell. Either do something about it or stop your bellyaching. You're ruining the best part of the movie."

"Why can't everyone mind their own damn business?" he yelled.

Maureen glared at him as she pulled her earbuds from their charger and shoved them in her ears.

Simone shook her head. "Because it's not like you to start a relationship you know isn't going to work out. Especially with someone you'll likely run into for the *rest. Of. Your. Life.*"

"Is it possible we can simply be friends with benefits? I mean, Elle is good with that," he lied. She'd agreed not to talk about their future. To enjoy the here and now. But everything else had been left unsaid. "Why can't you be good with it, too?"

She took her time in answering. "Because you're not good with it," she announced before standing up and marching from the room.

EVERETT RUBBED the top of the old Smith Corona typewriter. "I learned to type on one of these relics in high school." Learned was perhaps an exaggeration, though, since he still had to look at the keys on his laptop.

"I don't think Garth used it much in the later years," Tim Lovell said. "He kept it more as a talisman. According to Garth, this wasn't a real newspaper office without the clackity-clack of typewriter keys and the ring of the carriage return. He still comes in here and plays with the old thing every now and then."

"This place seems rather small to have housed a newspaper," he said.

"The size of the operation kept shrinking as the paper did," Tim explained. "In the end, it was just Garth. He was literally a one-man show. He still owns the building. I've expanded into some of the old newsroom's space to add another hygienist, but I don't need any more room. As you can see, this month, we are using the newspaper office to store the toys Hayden's veteran's group has already collected for the Angel Tree the youth center is sponsoring."

Everett added the few items he and Kitty bought to the growing pile of gifts. "I didn't mean to pull you away from your patients," he said. "I have someplace to be later. When Kitty mentioned this was the drop-off spot for donations, I figured I'd deliver them since I was already passing by."

Tim kicked something invisible with his shoe. "You and Kitty seem to be spending a lot of time together."

Not as much as I would like to be.

Knotical was busy this time of year with the influx of tourists. Not to mention Kitty led multiple groups that met after hours at the store to work on their projects for the Christmas Sidewalk Bazaar. The bazaar kicked off this weekend and would run through Christmas Eve.

"She's a very busy lady," he replied. "I'm grateful for whatever time I get to spend with her."

"Mm." If Kitty's brother-in-law suspected she'd been spending her nights with Everett in his bed at the inn, he didn't bring it up.

"Claire mentioned that Kitty seems much . . . lighter lately," Tim remarked. "I hope she stays that way."

The dentist may have spoken the words casually, but Everett didn't mistake the implied warning.

He nodded. "Message received. I have no plans for anything after the holiday season." Although one was beginning to hatch. "Nothing that will immediately take me away from your idyllic little town, anyway."

Tim's shoulders relaxed. "Good to know. Things are easier at the store when Claire doesn't have to worry about saying or doing something that will send her sister back into the doldrums."

"Kitty is lucky to have you both looking out for her." Everett pressed one of the typewriter's keys. "Your wife is very protective of the people in her orbit."

The other man hung his head with a sigh. "I'm sorry you had to see that the other night. Claire is a bit irrational when it comes to Elle McAlister. She's angry that our son didn't get the life he wanted."

"Who says he didn't get the life he wanted?"

Tim's eyes snapped up to meet Everett's. "You get a pass since you are new in town, but you don't know what you're talking about."

Everett held his hands up in front of his chest. "Pardon me. I didn't mean to offend. I only wanted to point out that life doesn't always work out the way we want. It's what we do with the curveballs that get thrown at us that shapes us. Your son seems like a solid guy. One who is happy with the path he's on. It may not be the one he envisioned at seventeen. Still, he's making the best of it." He looked out the window toward the Ship's Iron Gym. "He came out of the other side not just a survivor, but also as a man who has thrived. I envy him."

"You make it sound easy. Hayden had a lot of people helping him."

"Manning up and accepting that help is half the battle," Everett murmured. "And if you'll excuse me, I think it's long past time I man up."

He walked across Water Street and into the gym. The place was busy for a weeknight. Upbeat holiday music blared from the sound system. The Christmas tree in the corner was white with flocking. Ornaments shaped like exercise equipment dangled from its branches.

"Welcome," the teenager behind the desk said. "Are you looking to work out? We offer complimentary onetime guest passes." He held out a candy cane to Everett. "And these are free for stopping in."

"Candy? At a gym?" Everett shook his head. "Actually, I was told the veteran's group meets here."

"Oh, yeah, sure. They meet downstairs." He stood and pointed toward the back of the gym. "Through that door behind the ellipticals."

"I'll show him, Kyle," the sheriff offered as he entered the gym. If he was surprised to see Everett asking about the meeting, he didn't let it show.

Everett reached into the bowl of candy canes and grabbed a handful. "I think I'm going to need these. I have some bridges to mend," he explained to a wide-eyed Kyle.

The two men walked to the back of the gym in silence. Xander met them at the bottom of the stairs. The gym owner wasn't as adept at controlling his expression. He looked at the sheriff, then back at Everett. His lips formed a mulish line.

"If you're here to mock our members, you can turn around and head right back up those stairs."

The sheriff stepped between the two of them. "Xander—"

"It's okay, Sheriff," Everett interrupted. "He's right to assume that I might be here under false pretenses after everything I said the other night." He shook his head. "Or judging from the parts of my book that have been excerpted, I would react the same way." The sheriff turned around so both men were looking at him. Everett swallowed roughly. "I have some work to do on myself. And I was told the best place to start was in that room."

The silence stretched until the sheriff reached over and turned the door handle to the meeting space. He gestured for Everett to enter first.

Forgive me, Keeley, but it's time to let you go.

"SORRY, Livi, but you're still recovering from four days with a high fever," Kate said as she poured gingerbread martinis into a row of glasses. "You're going to have to settle for a cranberry mocktail tonight."

"Just like me!" Emily waved her arm and nearly spilled her drink all over the island in the inn's kitchen.

"Me too." Lori balanced a glass on her belly.

It was cookie decorating night at the Tide Me Over Inn. An annual tradition that Elle had missed for the past several years. With two new sisters-in-law, a new stepsister, and now a sister-in-law-to-be, the number of decorators in the kitchen had certainly grown. Since Livi's illness, Elle's mom had taken her under her wing, including her in tonight's activities.

"Really, I'm fine with water," Livi replied.

"Me too," Whitney chirped.

Paige kissed the little girl on the cheek. "Have I told you that I love the sound of your voice?"

"When Whitney first arrived in town last summer, she kept her thoughts and her words to herself," Elle's mom explained for Livi's benefit.

"What I wouldn't give for a little of that quiet when she is chatting up a storm at six o'clock on Sunday mornings," Whitney's mother, Donella, teased.

Ginger handed out Santa hats to everyone. "I brought props from the dance studio. We'll look festive for any video Elle might want to shoot."

Elle set the hat on her head. "Is that all I am to you guys? The videographer?"

"And the dog whisperer," Jane quipped. "Kringle's ego is getting so big, he refused to eat his dinner from his plastic dish tonight. He would only touch it once we put it on a plate from my grandmother's china."

"Ha ha. Very funny," Elle replied as the rest of the women laughed.

"Seriously, though. Thanks for the interview stipend. We're going to put it in Henry's college fund," Jane said.

Ginger clapped her hands together. "Ooo, I know. You could set up a photo booth with Kringle at the bazaar this weekend. I guarantee there will be tourists willing to pony up some cash to take a picture with him."

"Dr. Lovell did mention Henry might need braces. It's never too early to start saving for those," Jane joked.

"Speaking of Dr. Lovell, has anyone seen Hayden around town?" Livi asked.

Elle kept her eyes on the bowl of cookie dough in front of her, hoping the question wasn't directed at her. She focused on scooping out some of the peanut butter dough and rolling it up into a ball before putting it on the cookie sheet.

"He's been working on a kitchen table for our new house," Ginger chimed in. "My husband and Paige's fiancé are designing a new golf community together. We are moving into one of the new homes Gavin is building this spring. I'm leaving all of Gavin's bachelor furniture in the loft."

"Probably a good idea," Kate agreed. "Lord knows what stories that stuff would tell if it could talk."

"Like bedtime stories?" Whitney asked.

Everyone except Ginger laughed.

"Something like that." Kate's words were met with more laughter. "Sorry, Ginger."

Elle's mother mimed putting her fingers in her ears. "I'd prefer not to know any of this." She looked over at Livi. "The deputies are all taking turns filling in for Deputy Pettyjohn. He got bit by the flu bug, too. I believe tonight is Hayden's turn to cover his shift."

Her mom was correct. It was Hayden's turn tonight. Not that Elle was going to confirm anything. Mostly because she felt uncomfortable about Livi's interest in the guy Elle was sleeping with. Hayden had repeatedly assured Elle that nothing was going on between him and the designer, and she believed him. He insisted he would set Livi straight as soon as the other woman felt better, and he could do it in person. That wasn't going to happen tonight, though. Which meant Elle would remain mum.

She wasn't looking forward to spending the night alone in her big bed upstairs, especially when she'd been sleeping so much better with Hayden by her side. Waking up feeling refreshed and human again was something she could get used to.

Next to her, Kate began to unwrap the chocolate kiss candies that would be pressed into the warm peanut butter balls once they came out of the oven.

"Sucks for you. Who is gonna keep you warm tonight?"

Kate's softly uttered words had Elle dropping one of the peanut butter balls onto the floor. When she bent down to retrieve it, her sister followed.

"Wow. Direct hit. Gabby mentioned she saw Hayden sneaking in the other night when she came to check on Livi," Kate whispered. "Not that she was surprised after his odd behavior the day of the Turkey Trot."

Elle could feel her face flaming. "Isn't that some sort of HIPAA violation or something?" she hissed.

"Nah. This is just run-of-the-mill hospital gossip."

"People at the hospital are gossiping about me?" Elle croaked.

"Just me and Gabby." Kate winked at her. "For now."

"You're the head of the hospital. Act like it, for crying out loud."

Elle reached for the ball of dough, but her sister already had it between her fingers.

"Interesting. I figured you'd claim his nocturnal visits were innocent. That you two are *just friends* who were playing backgammon or something."

Dammit. Why didn't I think of that?

Her sister sighed and seemed to lose some of her snarky bluster. "It's none of my business—"

"You're right. It isn't."

They stared at each other in stony silence for a few beats, until Elle's leg grew numb from maintaining her crouch.

"My offer still stands," Kate said eventually. "I'm here if you need to talk."

Elle felt like the biggest brat. As overwhelming as her siblings' achievements were, they never lost sight that they were family. They always had each other's backs. It was something Elle never wanted to take for granted. But how could she explain things to her sister when she didn't understand them herself?

Jane peeked around the corner of the kitchen island. "Hey, you two. What's going on down there?"

Elle wobbled slightly when she stood back up. "Just a runaway cookie."

"Like the gingerbread man," Emily exclaimed.

"Mm. And look what happened to him," Kate mumbled just low enough that only Elle could hear. "He didn't just get his heart broken. He got eaten alive."

The others began chatting about their favorite Christmas stories. Elle went back to scooping the dough into balls. There was no risk to either of their hearts breaking. She and Hayden would figure things out. At least she hoped so because the alternative made her uneasy. If they couldn't figure things out, she would lose him forever. And that would break her heart.

"I love you," Kate whispered.

Elle suddenly had difficulty swallowing. "Right back at you," she managed to push out.

When she looked up, their mother was studying them intently, her head canted slightly to the side. Elle may come out of this holiday season minus a best friend, but the people in this room would always be there for her. It would hurt. Immensely. She was a McAlister, though. And that had to count for something.

CHAPTER FIFTEEN

THE FOLLOWING AFTERNOON, Hayden was gliding the sander over the table Gavin and Ginger commissioned him to build when Elle's soft voice interrupted him.

"My God, Hayden. It's a work of art." Her tone was almost reverent.

He turned and smiled in gratitude. Not just for her comment, although he appreciated that her praise was genuine. What he felt was a profound wonder that after months of dreaming about it, their relationship was finally more than "just friends."

Not only that, but she was sexy as hell seated cross-legged on the chintz loveseat that used to be in his grandparent's living room. From his angle above her, he had a bird's-eye view down the V-neck of her soft sweater. The sweater was decorated with Santas complete with puffy beards. All Hayden saw, though, was her soft, creamy skin. Just a peek at the top of her breasts had the zipper on his jeans growing painfully tight.

Her hair was piled up in a messy bun. A single strand stuck to her cheek. The dark circles beneath her eyes had disappeared, only to be replaced by a glowing warmth in her cheeks.

She had her laptop balanced on her thighs, typing away at one of the blogs for Chances Inlet, he assumed. Her bottom lip was shiny from her chewing on it while she wrote. He had to work to keep himself from turning into a Neanderthal and ravishing her right there on the sofa where his grandmother used to sit and watch *Wheel of Fortune* every night.

"Is that for my brother?"

Hayden was grateful for her question. It redirected his thoughts to more appropriate ones.

"It is. With its leaf, it will seat eight. Seems like overkill for a kitchen table." He shrugged. "I guess they're planning on a family the size of yours."

"It's weird to think of Gavin not living in his loft," she said. "I mean, it was the prototype for the lofts he became famous for building in Tribeca. Now, he'll be living on a golf course ten miles outside of Chances Inlet."

"Considering he never intended to return to Chances Inlet at all, I'd say that him living ten miles away isn't so bad." Hayden swept the sawdust off the big table. "Come to think of it, none of your siblings ever wanted to make their home in the town where they grew up. Yet here they all are."

It was her turn to shrug. "After they all made a name for themselves," she said, dashing the kernel of hope blossoming in his chest.

Beula weaved around his legs as if to offer some comfort. Or to urge him to keep pressing her. The cat was fickle most days.

"You never planned on returning home, either," Elle challenged.

She wasn't lying. His plan was to head to Oregon after college to train with the elite distance runners. Hopefully, go to the Olympics. He'd come back to Chances Inlet for one of those cheesy parades after he won a medal. Maybe they'd name the high school track in his honor.

Instead, he was sent to a dusty, dangerous hellhole. Then to Texas to rehab his body and his mind. Returning to Chances Inlet felt like paradise after all he'd been through. Eight years later, it was the place he felt the most comfortable. Safe. No one asked him about his trauma. Best of all, he knew what to expect most days. Some people might call it boring, but Hayden wore that predictability like a suit of protective armor.

"We both had goals once," he remarked.

She snorted. He was a perv because he found the sound to be incredibly sexy.

"Not me. Remember? I couldn't come up with one besides making my family proud."

"Your family has always been proud of you."

"But not for something I've accomplished." She held up her hand to stop his protest. "West called me a nepo baby when we first met. And as much as I hate to admit it, he's right. My reputation is based on the achievements of my family. The Fab Four. Is it so wrong to want to make a name for myself as Elle McAlister? Not just as one of 'the McAlisters'?"

He shook his head. "You are making a name for yourself as a journalist. You already had several freelance articles published nationally when you were in college. You're about to become a lifestyles columnist at *Vantage*. What am I missing?"

"It's more about what *I'm* missing." Elle sighed. "I'm not like Kate and Miles who knew what they wanted to do with their lives on the first day of kindergarten. Or Ryan with his ridiculous athletic ability. Or even Gavin, who made being a math geek cool. There was never anything that I just *had* to be doing to make myself happy." She shrugged. "Writing has always come easy to me. But it was just something I did, you know? Tell stories. It's not like I'm contributing to anything big in the grand scheme of things."

He growled in frustration. "Your letters were the only things keeping me sane most days," he told her. "When I was deployed and . . . those long months after."

Her lips parted in surprise. "You never told me that," she whispered. "You barely acknowledged that you even got them."

Hayden walked over to the file cabinet he kept in the corner of the workshop. He pulled open the bottom drawer and took out an old shoebox. She had risen from the loveseat and stood right behind him when he turned around. He lifted the lid.

Elle gasped. "Are those my letters?"

"Mm-hmm."

She fingered the envelopes carefully. "I—I . . ." Her eyes were shiny and stunned when they met his. "You kept them? All of them?"

"Yeah. I liked to reread them on days when . . ." Words failed him. There was only so much vulnerability he could show her.

On days when I didn't want to try anymore.

On days when it felt like you were my only friend.

On days when I miss you so much, it hurts.

He had a sinking feeling he would be in for a lot of those days come the New Year.

She opened her mouth, but no words came out. Instead, she took the box from his hands and carefully placed it on top of the file cabinet. Tentatively, she placed her palms on his chest. She sank her teeth into her bottom lip. He fought to contain his groan. Her hands slid up to behind his neck.

"Oh, Hayden," she murmured before stretching up on her toes and pressing her lips to his.

She kissed him tenderly, as though he might shatter. He didn't want her gentleness. Not when it felt too much like pity.

He bit down on her lip before soothing it with his tongue. His fingers gripped her waist tightly as he walked her backward toward the table he'd just finished sanding. She gasped when her legs hit the edge of it. He slipped his palm under her sweater. His fingers traced the warm flush beginning to spread over her skin.

Nothing about her kiss was tender now. A wild keening sound slipped from the back of her throat when his thumb grazed her hard nipple. She pressed her hips against his. He lifted her onto the table as he pulled his mouth from hers.

Her eyes were wild, and her lips swollen when she reached for the hem of his T-shirt. Their arms tangled as he struggled with her sweater while she tried to work his shirt over his head. After some maneuvering, both pieces of clothing landed on the table beside her.

Elle kicked off her shoes as she fingered the button of his jeans. She froze when Hayden leaned down to suck her nipple pebbled against the satin of her bra. Her legs suddenly gripped his waist tightly. When she rubbed her core against his crotch, he nearly exploded right then and there.

He worked her bra over her head before leaning her back and laying her out on the table like a feast. Her long legs still had him in a vise grip. She panted frustrated breaths. Hayden pressed a kiss between her breasts. Her pulse pounded beneath his lips. He tugged at her leggings, but it was no use.

"Elle," he pleaded. "Pants."

She loosened her legs while sitting up to reach for the zipper of his jeans. He let out a pained hiss as she worked him free. With a breathy sigh, she shoved his briefs down below his ass, then shimmied out of her leggings and panties.

Hayden groaned like a wounded beast when she wrapped her fingers around his length and began to stroke him. Her legs were back around his waist, guiding him closer. He watched like some voyeur as she angled his length inside her. Her delighted moan was his undoing. Swearing violently, he pressed her back down onto the table with his body before ruthlessly pushing into her.

"Yes!" she cried.

Strands of her long hair were coming undone, their tips stirring up bits of sawdust as her head thrashed from side to side.

"Please, Hayden." She clawed at the tabletop.

The pleasure built, and her muscles contracted around him. When he reached beneath her ass and tilted it to increase the friction, she shrieked. Her hips bucked frantically right before a silent scream left her lips, and she went limp. Elle was always beautiful to him, but he was suddenly in awe of how much more gorgeous she was when she came.

"Belle," he whispered reverently.

Her eyes fluttered open. She gifted him with a grin that looked spellbound. "I love it when you call me that," she whispered back.

It was as if she'd unlocked a secret vault of feelings that Hayden didn't know existed. Or how to process. He was struggling to wrap his head around them when she squeezed her core tightly. His other head demanded he stop thinking and start acting. Propping his elbows on the table, he leaned over her.

"My Belle," he grunted next to her ear.

She sighed words of agreement as he thrust into her several more times.

"My Belle!" he shouted as he finally came in a satisfying rush.

They were both breathing hard when the room began to come back into focus. Bits of sawdust clung to Elle's skin. She giggled when he tried to brush them off her.

"I'll never be able to eat a meal at Gavin and Ginger's house after this," she joked.

He touched his nose to hers. "Knowing Ginger's lack of kitchen skills, that's probably a good thing."

They both laughed before a heavy silence settled over the room. She sank her teeth into her bottom lip. He instantly recognized her tell. She was anxious about something. And he had a sneaking suspicion she was also having trouble making sense of the emotions swirling around them.

Elle brushed a piece of hair back from his forehead. "Hayden—"

He distracted her with a kiss. "Let's go inside and shower all that sawdust off you," he murmured against her lips.

Her hands stilled against his back, and he said a little prayer she'd drop it for now. He sighed in relief when she dragged her fingers along his side.

"A shower sounds wonderful."

HAYDEN WAS STRETCHED out on the bed an hour later, watching Elle braid her wet hair, when a chime echoed throughout the house.

"Someone's at the workshop." He reluctantly got up, cursing whoever was interrupting them. "It's probably Xander or Simone. I'll get rid of them. I have plans for you this evening." He nuzzled the spot on her neck where he'd left his mark earlier.

Her sigh was filled with relief. "I'm glad you went down and grabbed our clothes. I wouldn't want a potential client finding my elf panties hanging from one of the chairs."

He winked at her. "You have no idea how much those elf panties turn me on."

The chime sounded again, and Elle swatted him on the ass. "Go get rid of whoever it is and put out the closed sign. Or else my elf panties are taking a walk."

Hayden scrambled out the kitchen door and over to his workshop. Dusk was just beginning to blanket the little town. The Christmas lights he'd hung from the eaves of the old outbuilding glowed festive and welcoming against the weathered wood.

Perhaps he and Elle would get a Christmas tree tonight. He'd never bothered to put one up in previous years. But this Christmas felt a little different. Visions of them snuggling beside a twinkling tree, while watching holiday movies danced in his head.

He was whistling "Have Yourself A Merry Little Christmas" when he opened the door. The tune died on his lips as soon as he saw who waited there.

"Livi."

She aimed a bright smile at him. As usual, she was dressed impeccably in a pair of white wool pants and a matching sweater that featured a giant gold snowflake. Chunky gold jewelry complemented the look.

"It's good to see you up and about," he told her. And he meant it. He liked Livi. Just not the way he "liked" Elle. "What brings you by?"

Her expression dimmed a smidge. Had she expected a more exuberant greeting? *Probably.* He dragged his fingers through his hair. The last thing he wanted was to hurt this woman.

"I have a few potential clients for you," she announced.

The news had him rocking back on his heels.

Livi pulled several pieces of paper from her leather satchel. She hesitated for a long moment before placing them on the table in the center of the room. Hayden held his breath, hoping there wasn't an obvious butt print on the table's edge.

"Um. One person is looking for a desk similar to the one I bought," she said. "They want it made from walnut, however. Here are the dimensions they need. The other client would like a kitchen table." She paused again as she gestured to Gavin and Ginger's piece. "Modern farmhouse like this one."

"Wow. Thanks."

She smiled at him again. "You can work up the price estimates and get back to me."

"Sure."

They stood staring at each other, the strained silence becoming more awkward.

"Livi—" he began.

"Are we still on for the snowman-in-the-sand contest?" she asked at the same time.

"Uh . . ."

"You know what? You don't have to answer me now. Patricia said you are pulling double duty while one of the deputies is sick." She glanced down at her watch. "I have to get up to Wilmington. I'm headed back to Atlanta tonight to meet with the developers. I'll be back in time for the contest next week. If you can't make it, no worries."

"Livi," he repeated. He needed to tell her that friendship was the best he could offer her.

Except she wasn't inclined to hear it. Almost as if she knew what was coming, she rushed over to him and planted a kiss on his cheek. "Gotta jet. See you when I get back into town."

She was nearly to the door when she stopped short in front of the sofa. She pointed at the laptop on its cushion. "Is Elle here?"

Hayden's palms began to sweat. There was no way he could deny the computer belonged to Elle. She'd decorated it with stickers that read "Hot Girls Read" and "Bookmarks Are For Quitters."

"Um, no. She must have left it when she stopped by earlier," he hedged.

Livi nodded while avoiding his eyes. "I've been looking all over town for her today. I had a tip on a shoe sale I wanted to share with her." Her smile was a little forlorn when she finally did look back up. "If you see her, tell her I'll catch up with her next week."

With a stilted wave, she hurried out the door. Hayden blew out a breath. He spied the shoebox of Elle's letters and quickly returned them to the file cabinet drawer. When he went to close Elle's computer, his finger brushed the mouse pad, and the screen lit up. A website titled Lovell Woodworking filled the screen.

What the . . .?

Hayden slumped down onto the sofa and pulled the computer onto his lap. He scrolled through the site. There were photos of his workshop and several pieces of furniture he'd made for friends and family. A picture of the captain's desk, front and center in his mother's shop, served as the banner. There was even a testimonial from "a very satisfied customer, interior designer, Olivia Turner."

"Was that Livi?"

Elle's question startled him. He'd been so transfixed by whatever this was on her computer that he hadn't heard her come in.

"What is this?" He turned the computer so she could see the screen.

Her cheeks went immediately pink. She rushed over to where he sat, trying to grab her laptop. Hayden held it out of reach.

"You're not supposed to see that yet," she insisted. "It's your Christmas present."

"What gave you the idea I wanted a website for Christmas?"

She plopped down beside him. "Actually, it was Livi's idea."

Was she serious right now? "Livi is doing just fine bringing me clients without a website. She just showed up with two furniture requests."

Elle's face lit up with delight. "She did? That's fantastic." She scooched up next to him. "With a bit of good promotion, this doesn't have to be something you do in your spare time. You can become a full-time artisan and make your living crafting furniture. You can grow it over time. Maybe expand to a bigger workshop somewhere else."

So that's where this was going.

His heart sank. "Somewhere else?"

Elle squirmed a little. "Well, yeah. I mean, you don't have to necessarily stay here in Chances Inlet . . ."

Hayden sighed heavily. He closed the computer and placed it on a cabinet beside them before taking both her hands in his.

"Belle," he said gently, "I don't want to live anywhere else. I'm satisfied with my life here in Chances Inlet. It's what I know. And I don't need to become a famous artisan to prove to anyone that I'm worthy. And for the record, neither do you."

He could see the disappointment settle in her eyes before she snuffed it out and adopted a too-cheery, fake smile. "Of course I don't. Furniture making is not *my* passion."

Hayden resisted rolling his eyes at her clever attempt to

deflect the discussion away from her hang-ups. Her ridiculous need to prove herself to her family.

"I don't know. You were pretty passionate *on* the furniture a little while ago," he teased.

Elle draped her arms around his neck. "Maybe I should add something to the website alluding to your thorough testing of the furniture before it's delivered."

He laughed, thankful they navigated the conversation away from the emotional landmines. She kissed him then. It was enthusiastic and sensuous. But he could taste the hint of disappointment that lingered.

Hayden laid her down on the sofa, desperate to erase any dejection she might be feeling. He ignored the insistent voice in the back of his head telling him he was out of his mind. Convincing Elle to stay in Chances Inlet was a fool's errand. Believing he could live without her was even more foolish.

CHAPTER SIXTEEN

"CAN WE GET SOME POPCORN, Aunt Elle?" Emily pointed at the old-fashioned popcorn cart in front of the Foghorn Deli.

"Why not?" The words had barely left Elle's lips before her niece was tugging them across the town square.

Opening day of the Christmas Bazaar had dawned bright and sunny, with a promised high of a balmy sixty degrees. Perfect weather to attract a throng of tourists to downtown Chances Inlet. The merchants throughout the town greeted Elle with a warm smile and a wave. They'd been showering her with gratitude all week as though she'd somehow single-handedly lured customers into their shops.

"Don't be surprised if they give you the key to the city next," Hayden joked as he kept pace next to her.

"I didn't do anything other than post a few videos and blogs," she argued.

The owner of the deli handed Emily a bag of popcorn. "This one is on the house. Payback for your aunt's help with getting my social media some traction." He beamed at Elle. "Don't discount your talents, young lady. We wouldn't have gotten this kind of boon in business without you."

Elle offered him a gracious smile. "I would argue that Mother Nature played a bigger hand in this than I did, but thank you. I'm glad people are finding our town."

Emily scampered ahead toward the toy store.

"DID you hear what you just said?" Hayden asked as they walked behind Emily. "You called it 'our town.'"

The hope in his voice wasn't hard to miss. They'd both been avoiding any talk about their future. It came as no surprise that he wanted her to find her way back to their hometown permanently. Especially since he'd made it clear he wasn't interested in leaving Chances Inlet.

She got it. This quirky little town was his safety net. His comfort zone. Hayden no longer had to prove himself to anyone. He'd faced down several of life's greatest challenges and won. Accomplishments met and exceeded.

Too bad Elle couldn't say the same.

"This is my town, too," she told him. "In case you forgot, I was born here." Linking her arm through his, she rested her cheek against his shoulder. "No matter where I live, Chances Inlet will always be home. After all, the most important people in my life live here."

He heaved a weary sigh.

"Timothy Hayden Lovell."

Claire Lovell's voice had Elle shrugging her arm out from under Hayden's in order to put some distance between their bodies.

"No need to be so formal, Mom." Hayden reached out an arm and gave his mother a side-hug. "Wow. This looks great." He gestured to the rows of tables displaying the various crafts Knotical's knitting club was offering for sale.

Elle reached for one of the Santa Claus knit doorknob covers. "We had some of these growing up. I always loved them. I wonder what my mom did with them when she moved to the inn? Maybe I should get some new ones of my own."

Hayden's mother made a sound of disgust before snatching up the remaining four Santas and slipping them into a plastic bag. "This is my last set, and Livi mentioned she'd enjoy having them. I've invited her to dinner next week. You can give them to her then, Hayden."

The glare she aimed at Elle said "checkmate." Elle bit back her gasp. For the past ten years, Claire Lovell made no secret of her loathing. One would have thought she'd be used to the other woman's animosity by now.

Except she wasn't. The woman standing before her was once like a second mother to Elle. Hayden's mother's hatred cut deeply every time their paths crossed. If Elle needed another reason why she and Hayden weren't meant for the long haul, Claire Lovell was it.

"Mother," Hayden snapped.

Elle pressed a hand to his arm. "It's fine. I didn't realize Livi wanted them, too. Of course she should have them. I'm sure my mom has her set somewhere. I'll ask her about them later." She'd never endured a more painful smile than the one she gave to Claire. "I hope you have a successful bazaar," she managed to say before turning and taking Emily's hand. "Come on, Ems. Let's go get our picture taken with Kringle."

She didn't bother waiting for Hayden to finish his whispered, heated exchange with his mother.

Kate suddenly appeared by her side. "Honestly, that woman needs to get a serious grip."

Elle tried to shrug it off, but her sister was having none of it.

"I'm serious, Elle. Don't you dare let that woman get to you. She has no right to treat you that way."

"I run into her once or twice a year. It's easy to let it roll off me," she lied.

Kate stepped in front of Elle, halting their progress. "Emily,

Daddy is over at the Bed and Biscuit helping with Kringle's photo booth. You go ahead, and we'll meet you there in a minute."

With a cheery "Okay," Emily dropped Elle's hand and skipped away.

"It's fine, Kate. Really," Elle insisted.

Of course, Kate ignored her. "Once or twice a year? What you're saying then is that whatever is going on between you and Hayden is a simple case of friends with benefits?"

Elle took the easy out her sister was unintentionally offering. "Yeah, sure."

It wasn't technically a lie. She and Hayden had been dancing around the relationship status discussion for over a week. Yet, given all the obstacles in their relationship, friends with benefits might be the only option that worked for them.

The very thought made Elle's throat tight, though.

"Bullshit." Kate glared at her from behind her glasses. "This"— she gestured at Elle and presumably toward Hayden somewhere behind them— "has been building for a very long time. It's not some casual fling. You are each other's destiny. And don't you dare insult me—or yourself—by pretending it's anything else." Her sister's voice cracked. "If that woman is the reason you two aren't going to make a go of this, I swear, I'll—"

Elle stopped her sister's tirade with a hug. Her throat was so clogged with emotion, it hurt to speak. "If only it were that simple," she managed to say.

"Love is supposed to be simple," Kate murmured against Elle's hair. "I wish it could be that way for you. I want you to have everything you've always dreamed of."

Her sister's words hit Elle square in the chest. How could she explain that she wasn't like Kate? That she'd never really "dreamed" of a specific future? That her only goal was to live up to the family name, except she had no idea how to accomplish that? Kate would think she was being ridiculous.

"Elle?" Hayden came up beside them.

Kate brushed back a piece of Elle's hair as she stepped out of their embrace. She offered up a wane smile. "At the risk of repeating myself, I'm here whenever you need to talk." With a nod to Hayden, she wandered off in the direction Emily had taken.

"I'm so sorry, Elle. I don't understand why my mom continues to behave the way she does."

She waved his apology away. "It's okay." The lies just kept on coming.

He opened his mouth to say more, but a call came over his radio. Something about someone burning trash without a permit.

Hayden groaned. "Guess my lunch break is over early."

Elle patted him on the chest. "Go protect and serve."

"See you tonight?"

"Of course." She was like a moth to a flame.

He made a move as if he were going to kiss her, but Elle stepped back and shook her head.

Hayden let out another one of those weary sighs of his. "Yeah. Sorry. I wasn't thinking."

"Save it for tonight, Deputy." She hoped the words came out more playful than she felt right now. Her head swam with so many conflicting emotions that maintaining her composure proved difficult. Without waiting on his response, she turned on her heel and headed for the Bed and Biscuit.

You are each other's destiny.

Why did Kate have to be so dramatic? She was a woman of science, for crying out loud. Besides, hadn't everyone once thought Jeremy was her destiny? Look how that turned out.

Except losing Jeremy hadn't hurt the way she knew losing Hayden would. The misery she'd gone through this past year wasn't brought on by her boyfriend cheating on her. It was because she thought she'd messed up her relationship with her best friend.

It's not some casual fling.

Her sister's words made her dizzy. Mainly because Kate was right. Nothing about her relationship with Hayden was casual. And now they'd gone and complicated it with sex. Losing him was not an option. Elle just needed to find another way for them to make this work. And soon. The end of the year—and her stay in Chances Inlet—was two and a half weeks away.

EVERETT TOOK a sip of his coffee while covertly watching Elle march toward the photo booth constructed for the little white dog everyone seemed to be fixated on.

"Claire must have said something to rain on her parade," Kitty remarked beside him.

Kitty was handling the knit shop while her sister worked the tables on the sidewalk. Everett snuck in the back door, bringing with him coffee and a passionate kiss for her. Unfortunately, the store was overrun with customers, and both had to wait. The situation would have normally made him testy with impatience. Yet, after a couple of weeks in this town—and with Kitty in his bed—more and more things that used to irritate him seemed to roll off his back now.

He wasn't naïve enough to think he still didn't have a long way to go to shed the anger shadowing him. Thankfully, his session with the veteran's group earlier in the week went better than expected. After a few tense minutes, the men and women accepted him without the malice he likely deserved. Since the meeting, he'd enjoyed several lunches with the sheriff and a former Navy SEAL who founded the group. He was right in thinking he and Lamar Hollister could become friends if Everett could just get rid of the devil on his shoulder.

One step at a time.

Now, though, he had a roadmap for how to get on with the

rest of his life. And if all his plans fell into place, it began right here in Chances Inlet.

"Your sister will have to learn to deal with it because those two are mad about each other." He took another sip of his coffee.

Kitty's sigh sounded desolate. When he glanced over, her expression matched.

"What?" he demanded.

She shook her head. "They are both on different paths. Hayden enjoys the comfort and stability of this small town. He's had enough excitement to last a lifetime. Elle is still chasing her dream." She shrugged. "Maybe she'll find her way back. Maybe she won't."

"That's the dumbest thing I've ever heard. Why can't her dream be a cozy place to live with a man who obviously adores her? Why risk everything just to feel like she's done something important?" he snapped.

Kitty eyed him curiously. "Are we still talking about Elle and Hayden here? Or you and your late wife?"

He slammed his eyes shut and practiced the breathing his shrink had taught him two years ago. It never worked before, but he needed to master it now. The last thing he wanted to do was snipe at Kitty.

Especially when she was right.

She tentatively placed her hand on his back and began rubbing in circles. "I'm sorry. That wasn't fair."

"No. I'm sorry," he murmured. "Your words were spot-on." Sucking in a deep breath, he opened his eyes. "I just hate to see little Gidget make a similar mistake."

"Mm. Well, you are her Ghost of Christmas Future."

"What do you mean?"

"You really don't know?"

Everett could feel the little devil on his shoulder waking up. "No."

Kitty sighed. "Hayden told me that Elle's been promised a big promotion at *Vantage* when she gets back to New York."

"I can't say I'm surprised. She's a fabulous writer." He shot her a guilty grin. "Bernice hinted that Donald McAlister kept a file with his daughter's freelance work. I was curious, so I took a look. The kid wrote some terrific pieces when she was first out of college. She'll be an asset to the magazine."

"If she gets the chance. The promotion hinges on you turning your book in on time."

Kitty's revelation had him swaying on his feet. It all made sense to him now. This little sojourn to the Tide Me Over Inn with Gidget as his taskmaster. No wonder she'd been so dogmatic about him finishing his memoir.

"That bitch," he grumbled.

Kitty's eyes went wide before her expression grew defensive.

"Helen Keneally. Our mutual publisher," he explained. "She can't help pretending she's an omnipotent chess master toying with her minions' livelihoods. Helen was always pulling Keeley's strings. She's the one who lured Keeley back to Afghanistan to rescue the interpreters. Helen is all about selling magazines no matter what the risk."

"Wow. Maybe you shouldn't finish your book. I'm not sure I like the idea of Elle being in that woman's clutches."

Everett swallowed around the sour taste in his mouth. He didn't like it, either. Not one bit.

CHAPTER SEVENTEEN

THE LINE at Kringle's photobooth stretched around the corner. Addison Lockheart, the owner of the Bed and Biscuit dog hotel and groomers, wore a pair of fur antlers over her blonde hair and necklace of flashing Christmas bulbs. Joking with the crowd, she worked the line selling the organic dog biscuits she made in her shop. She'd also created a cutout Instagram slide for customers to stand behind while taking photos with the dog.

Kringle let out a bark of recognition when Elle walked up. His entire body shook with excitement, dislodging the little green elf's hat tied to his head. Ryan posed for a few selfies with fans while Jane readjusted the dog's hat.

"Wow. This is sick." Elle lowered her voice so only Jane would hear. "At this rate you'll be able to afford braces not just for Henry, but all your future kids."

Jane blushed as she pointed at a sign near the booth. "The profits are being donated to the local SPCA."

Elle pulled out her phone. "Aww. That makes the story even more uplifting. I'm going to interview some of the people in line. I can use it for the town's website."

She recorded her conversation with a family from Myrtle

Beach and a couple from Wilmington. It was their first time in Chances Inlet.

"We are so glad you're here," Elle told them. "I hope you'll check out the Christmas Bazaar while you're in town. And don't forget to grab a bite at one of our unique eateries."

"My grandson says the afternoon tea at the Tide Me Over Inn is to die for," a familiar voice said behind her.

Elle spun around to find Helen Keneally standing there. The woman looked ridiculously out of place. Her oversized Chanel sunglasses and Burberry coat were more suited for the Hamptons than a balmy December afternoon in coastal Carolina.

"M—Mrs. Keneally. What are you doing here?" Elle was proud of herself for not asking if a hurricane had blown the woman's private jet off course.

"I'm on my way to spend the holidays in Palm Beach." She glanced around. "I thought I'd stop in to see what all the fuss is about."

Elle braced herself for condescending remarks like the ones her grandson made the last time he'd come home with her.

"I must say this is even more charming than those small towns you see in the television Christmas movies." Helen pushed her sunglasses up on top of her head. "No wonder Jeremy recommended it so highly."

The mystery of why Jeremy advocated Chances Inlet to his grandmother hadn't been solved. But Elle knew it wasn't because he thought her hometown was "charming." Not that she would argue the point with her boss' boss. She leaned on her manners, instead.

"You've come on a good day. The Christmas Bazaar is always a fun time."

"Is that Santa's dog?"

"Um, yes. Well, sort of. He belongs to my brother's stepson-to-be now."

"That was a very moving piece you wrote about him." Helen

tapped her chest right over her heart. "Very moving. You are going to make a wonderful columnist, Elinor."

Funny how the words didn't sound as appealing as they did a couple of weeks ago.

"I was hoping to catch West while I was in town. There was no sign of him when I stopped by the inn. That's very troubling to me, Elinor. Since I don't have the completed manuscript in my hands, I have to assume he's still writing it. The question is, where?"

Elle's mouth went dry. "Uh—"

Helen tilted her head to the side. "Madelaine has been conveying your updates to me. You've told her the book is almost complete. Is that not true?"

Well, shit.

If Elle's career wasn't on the line, she'd grab Emily and Henry to share a teachable moment about lying. As in, *don't do it. You only get caught in the end.*

She'd been keeping out of West's way for days now. Maybe he'd surprise her by producing a Christmas miracle of a completed manuscript. Of course, he could just as easily be spending his days locked up in the study designing a snowman built out of sand.

Helen's eyes narrowed. The older woman could probably smell the fear wafting off her.

"Is West even in this town?"

"Yes. Of course. He likes to work at the bookstore some days. For inspiration. Or something like that . . ." Elle's voice trailed off.

Helen's shoulders relaxed. Like Elle, the woman had a lot riding on West finishing his book. "Thank God for that. And thank God he's not at the bar. Let's go find our renegade author, shall we?"

Elle said a silent prayer West wasn't holding down a seat at Pier Pressure. With Helen trudging across the town square alongside her, she couldn't even text the man to see where he might be. Not that he ever answered. His texts seemed to go only one way, drat him.

Helen stopped short when they entered the bookshop.

"Oh, my. I can see why West prefers to work here." She took in the colorful displays, stopping at the new releases table to peruse for titles she'd published, Elle presumed.

Elle tried to flag down Paige, but the store was bursting at the seams with customers. Tanner was helping her out by working the point-of-sale computer at the front of the store.

"I'll just go check for West." Elle hurried to the back of the store, hoping to have a moment to warn the dratted man, only Helen was right on her heels.

Of course, he wasn't there. Elle was never that lucky.

EVERETT WAS sure he had to be hallucinating. That couldn't be Helen Keneally trailing in Gidget's wake as they made their way across The Green. He wasn't aware he had the power to make someone appear just by mentioning them. If he did, Keeley would have returned to him two years ago.

"Well, I'll be damned," he muttered.

"Who is that?" Kitty asked.

He huffed out a surprised laugh. "Believe it or not, that is the dragon lady herself. Helen Keneally."

"The publisher you just mentioned?"

"One and the same."

Kitty stared out the window, watching the two women approach the bookshop next door. "What's she doing in Chances Inlet?"

Given that they were striding toward his favorite hiding space, he had to guess Helen was looking for him. That could only mean one thing: part of his plan was already in motion.

"Not sure," he told Kitty. "But I'm going to find out."

He left through Knotical's back door and hurried in through the delivery entrance of the bookstore. The storage room butted up to the small reading nook Everett had commandeered the past couple of weeks. He stood behind the curtain separating the two rooms and listened.

"It's pretty crowded here today." Gidget was trying her best to cover for him. "He might have gone back to the inn to work."

He swore he could hear Helen grinding her teeth.

"I just left there. No one has seen him all day. Or yesterday, for that matter."

"West prefers to work at his own pace. You really don't have anything to worry about, though, Mrs. Keneally. He's assured me he'll be done by the end of the year, and I believe him."

Peeking through the crack in the drapes, he could see Gidget crossing her fingers behind her back.

"That's your first mistake." Helen snorted. "I believed him when he said he'd have the book to me two months ago. Now he's reneging on his option for a second book. The man's word is no good." She pointed a finger at Gidget. "You had one job. That was to make sure the man delivers his book on time."

"And I will."

Helen's laugh lacked any humor. "You don't even know where the damn man is! I should listen to my lawyers and sue the idiot. He's lost his mojo. West is never going to finish that book."

"He hasn't lost his mojo."

Everett was so stunned by Gidget's staunch defense of him, he froze in place.

"In fact, the book is finished," she lied. "He's taking these last few weeks to polish it up."

A charged silence fell over the nook.

"He told you this?" Helen asked. Her tone indicated she didn't believe one word her employee said.

Gidget nodded. "Even better. I've read through the final chapters. They are as captivating as the rest of the book. You'll be pleased. So will your readers."

Some of the steam seemed to leave Helen. "You do realize what you stand to lose here, Elinor?"

"I'm a McAlister, Mrs. Keneally. We don't lose."

Everett resisted the urge to jump from behind the curtain and applaud her bravado. Or chastise her for her ill-advised recklessness. He suspected it was the latter and not the former making her spout her nonsense. Gidget was desperate for the carrot Helen dangled on a string. She'd rather chase a promotion than settle for love.

He hated how much that disappointed him.

Still, there was no excuse for letting her cover for him by lying to Helen. His beef was with the publisher. There was no reason Gidget's career should be collateral damage, whether he thought it was the right choice or not. He was just about to step through the curtain when she spoke up again.

"You mentioned afternoon tea at the inn. It's just about that time. I know my mother would love to thank you in person for sending me home for the holidays."

Well played, Gidget. Well played.

It was uncanny how similar in behavior she was to Keeley. His late wife had always been an enchantress at persuasion. Keeley led with her big heart, too. His gut clenched.

And look where that got her.

He shook his head trying to refocus his attention on the conversation on the other side of the curtain. Helen hesitated, likely weighing Gidget's sincerity. The publisher had no alternative but to trust her, though. Especially since Everett had backed Helen against the proverbial wall. He pondered his next move while the two women walked out of the bookstore.

ELLE'S MOTHER was still practically levitating a half hour after Helen left the inn.

"You didn't tell us you were being promoted." She gave Elle a hug, the fourth one in the past fifteen minutes. "I'm so thrilled for you. You are a beautiful writer. It's nice to see you getting the recognition you deserve. What an accomplishment."

"Thanks."

She didn't have the heart to tell her mother the promotion wasn't a done deal. Helen made it sound that way while she sang Elle's praises to everyone enjoying afternoon tea. It was almost as if Jeremy's grandmother was raising the stakes. Had she guessed Elle was lying about West and his manuscript?

I'm so screwed.

Still, she didn't regret her actions. West had been given until the end of the year to turn in the final manuscript. He didn't respond well to helicopter editing. Helen showing up would only make him dig in his heels even more.

Not only that, but Elle sensed it was costing him to write those last few chapters. As irritating as the man was, she wouldn't force him to do something that might be upsetting. It wasn't right.

Which meant she *was* royally screwed.

"We should have everyone over to celebrate," her mom was saying.

"No!"

Her reaction had her mother cocking her head to the side.

"I don't want to jinx it," Elle told her. "We can celebrate in January when everything is official."

Of course, I could be unemployed. What a party that would be.

"Besides, I don't want to rain on Ryan and Jane's parade," she continued. "They just got engaged. Let them have their moment before we move on to the next thing. In fact, let's keep my promotion between you and me for the time being."

Elle's mother was still looking at her funny when the ringing of a cell phone saved her from continuing the awkward conversation. While her mom answered, Elle hurried into the kitchen to load the dishes into the dishwasher.

"I need to take Midas back to Gavin and Ginger's loft," her mom said when she joined her. "They left him here while they showed their place to a prospective buyer. Gavin is just now putting Hazel down for a nap. Ginger has a meeting at the auditorium to prepare for *The Nutcracker* performance." Her mother sighed as she glanced around the messy kitchen. "The traffic will be crazy with so many people in town for the bazaar. It could take thirty minutes to get there and back."

"I'll take him," Elle offered. "We can walk. I didn't get a chance to check out all the booths earlier."

"Are you sure?"

Elle grabbed the dog leash from a hook by the door. "I'm not getting nearly the same number of steps here as I do in New York."

"Make sure you avoid downtown. Midas is still persona non gratis. Bernice claims there are Most Wanted posters with the dog's picture on it hanging in a few shop windows."

"Midas is at the top of Santa's naughty list, that's for sure," Elle said with a chuckle as she hurried out the door in search of her brother's dog.

She found him standing as still as a statue beside the garden house where he'd cornered a squirrel. Both animals were in the middle of an intense stare down when Elle went to attach the leash.

"Come on, you nutty dog. You've got a perfectly good dinner waiting for you at home."

The mention of dinner had Midas spinning in a circle, tangling them both up in the leash.

"Whoa," Lamar said as he grabbed the dog before Midas took her down. "Sit, Midas."

For once, the dog did as he was told, allowing Elle to step out from the confines of the leash. She smiled up at her stepfather. "Thanks for the rescue."

"All in the line of duty. Lucky for you, I stopped by to tell your mom it's all hands on deck tonight."

"More flu?"

He nodded. "Coupled with the crowd in town, Hayden, Simone and I have our work cut out for us. It's going to be a late night."

So much for her and Hayden sneaking up to Wilmington for a dinner date away from the prying eyes of everyone in town. This day was really beginning to suck.

"Oh, by the way," he said, interrupting her pity party. "You were right about West."

She didn't see that coming.

"How so?" Hopefully, her suspicions about him not working on the book weren't what he was alluding to.

"About him dealing with a lot of baggage. He showed up at our meeting earlier this week. West is working to address the issues haunting him."

"Oh my gosh! That's great. Thank you for inviting him."

He put a hand on her shoulder and gave it a gentle squeeze. "You're the one who put him on my radar. Any credit goes to you for caring."

Elle had a little skip to her step as she headed into town. Perhaps West would finish his book after all. Her promotion was in reach. Finally, she'd have an accomplishment worthy of the McAlister name. She couldn't wait to see the look on Helen Keneally's face when she returned to New York a success.

Returned to New York.

Why did the thought make her stomach drop? The answer to her question sped by in one of the sheriff department's cruisers, headed north toward the highway. She sighed.

"Why is life so complicated?" she asked the dog.

Midas responded with a nudge to her leg and a swish of his tail.

"Oh, you're no help. You've only got one thing on your mind—dinner."

As if to agree, the dog tugged on his leash, eager to get home to his waiting bowl of kibble. Elle took her mother's advice, circumventing the town square and following the more direct route down Water Street toward the old torpedo factory that housed Gavin's second-floor loft. The century-old brick warehouse was on the water, blocks away from the city pier. Gavin's loft featured panoramic views of the town and the point where the Cape Fear River met the Atlantic Ocean.

Her father bought the building long before Elle was born. The bottom floor housed the offices of McAlister Construction and Engineering. Miles and his congressional staff now used that space for his local office. Across the hall was the Tiny Dancer Ballet studio. Elle's childhood dance teacher, Audra Greaves, still owned it, but Ginger and Donella—both professional dancers—did most of the instruction now.

When she pushed open the double doors, Midas bolted up the stairs and through the doggie door without a backward glance.

"Love you, too," Elle called after him.

She chuckled to herself as she turned to make her way back to the inn. A movement in the dance studio caught her eye. West was inside . . . wielding a tape measure?

Elle pushed through the glass doors. "Thinking of taking up dance while you're in town?"

If her interruption of whatever the heck he was doing surprised him, he didn't let on. "Your sister-in-law mentioned she could use an extra party guest or two for this week's performance. Who am I to turn down an opportunity to take part in *The Nutcracker*?"

She didn't doubt his sincerity for one minute. "Mm. You don't want to miss a chance to cross something off your list of cheesy Christmas experiences."

The man smiled at her. A genuine smile like the ones that made Lois and Bernice blush. Heck, it was so unexpected, it almost made Elle blush.

"What are you really doing here?" she demanded.

His grin turned wily. "Working on a project."

Elle slammed her eyes shut while she began silently counting to ten. The man had a project to work on, *dammit*. His memoir!

She snapped her eyelids up. "Helen Keneally was here today."

Neither her announcement nor her tone seemed to faze him. He stretched the measuring tape across the floor.

"Do you even care, West?"

"Helen's travel exploits are of no interest to me."

"She was here looking for *you*."

A loud snap echoed off the high walls when he retracted the measuring tape.

"So I heard."

"Wait? You knew she was here looking for you, and you didn't even bother to show your face?"

"I figured since you are my handler, you could"—he twirled his index finger in the air— "handle it."

Elle was sure she was going to explode. "Oh, don't you worry. I handled it. And now both our necks are on the line."

He deigned to look at her. His green eyes were thoughtful. "Mm. I know. Thank you for that, by the way."

Was he serious right now?

Was this man ever serious?

It was no use. Elle didn't have the emotional wherewithal to deal with West any more today. She spun on her heel to march out.

"Elinor."

The shock of hearing her name come from his lips had her wheeling around swiftly. West stood in the center of the room holding something out to her. From this distance it appeared to be a small rectangle of plastic.

"What's that?" she asked.

He tossed it to her. She caught it right before it landed on the parquet floor. It was a jump drive.

"My memoir."

Elle was suddenly lightheaded. "Wh—what?"

"Complete and ready for Helen to let out into the world."

No surprise, she was having trouble making sense of the man. "You could have given it to her yourself today."

West shrugged. "She tasked you with riding my ass for it. I figured I'd give you the glory of delivering it to her."

"I—I . . ." Words failed her.

He went back to taking measurements.

Elle was now more confused than ever. "When did you complete it?"

The man had the nerve to chuckle. "Sometime in August."

"*Sometime in August!*" Her shout was loud in the cavernous room. "And you couldn't be bothered to turn it in on time?"

He shook his head. "Helen would have pressed me to start working on the next book. And I wasn't ready to write it. I'm not sure I ever will be."

Something the publisher said earlier swam through Elle's mind. "She mentioned you reneged on the option for a second book."

He scoffed. "I guess you could say I did. The contract for the second book is null and void if I miss any deadlines with book one." He shot her a wicked grin. "I simply had my agent remind her of that. She showed up today because she's worried I'll sell it to another publisher. I won't. Not anytime soon, anyway."

Holy crap.

West had been sitting on his book in order to execute some power play against Helen. Elle ought to be furious that he'd involved her in his antics. Except she was getting her promotion out of it. She fingered the jump drive in her hand.

"It must be a hell of a story to warrant Helen coming all the way to Chances Inlet," she said.

He was quiet for a long moment. "Mm. It's a book based on my late wife's journals."

Whoa!

"They are telling. Written as only someone with Keeley's heart could write them." His tone was almost reverent. "But I'm too close to the subject matter to do them justice. Someone else will write the book one day."

The fine lines bracketing his eyes and his mouth were suddenly more pronounced. Elle guessed memories of the tragic way he'd lost his wife were sneaking up on him. She tried to lighten the mood.

"Don't tell me. Rather than writing a book, you're going to build a ballet studio somewhere instead?"

His responding laugh was rich and deep. And sexy. Her sisters-in-law had called the man dreamy when he first arrived. Witnessing this side of Everett West, Elle had to agree.

"Now there's an idea," he replied, keeping his secrets close to the vest as usual.

Elle leaned her shoulder against one of the pillars surrounding the room. "My father built this place for me."

That got his attention. He shot her a curious look.

"Well, sort of. I suspect he built it more for himself than for me. After four kids, he was sick of schlepping one or the other of us to practice. The closest dance studio was in Wilmington." She shrugged.

West's smile held a hint of amazement. "Still a sweet thing for him to do."

"Mm. The sad truth is, I got bored with ballet after a year."

His eyebrows crawled up his forehead.

"I couldn't tell him that, though. I danced for six more years because I didn't want to disappoint him."

Funny, Hayden was the only other person in the world who knew that fun fact.

He shook his head. "Why does that not surprise me?"

She shifted away from the pillar. Was he making fun of her again?

West shoved the tape measure into his jacket pocket and walked toward the door. "You do a lot of things you'd rather not do simply to avoid hurting other people," he called over his shoulder. "Don't you think it's about time you did something just for you, Elinor?"

His cryptic words hung in the air even after he was long gone. Elle studied the jump drive in her palm. It was her ticket to success. A smarter woman would be emailing the manuscript to Madelaine and Helen immediately. Suni had been texting her all week about the fabulous holiday party *Vantage* had planned.

Christmas was a whole nine days away. She could fly back to New York, enjoy the party with her friends, get a jumpstart on her new position and still return to celebrate the holiday with her family.

That would mean leaving Hayden, however. They hadn't yet worked out the logistics of their relationship. And things were good right now. Perfect even. Why waste this time in New York? She doubted she'd enjoy the party without him. And the job would still be there in January. This thing with Hayden might not be.

She shoved the jump drive into the pocket of her jeans. It was the weekend. The *Vantage* offices would be empty anyway. West's memoir could wait until Monday to land in her editor's in-box. She wandered out of the dance studio to check out the rest of the bazaar.

CHAPTER EIGHTEEN

Hayden looked over the contracts Livi had emailed to him last night. The fees her clients were willing to pay were more than double what he thought they should be. Even better, the agreed-upon due dates were several months down the road. He could take his time and make both pieces unique.

"Wow," Simone said from over his shoulder. "That's a sweet chunk of change."

He flipped the papers over. "Do you mind?"

She plopped down into the chair beside his desk. "Can I help it if I'm worried I'm going to lose my partner to the lure of the almighty dollar? And who knew upmarket woodworking was so lucrative?"

"You're not getting rid of me that easily, Simone. I'm not going anywhere." He shoved the contracts into his desk drawer and stood. "Except to the elementary school. Today is the holiday concert, and we've been assigned to help direct traffic." He handed Simone her jacket. "We need to hustle."

"I'm glad your furniture making is becoming more than a stress-relieving hobby," she said as they walked across the town square. "If you put a little promotional effort in, maybe you could grow your business into a full-time gig."

"You sound like Elle."

"Aha! So we've discussed a future together, have we?"

Hayden stopped at the corner to let the Amazon truck go by. The driver was dressed in full Santa garb. He gave them a loud "Ho, ho, ho" as he passed by.

"No talk of the future. We're living in the here and now. Not that it's any of your business." He gave her a pointed look. "She got some crazy idea to build me a website as a Christmas present."

"At least one of you is thinking about your future," she muttered as she stepped past him. She turned around and walked backward so she was facing him. "Have you at least told her that you love her?"

He ignored her as he zipped around her on his way to the school.

Simone grabbed his arm and pulled him toward a bench in front of the town's library. "Whoa there, Deputy Dog. You're not going any farther until you tell me the game plan."

"The game plan is for you to take the entrance to the parking lot on Water Street while I take the one on Oak."

She made a growling sound deep in her throat. "I meant the game plan with Elle, wiseass. You love her. She obviously makes you happy because you've been wearing a shit-eating grin for days now. And, seeing as you are one of the most important people in my life, I want *you* to be happy." She put her hands on her hips. "Are you going to do the smart thing and ask her to stay in Chances Inlet?"

Hayden focused his gaze over her shoulder. The library's front window was painted with an elaborate mural of Santa flying his sleigh, dropping books into the outstretched hands of eager children below. The artwork was courtesy of a local artist who'd set up a gallery in town. In her application for the commission for the window, she told the city council she'd come to Chances Inlet for the sole purpose of finding her passion and sharing it with others. He sucked in a deep breath. Too bad Elle couldn't find her passion in their hometown.

He looked Simone in the eye. "No. I'm not asking her that." He started walking again.

"Why the hell not?" she demanded as she raced to catch up with him. "And don't give me that bullshit about 'if you love someone, set them free.'"

If it's meant to be, they'll come back to you.

Or something like that.

It seemed Hayden was constantly "setting Elle free." She did always come home. Just never to him specifically.

"That plot point seems to work just fine in your grandmother's romance books you're always waxing on and on about," he said.

"Are you kidding me?" She threw up her hands. "What is your problem? Just tell her."

Hayden turned on his heel so fast, Simone lurched into him.

"Okay. I tell her. And she agrees to give up her dreams for me. What happens five years from now when she regrets missing out on her big chance because she chose me out of pity? Or guilt?" he yelled. "When she realizes she's stuck in the town she couldn't wait to escape from because I'm too effing messed up to live out there in the real world? Where will I be then, huh?"

Simone shook her head. "Where is this coming from?"

He heaved a sigh. "From real life. My real life. And Elle's. We both had big dreams once. One of us should get to achieve theirs."

"Oh, Hayden, what if *you* are her big dream?"

Her words hurt to even contemplate. "I told her why I can't leave. That this is my home. And she knows I love her—"

"Have you told her that? Actually said those three words? Out loud?"

He'd said those three words to her countless times over the years. So maybe the words meant something different now. But he'd shown her with his body what she meant to him. There was no way she didn't know.

"I won't beg her to stay. Call it bullshit if you want, but if she chooses New York over me, I'll set her free."

Simone stared at him, wide-eyed and breathing heavy. A car pulled up beside them, and a throat cleared.

"Everything okay, kids?" Sheriff Hollister asked from the front seat of his Bronco.

Hayden found his composure first. "Yessir. We are on our way to direct traffic."

The sheriff looked between them as if he didn't believe Hayden. After a strained thirty seconds, he let it drop.

"I'm going to watch the concert," he said. "Come inside when the parking lot is clear again. There are always lots of baked goods left over."

He drove off toward the school as Simone hurried around Hayden.

"He had me at baked goods," she quipped.

"Simone."

She stopped and looked over at him. Hayden wrapped an arm around her shoulders.

"Thank you for having my six," he told her. "And for being one of the most important people in *my* life."

"I still think you're focused on the wrong thing here. But if my grandmother's books have taught me anything, it's that men are idiots about love." She nudged him in the side. "You gotta do you, though. Good thing I know a doctor. She can sew up the pieces of your heart come New Year's."

"Dɪᴅ ʏᴏᴜ ɢᴇᴛ 'ᴇᴍ?" little Emily whispered when she and her two partners in crime slipped into the back room of the book shop that afternoon.

Everett nodded.

"Yes!" Henry whooped.

"Shh," Emily and Whitney hissed.

It was all Everett could do to maintain a straight face. He hadn't had much interaction with kids during his adult life. Not that he felt like he was missing out. Yet, over the past couple of weeks, these three had wormed their way into his afternoons until he looked forward to their grimy faces and silly stories each day.

Emily held out her hand. "Lemme see." She opened and closed her palm. The eldest McAlister granddaughter was the undisputed ringleader of the trio. The girl would be a force to be reckoned with when she was older.

He pulled the crocheted snowflakes from his bag. All three were unique and crafted by Kitty. She thought it was adorable that he wanted to give them to his "fan club" as she called them. Technically, they weren't gifts. They were a bribe to keep the kids from interrupting while he worked. They could stay, but only if they were silent.

He held them out of Emily's reach. "We have a deal?"

"Yes." She wiggled her fingers again. "We have a deal."

All three kids nodded solemnly. He almost laughed at their earnestness. He didn't have huge expectations that this would work. Emily couldn't help bossing the other two around. And Henry was a wiggle worm who "forgot" he was supposed to be quiet most days. Not that it mattered. West had finished all his research. Now, all he could do was wait.

He handed them each one of the snowflakes. "Here's my end of the bargain. Now each of you can give your mom a special gift for Christmas."

"But I have two moms," Whitney moaned.

"That's right." He made a show of patting his pockets before pulling a fourth one from his bag. "Here you go."

The little girl's blue-green eyes lit up. "Thank you," she whispered.

"We need to wrap them so I can put mine under the tree. That way, my mom won't see it until Christmas," Henry said.

"I'm way ahead of you." West pulled out a roll of wrapping paper from behind his chair.

Emily frowned. "But we don't have scissors. Or tape."

"In my satchel." Everett reached for his bag, but Emily beat him to it. No surprise, she was rifling through it before he could stop her. She yanked the scissors and tape from the bag and put them on the table.

He hoped she'd stop her snooping there, but of course she didn't.

"Hey. What are these?" She pulled out Keeley's journals. "They are pretty."

His heart smashed against his chest as he watched her finger the precious books. He reached across the table and grabbed them from her hands. "Those are private," he said with more force than necessary.

Emily's blue eyes were instantly shiny, and her bottom lip began to quiver.

"You can't touch other people's things without asking, Em," Whitney chastised Emily before wrapping an arm over the girl's shoulders. The littlest one was the empath of the group.

"I'm sorry." Emily's lip was still wobbling.

Everett felt like a beast. He reached over and gently cupped Emily's chin.

"I'm sorry for snapping at you. These notebooks are very important," he explained. "These are very pretty, aren't they?"

He was glad to see her regain her composure almost instantly.

"Where did you get them?" she demanded. "Are they yours?"

All three children moved closer to get a look at the leather-bound journals in his lap. They were tied together with a piece of red-and-green ribbon he'd found at the inn.

"They belonged to my wife."

"You're married?!" they all seemed to say at the same time.

"I was. Once."

Henry's face went pale. "Did she die?" he whispered.

Everett didn't know much about kids. He believed it was best to lead with the truth, though. At any age.

"She did," he replied.

He watched as Henry swallowed roughly. "My dad died, too."

"I didn't know that," Everett replied. Perhaps he should have thought this conversation through a bit more. "I'm sorry."

The little boy nodded. "Do you still miss her?"

Everett returned the nod. "Every day."

"My dad died before I was born, but I miss him." Emily and Whitney each took one of Henry's hands.

Christ. Everett had waded into a minefield.

Henry flicked his chin toward the journals. "I keep the flag from my dad's funeral in my bedroom. It's good to have something of theirs 'cos then they are a part of you still."

Now, it was Everett's turn for a painful swallow. The little boy was likely parroting words the adults in his life had fed him. Still, Henry was spot-on.

"It is."

"She must have been really special," Whitney said.

Out of the mouths of babes.

Unbidden tears burned the back of Everett's eyes. "She was."

"Did she write books like you?" Emily, ever the inquisitor, asked.

"She wrote stories for magazines and newspapers."

"Like Aunt Elle," Emily said.

"Exactly like your aunt Elle." He placed his palm on the top notebook. "These are her books that tell the story of her life."

"Are you going to let other people read them?" Henry asked.

Let other people read them . . .

That was the million-dollar question. Everett had only gotten the courage to read them himself this past week. They were eloquent and brilliant and so transparent, it hurt. They also told her story of why she was so determined to free her interpreter and the many others who aided Western journalists.

Other people needed to read the message of her grit and devotion. He just didn't have the guts to take on the job himself. But he was beginning to get an idea of who might be best for the task.

"Yes, Emily. Someday, I will. I'm not ready to share her with the world just yet."

All three children lunged toward him. Their arms crawling around his neck as they burrowed in closer.

"It's okay," Henry said. "You take all the time you need."

Everett felt a sob lodge in his throat. He wrapped his arms around the three kids. As angry as he was with Helen Keneally, she'd never know the huge favor she'd done by banishing him to Chances Inlet.

"This looks . . . interesting," Xander Fisk said from the doorway. "You aren't trying to shove these kids into an oven you have hidden back here, are you, West?"

Emily and Whitney squealed as they pulled free. Henry let go and raced toward the gym owner.

"Xander!" Henry wrapped his arms around the man's knees. "You promised you'd let me try the rock wall over break. Today was the last day of school. Can I come climb it tomorrow?"

Whitney was already back at the table, carefully wrapping her two snowflakes. Emily sat down beside her and did the same.

"It's up to your mom." Xander ruffled Henry's hair. "If she says yes, then sure."

"Aw." Henry dropped his arms and threw himself into a chair with extra dramatic flair. "She said I have to be sixteen."

"I'll work on her for you, sport," Xander said. "Maybe we can get her down to twelve."

Henry sighed as he rolled down into a sitting position at the table and wrapped his own snowflake.

"Are you almost done with" —Xander waved his hand toward the kids— "whatever this is?"

"I'm not interested in climbing the rock wall," Everett quipped.

"Har, har. The Rotary Club holiday cocktail party starts in twenty minutes. The sheriff said the individual you'd be interested in meeting will be there. Whatever that means."

Finally.

"Excellent. What's the address?"

"I can't tell you that. It's invite only."

Everett cocked an eyebrow.

Xander laughed. "You're going as my plus-one. When you're finished babysitting, come find me out front."

The three kids quietly finished wrapping their gifts. Everett picked up the pile of journals and rolled out some wrapping paper.

Whitney eyed him carefully. "What are you doing, Mr. West?"

"I want to wrap these because they are a gift from my wife. To me."

"Can we help?" Henry asked.

"How about you three do it for me? That would make it extra special."

He sat back and watched as the children worked together to carefully wrap the bundle of journals. His plan was coming together. If all went well at the cocktail party, he'd share his ideas with his agent. Not that he cared if the guy objected. Everett could always find another agent. Kitty was already onboard. And she was the most important piece of the puzzle.

CHAPTER NINETEEN

ELLE HUNCHED over and held her nephew's hands while he bounced on his toes and rocked his body toward the Christmas tree across the room.

"Max doesn't seem to have any interest in walking," she said to Kate.

Her sister stood at her kitchen island, arranging a charcuterie board. Kate and her husband, Alden, always hosted a dinner during the holidays when the McAlisters got together to draw names for Christmas gifts.

"Why walk when you can look adorable and have everyone else do your bidding?" Kate said. "And I'm in no hurry for him to start toddling. I can still plop him down with some toys or a board book while I enjoy a glass of wine after work. Once he finds his sea legs, all bets are off."

Elle grunted as she lifted Max and took him over to admire the tree. "What are you feeding this kid? He's built like a tank."

"According to his pediatrician, he's going to be 'a freak of a rugby player.'" Kate's imitation of her husband's British accent was perfect.

Max reached for an ornament. Elle tickled his belly to distract him. The baby's laughter had her giggling along with him. "There is no greater sound in the world. Someone should add it to those stress relief apps. It would work wonders."

"Speaking of stress relief," Kate said as she carried the platter to the bar area in her great room. "You look like you're sleeping a lot better."

"Mm." Elle decided not to take the bait.

Kate sighed. "Well, I'm glad to see you've worked through your issues."

She hadn't. Not really. Elle suspected she was sleeping better because Hayden wrapped his warm body around hers every night, protecting her.

Of course, the sex might have something to do with it, too. It was still off-the-charts fantastic. So good that she could hardly move her limbs afterward. No wonder she slept like the dead.

Yet another reason she was still holding on to West's memoirs. She wasn't ready to face sleeping alone in her New York apartment again just yet. Part of her worried the demons would show up again, perhaps even louder than before.

Monday came and went days ago without Elle alerting Madelaine or Helen that the book was complete. She worried they'd cut her stay in Chances Inlet short and insist she return to the office. And she wasn't ready to go yet. She wasn't ready to face those demons.

At least, that was how she justified it to herself.

"I still sleep with my clothes, shoes and phone piled on my nightstand," she admitted to her sister.

Kate paused briefly as she pulled wineglasses from a cabinet. "There's no shame in that. That's a mature coping mechanism."

Elle snorted. "Jeremy used to say I was being a baby."

"Jeremy was a twat."

Max squirmed in Elle's arms. She put him in his bouncy harness. He shrieked a laugh every time he jumped.

"What does Hayden say about it?" Kate asked.

Her sister was tenacious, she had to give her that.

"He was the one who gave me the idea. I couldn't sleep at all when I got back from Croatia." Elle shrugged. "Hayden has a lot more experience with, and knowledge about, post-traumatic stress."

Kate smiled softly. "He does. And he cares about you."

Elle wandered over to peruse the holiday cards Kate had displayed on her mantel.

"I'm going back to New York, Kate. I've been offered my own column at *Vantage*."

Her sister nodded.

"You already knew." Elle scoffed.

"Don't blame Mom." Kate offered her a guilty shrug. "What can I say? I have a knack for knowing how to drag these things out of our mother. Her face always gives it away when she has a secret she's excited about."

"Yeah, because she finally has something to be proud of me for."

"Don't be ridiculous." Kate snapped a dish towel at Elle. "Mom has always been proud of you."

"Oh, right. She's so proud of her unfocused child who keeps ping-ponging from one career choice to the next while the rest of her kids are wildly successful at the first thing they chose."

Kate recoiled as if Elle had punched her. "What the heck is going on inside that head of yours? And who says you're unfocused? You're months away from turning twenty-eight. No rule says you need to have it all figured out by now."

"You did!"

Her sister groaned. "Yes, but I'm a bit of a type A personality that way. Actually, more like a type A plus plus if we are being fair. That doesn't mean my way is the right way. Heck, Elle, I spent my twenties buried in boring textbooks while you've spent yours trying things out for size. Exploring the world. Finding your niche." Kate took Elle's hand in hers. "Truth be told, I'm a bit jealous that you have the freedom to do that."

"It's not all fun," Elle argued. "It can be scary. The rest of you had big-time careers by my age."

"There's more to life than big-time careers, little sister. And there are plenty of well-adjusted people in this world without one who are content with their lives."

"Name one."

"Bernice."

Both sisters laughed. Max joined in.

"Although, I wouldn't be surprised if that woman doesn't have her own Wikipedia page someday," Kate admitted as she retrieved her son from his jumping harness. "Please tell me you aren't taking the job in New York out of a sense of obligation to make Mom proud. To make any of us proud?"

Elle couldn't find the words. She shook her head instead.

"Promise?" Kate insisted.

Elle nodded just as Emily, Henry and Whitney sprinted in the door. The rest of their growing family followed. The room was instantly crowded and loud, making any more conversation with Kate impossible.

Several moments later, however, Kate slipped a folded sticky note into Elle's pocket.

"What's that?" Elle asked.

"It's the email address of a friend of mine. She's also an expert in post-traumatic stress. Just in case you need it when you get back to New York. Or if you begin to suffer symptoms of withdrawal from the remedy you are using now."

Elle had to chuckle at her sister's analogy. Kate's diagnosis was correct, though. "Withdrawal" from Hayden was going to hurt. A lot. And if she'd learned anything these past few weeks, the demons were easier to keep at bay if you didn't have to face them alone. Heck, wasn't West proof enough of that?

"Thank you," she said. "I will get in touch with her tomorrow to set something up."

Her sister's look said "Yeah, right."

"I mean it," Elle insisted.

Kate pulled her in for a tight hug. "Whatever you do with your life, you will be successful at it."

"Because I'm a McAlister," Elle replied.

"And we are all here to cheer you on."

They jumped apart when baby Hazel let out a shriek.

"Max pulled her hair," Emily announced.

"She doesn't have any hair," Henry argued.

Hazel was crying in earnest now as everyone tried to placate her. Not to be left out, Max joined in.

"There's a sleeper sofa at your place in New York, right?" Kate asked.

Elle nodded.

"Excellent. Sisters' weekend at your place. Soon. Very soon."

HAYDEN SAT on the corner of his bed, tugging on his uniform boots. Elle's contented sigh had him glancing over his shoulder at her. She was sprawled out on his sheets wearing a coy grin, and nothing else.

He groaned. "Could you maybe turn the sex appeal down a notch this morning? I have to pull a twelve-hour shift, and at this rate, I'll be doing it with a hard-on."

"Can I help it if my man thoroughly satisfied me last night? Multiple times, in fact."

He was on top of her in an instant. "Is that a fact?" he murmured against her ear.

"Mm. It might have been a record." She moaned when he fondled her breast. "In fact, I ought to add that to your website. *Overachiever in bed.*"

She broke out in a fit of giggles. Hayden silenced them with a possessive kiss. When she squirmed again, her thigh brushed against his arousal. He jumped off the bed before he made a fool of himself.

"Here." He tossed her the T-shirt he'd left on the floor the night before when they'd both been stripping off their clothing in haste. "Put that on so you don't keep distracting me. Please," he pleaded.

She made a show of stretching the tee over her torso, causing him more discomfort. When she was finally covered up, she lifted her hair from beneath the collar and swung it behind her. She sat up on her knees like a prim schoolgirl.

"Better?"

It wasn't. The shirt accentuated her pebbled nipples and the soft slope of one of her shoulders where it slid down her arm. He didn't think he'd be able to take his eyes off her and leave for the station.

"Yes," he croaked.

Hayden sucked in a breath to refocus his horny brain cells before mentally going through the checklist of things he needed to do before he reported for duty. It was critical he didn't miss a step. Possibly the difference between someone's life and death.

He opened the door to his closet and punched in the combination to his gun safe. His service revolver sat neatly inside, its ammo in a sleeve beside it. He retrieved them both and loaded his weapon. Once he'd ensured the safety was on, he slid the gun into the holster around his waist. He could feel Elle's eyes on him the entire time.

"I drew Lamar's name last night," she said, her voice soft.

"Huh?"

"Our family is so big that we each pull a name out of a hat and buy a Christmas gift for that one person. I got Lamar this year."

The delight and adoration in her eyes made his chest tight. The sheriff's assimilation into the McAlister family had been a bumpy one. Mostly because Miles decided he needed to be an overprotective jerk where his mother was concerned.

Elle had been cautious with her acceptance, too. Her late father meant so much to her. It seemed the tide was turning, though. Hayden couldn't be happier for all of them.

"Maybe you could help me come up with an idea?" she asked. "I want to get him something really special."

He nodded before leaning down and brushing his lips against hers. "We'll come up with something great."

"Hayden, honey, are you home?"

The sound of his mother's voice had them jumping apart.

"Oh my God," Elle mouthed. Her wide eyes darted around the room.

"I'll be right out," he called as he helped Elle scoop up her clothing from the floor.

His mother's heels were loud on the hardwood floor as she made her way down the hall.

"What on earth happened to this picture?" Her voice was getting closer.

Elle hurried into the open closet.

"Were you and your friends roughhousing inside the house?" his mom asked.

The woman still thought he was ten years old. Her comment had Elle fighting back another fit of giggles. Hayden put his finger to his lips before closing the closet door.

"Mom, could you wait in the kitchen? I'm getting dressed."

Too late, she was already charging into the room.

"You look dressed to me."

"That's because I just finished. And I'm on my way out the door. My shift starts in a few minutes."

She tsked in disgust. "Without making your bed? I know I raised you better than that. You know what they say? 'If you want to change the world, start off by making your bed.'"

His mother leaned down to pull up the sheets. Hayden rushed

forward when he spotted the heel of Elle's Ugg boot sticking out from under the bed, inches away from his mother's foot.

"Really, Mom, I got this." He kicked the boot out of sight before taking the sheet from her and quickly making his bed. "What are you doing up and out this early anyway?"

"Today is your father's breakfast for the dental reps. I thought I'd drop off the cat's heartworm medicine while I was driving by." She wandered over to his dresser and began to rearrange the photos he had there. "I have no idea when Kitty will remember to bring it over."

She lowered her voice as if they weren't the only ones in the room. Which they weren't. Thankfully, she didn't know that.

"Kitty is sleeping with Everett West, you know." There was a hint of glee in his mother's voice.

For crying out loud.

"None of my business." He thumped the pillows on the bed. "There. Now, can I buy you a cup of coffee at the Java Jolt?"

"Why would I want to do that? I'm about to have coffee at the breakfast." She bent over to pick up his socks off the floor.

The odds were high there was a condom wrapper somewhere in this room. He needed to get his mother out of here before she found it. Or decided to organize his closet.

"Your sister is coming in early for Christmas," she announced. "She'll be interested in the situation between Kitty and Mr. West."

He dragged his fingers through his hair absently. "That's great."

His mom reached up and smoothed down the strands he'd just mussed up. "*Annnnd*, she'll get to meet Livi."

Hayden froze. "What? Why?"

Her smile was smug as she hiked one shoulder in the air. "Why not?"

"Mom, nothing is going on between Livi and me."

She adjusted the collar on his uniform. "That's because you two have barely had a chance to spend any time together. She got back into town last night, and is here through Christmas Eve."

"How do you know this?" he asked even though he really didn't want to hear the answer.

"We talk. I adore her, Hayden. And I know something could be there if you just give it a chance. I'm not getting any younger." She patted his chest. "I want grandchildren."

Mother of God.

"Mom—"

Her phone chirping startled them both.

"That's your father," she said before she even looked at the screen. "He can't function one minute without me. I made Aunt Edith's rum cake last night. I'll stop by the station house later to drop it off. I need you to do something for me in return."

Hayden grimaced, knowing what was coming.

"Stop by the inn to say hello to Livi." She kissed him on the cheek. "I've invited her to our family dinner after the snowman-in-the-sand contest tomorrow night."

The click-click of her heels accompanied her from the house. Hayden sank down onto his bed. As soon as he heard her car pull away, he called out to Elle.

"She's gone."

Elle opened the door slowly. Rather than come out, she leaned a shoulder against the doorjamb, her long legs crossed at the ankles and the pile of her clothes still gathered against her midsection. The giggles were gone. A solemn expression replaced them.

He sighed. "I'll find some time to stop by the inn and talk to Livi. I hate to think about what my mom might be filling her head with."

She didn't reply.

"What?" he asked.

"Nothing." Elle shook her head. "It's cute, though. I mean that she wants to be a grandmother."

Hayden wasn't sure how to respond to that. She stepped out of the closet, moving in the direction of the door.

"I should get dressed and get gone in case she comes back," she said.

He reached for her elbow when she passed and guided her down to the bed. His stomach rolled at the sight of her shiny eyes.

"Belle." He kissed her forehead.

"We've been dancing around the elephant in the room for weeks now. But elephants are big creatures, Hayden. They are unavoidable. Even if my job were here, your mother would never accept me as her grandchildren's mother." The laugh that came out of her mouth lacked any humor. "She barely tolerates me being your friend."

Anger at his mother coursed through him. How dare she ruin this? "My mother doesn't figure into this."

She shook her head. "You say that now, but she's your mother, Hayden. She's important to you."

"So are you!" he shouted.

Elle pressed her palm to his cheek. "I know that. And you're very important to me. But—"

Hayden tried to ignore the lick of panic that raced down his spine.

"No buts!" He grabbed both her elbows. "We said we were going to live in the here and now until West finishes his damn book. He hasn't done that yet." He leaned his forehead against hers. "Let's not spoil this special thing we have by wondering about the what-ifs."

She dug her teeth into her bottom lip.

Hayden sighed. "I have to get to work. I'll see you tonight?"

Elle slowly nodded.

The relief he should have felt at her agreement was nowhere to be found. After kissing him on the cheek, she padded on bare feet down the hall. The sound of the door closing was like a gut punch. He swore violently.

What a mess.

Hayden had no regrets about taking their relationship to the next level. He loved Elle. Maybe even more than he realized. And he was beginning to realize he'd sooner give up his other leg than live without her. His mother would just have to get over it. If she didn't, so be it.

He hadn't changed his mind about begging her to stay in Chances Inlet. It had to be her idea. Only they were running out of time. Which meant he needed to come up with a backup plan. The clock was ticking.

Shit.

There was no time to come up with one right now. Hayden was going to be late. He snatched his jacket from the chair and hurried into the hall only to stop short. Beula sat in the middle of the floor blocking his way. The look she gave him was so much like his grandmother's "don't screw this up" look, he was taken aback.

"Don't look at me like that. I'm working on it," he told the cat.

The cat continued eyeing him in disbelief.

"I promise."

With a swish of her tail, the cat wandered off—message delivered. Hayden rushed out the door praying he could find a solution that would allow him to keep that promise.

CHAPTER TWENTY

IF HAYDEN HAD COME by the inn to set Livi straight, the woman was taking it exceptionally well.

"Elle," she gushed when Elle entered the inn's parlor later for afternoon tea. Livi patted the seat next to her. "I've been looking for you."

And I've been avoiding you.

"Things have been crazy busy helping West wrap up his memoir," Elle lied as she helped herself to a plate full of Christmas cookies and a cup of tea.

In truth, she and West hadn't spoken since he'd delivered his bombshell in the ballet studio several days ago. The man was still in Chances Inlet. She knew because she'd spied him at the diner enjoying lunch with several town council members the other day. Their paths had crossed at city hall, also. Elle couldn't fathom what West could want with the chamber of commerce.

"Is he almost finished writing it?" Livi gave her a speculative glance over the rim of her teacup. "I'm sure you're dying for him to hurry up so you can get back to New York."

Elle shrugged. "Christmas is four days away. There would be no point now."

"But you wouldn't stay for New Year's if he completes it before then, would you?"

Wow.

It sounded an awful lot like Livi wanted to get rid of her. Was she fantasizing about sharing a New Year's kiss with Hayden? A sharp pang of jealousy knotted in Elle's stomach.

Get used to it, she told herself. Even if they decided to continue their relationship as a long-distance one, women like Livi would constantly throw themselves at Hayden. And why wouldn't they? He was perfect.

Would he get tired of waiting for her to come home and take what Livi was offering? His mother certainly would support that. Her appetite vanished at the thought. She pushed the plate of cookies to the center of the table.

"I'll cross that bridge when West finishes," Elle said.

"When West finishes what?" The damn man would pick that moment to enter the parlor. He strode over to their table and helped himself to one of Elle's cookies.

Elle's palms began to sweat. She believed they'd had a breakthrough in their relationship the other day when he'd given her the jump drive. He'd told her it was up to her when she turned it in. She presumed that meant he didn't care that she wasn't racing back to New York. Still, she had no idea if he'd cover for her right now.

"Your memoir, silly," Livi told him. "I was asking Elle if you finish before the end of the year, will you both be returning to New York?"

Elle didn't dare meet the man's eyes. She could feel them boring into her, though. A painful moment stretched before he put her out of her misery.

"I have no plans to return to New York," he declared as he ambled over to the coffee urn.

Livi looked as shocked by his words as Elle felt. Although, when she thought about it, his announcement made sense. There was something going on between him and Kitty. She was sure of it. And he was showing a lot of interest in the works of her town for some reason.

"Where will you go?" Livi asked. "Back to reporting from a war zone?"

He winced ever so slightly before he answered. "No. I have something more fun in mind."

"You're being very mysterious, Mr. West." Livi tried to charm the man with her dazzling smile. "Won't you let us in on your secret?"

West laughed before taking a sip of his coffee. He leaned a hip against the sideboard and aimed his gaze directly at Elle. "As soon as I get all the players onboard."

"Will you be writing another book?" Livi asked.

Elle thought of the notebooks he'd been carrying around with him all this time. The journals written by his late wife. She wondered at the stories contained within them.

"I hope you do," Elle surprised herself by saying.

One corner of his mouth turned up. "Do you?"

Were they back to this again?

"Yes. I do," she stated emphatically.

His lips curved into a wide smile at her words. "Good." He nodded to Livi. "Enjoy the rest of your tea, ladies."

Two of the guests stopped him for a selfie on his way out. West obliged them before heading back down the hall to the study.

"What was that all about?" Livi asked.

Darned if she knew. But she was going to find out. Right now.

Elle stood from the table. "I'd better get back to work, too," she said, spinning yet another fib. "I'm sure he needs some emails answered."

Livi quickly stood to block her path. "Wait. I need your help with something."

"You need *my* help?"

"Yes." Livi's lips formed a obstinate line. "I'd like to get Hayden a Christmas gift."

Elle's stomach was really burning now. "I'm sure he'd say it isn't necessary."

Something flashed in the other woman's eyes. "Of course it's not necessary. I want to anyway. I was hoping that, as his *best friend*, you could give me some ideas."

"Did you ask his mom?" Elle regretted the words as soon as they were out of her mouth. She wasn't being fair. And she certainly shouldn't let on that she was aware of the friendship between Claire Lovell and Livi.

"I did. Everything she suggested was practical. I don't want to get him another pair of joggers or a vest to wear while he runs outside this winter. My gift needs to be something special. I want it to mean something."

It felt like the air had been sucked from the room all of a sudden.

I want it to mean something.

The devil on Elle's shoulder was telling her to give Livi an idea that was totally off base. Her conscience wouldn't let her, though.

"He likes puzzles," she said softly.

Livi arched her eyebrows. "Puzzles?"

Elle nodded. "Mm. Not just jigsaws. All kinds. Hayden likes the challenge of problem-solving and building things. Check at the bookstore. Paige has these cool three-dimensional ones of some of the famous buildings and sculptures around the world. She might also know if he has any of them already."

"You are the best. Thank you so much." Livi pulled her in for a hug before Elle had a chance to resist. "I can see why Hayden loves you so much."

It took everything Elle had not to pull out of the other woman's embrace and run screaming from the room. Hayden loved her. She knew that. He hadn't said the words, but he didn't have to. She felt it with all her being.

What she wasn't so sure of? Whether their love could go the distance. They were both on different paths. One person had to bend for them to have the forever love she so desperately wanted.

"What an awesome idea," Livi continued when she finally released Elle. "I'll go into town and check with Paige after we finish our tea."

"Great," Elle said a little less enthusiastically. "I can't stay, though." She was pretty sure those cookies would taste like sawdust in her mouth. "I need to get back to work."

"Sit with me at *The Nutcracker* tonight?" Livi asked. "Hayden won't be off work in time to go, and I don't know many other people in town."

She bit back a sigh. "Sure."

The study door was closed when Elle reached it. She knocked. After no one answered, she stormed in. West sat at the desk, wearing his headphones again, as he tapped the keys of his laptop. He pulled one side of the headphones away from his ear, and Mannheim Steamroller's version of "Carol of the Bells" blared throughout the room. He clicked something on his keyboard, and the music stopped.

"Do you need something from me, Elinor?"

Now that she was face-to-face with the man, she couldn't remember what she meant to ask him.

"Um, more like do you need any help from me?" she said.

"You were set free once you had the manuscript in your hands."

"Uh, yeah. Okay."

"Since my agent hasn't received a congratulatory note from Helen, I assume you haven't turned it in yet?"

"Hardly anyone is in the office this week," she hedged. "It's not like copy editing will be jumping right on it. Besides, I already read through it. It's pretty clean."

He leaned back in his chair. "But you could be back in New York City enjoying all the holiday glamour. Getting ready for your new job."

Elle snapped to attention. "You know about that?"

"Helen likes to toy with people. I figured there had to be a reason she sent you to ride shotgun. A little bird told me she'd bribed you with a promotion."

She was immediately defensive. "I proved myself for that promotion long before this ridiculous little field trip."

"Yes, Elinor, you did. You are a fantastic writer, and you deserve the column. My point is that Helen shouldn't have manipulated you that way." He shrugged. "Now you know her game, and you'll be able to see it coming next time. The knowledge will serve you well at *Vantage*."

His words shocked her. "You think I'm a good writer? Even though I only write 'bits and pieces for social media'?"

He had the good grace to blush. "Touché. But I did my homework and read some of your early work. Don't doubt yourself, Elinor. You *are* a talented writer."

She didn't know what to say. "Thank you. Coming from you, that's more than just a compliment. Your book is amazing, by the way. I think once veterans read it in its totality and get the whole story, they won't be as negative toward you."

"That's what I'm counting on. I learned early on that you can't please everyone, though. You've got to let some of that vitriol roll off your back."

"Mr. Weeeesst!" Emily cried as she zoomed into the study. "It's time to go to the auditorium for hair and makeup."

"You weren't kidding about appearing in *The Nutcracker*," Elle said with a chuckle. Not that she was surprised.

"He's a party guest," Emily explained as West gathered his garment bag from the back of the door. "And I get to dance with him at the end."

"Do you now?" Elle tweaked her niece under the chin. "That sounds like fun."

"It promises to be," West said. "Life is always fun when you do the things you want to do." The man winked at her. "See you after the show."

Emily tugged at his hand. "Come on. Uncle Gavin is waiting in the car for us." She blew a kiss to Elle. "Don't forget to clap for me, Aunt Elle."

"I wouldn't dare."

HAYDEN HESITATED on the front step of the inn. He really didn't like having to hurt Livi, but his mother was allowing things to get out of hand. And that left him in an awkward position.

Livi had given him a taste of what his furniture-building business could be like if he pursued it, and he was grateful to her for that. He was also thankful for her friendship. Hopefully, they could maintain a friendly professional working relationship after he cleared the air.

The front door swung open, and Emily came flying out. West followed on the little girl's heels.

"It's almost showtime, Deputy Hayden." Her excitement was palpable. "Are you coming?"

He ruffled her hair. "I'll be there in spirit. Someone has to work tonight, or else the sheriff wouldn't be able to see you dance."

"He's going to record it. You can watch it tomorrow," she told him.

"I will look forward to it."

She raced toward the car idling in the driveway. "Last one in the car is Santa's stinky socks," she cried.

West let her win, descending the steps at a more sedate pace. He had a garment bag slung over his shoulder.

"Making your big ballet debut tonight?" Hayden asked.

"Something like that," West replied. "Life is too short, Deputy, not to experience new things."

"Funny. My aunt said something similar yesterday."

The man's eyes actually twinkled as he walked past. His smile was probably like the one of Hayden's that Simone described as shit-eating. Ironically, his aunt's smile was just as vibrant these days.

"West," Hayden called after him.

The reporter stopped and turned around. "Hmm?"

Hayden cleared his throat. "I don't think I've ever seen my aunt this happy. Not even when Uncle Theo was alive. Thank you for putting a smile back on her face."

Neither of them said anything for a charged moment until West nodded. "The feeling is mutual."

Gavin honked the horn. West chuckled as he turned toward the car again. "My dance partner is demanding."

"One more thing before you go," Hayden added. "Don't you dare break her heart."

West waved with his free hand. "I don't intend to," he said as he got into the front passenger seat of the car.

"Bye!" Emily yelled out the window as Gavin drove away.

Hayden climbed the steps to the veranda, in a hurry now to accomplish his task. As luck would have it, Livi was gliding down the stairs when he walked in. Her face lit up with a smile. She tugged her black cashmere jacket around her shoulders as she met him at the bottom.

"What a treat," Livi remarked. "Your mother said you might drop by, but I know you don't have much control over your time when you are on duty. I'm glad you could make it."

Damn his mother.

She rose on her toes and pressed a kiss to his cheek. "You caught me as I'm leaving for a walk into town. Join me?"

Hayden drew his hat from his head. "Sorry. I can't. I came in my cruiser. I'm headed in the opposite direction."

"Oh."

"Do you have a minute? I've wanted to speak with you since you came by my workshop last week."

A hint of apprehension filled her eyes. "If it's about the contracts, we are all good to go. You should have already gotten the deposits in your bank account."

"I have. It's all good." He ushered her back toward the parlor, which was blessedly deserted. Empty teacups were still sitting out. Hayden didn't have too much time before someone would interrupt them when they came in to clean. "Can we sit for a minute?"

Livi hesitated briefly. With a resigned sigh and a stiff smile, she obliged.

Hayden placed his hat on the table. He took the chair beside her, turned it around so they could face each other, and sat. Perching his elbows on his knees, he leaned forward so their conversation had less of a chance of being overheard. "I wanted to talk to you because I think my mom has given you the wrong idea about something."

"Oh my gosh, Hayden. Your mom is such a sweetheart. My parents have been on this five-month cruise, and I haven't been able to talk to my mother as often as I'd like. Claire has been a godsend to me these past few weeks. You are so lucky to have her."

Her enthusiastic praise of his mom caught him off guard. It seemed their friendship went both ways. Although he was glad she could be there for Livi, even if she had an ulterior motive in mind. He made a mental note to rope his dad in on what was going on because his mother likely wouldn't take it well.

"Yes, I'm very lucky to have her. Except I think she's been giving you the wrong idea about me. About us."

"But she hasn't," Livi insisted. "Your mom is so proud of you and your talent at woodworking. She knows your furniture sales can take off. So do I. We are both going to work together to help you get your business off the ground."

Shit.

This conversation was leapfrogging into territory even he didn't see coming.

"This isn't about my woodworking," he told her. "Although I can see now I'm going to need to have a serious discussion with my mom because there is no way she's getting involved with my business."

"Oh, but you're wrong to shut her out. Claire has incredible business sense."

"Be that as it may, I'm a one-man show."

She dropped her hands to her lap. "You don't want to work together any longer?"

Hayden covered her hands with his. "I want to work with *you.* You have a good eye for what your clients' needs are and I appreciate the business you throw my way. I would love to keep that going."

"But?"

"But that's all our relationship will ever be. Friends who do business together. I'm afraid I can't offer you anything more than that."

He let his words sink in, bracing himself for any sort of reaction, praying she didn't cry.

"Ever?" she whispered.

"I'm sorry, Livi. I think my mom has been giving you the wrong idea."

She drew in a deep breath. "It's Elle, isn't it?"

Hayden withdrew his hands. "What do you mean?"

"You're in love with Elle."

"We're talking about us," he insisted.

"You just said there is no 'us.' Outside of business, that is. And that's fine. You make unique and beautiful furniture. I'm happy to steer clients your way. But don't insult me by denying that you're in love with Elle. Anyone who has ever been around the two of you can see it." It was her turn to pat his hand. "I like both of you. I hope you two can work things out."

Her candidness stunned him. "That's—that's really kind of you, Livi. Elle's and my relationship is . . . complicated right now."

"I'll say. And I think it just got even more so." She nodded to the hallway behind him.

Hayden turned to see Jeremy Keneally standing there, a dozen red roses in his hand and a smug smile on his face as he looked down the long hall. Elle approached him from the direction of the study.

"Jeremy?" she said.

"Oh, babe, am I glad to see you." Jeremy wrapped his arms around Elle as if he owned her. Then he buried his lips against her neck.

CHAPTER TWENTY-ONE

ELLE CRINGED beneath the weight of Jeremy's embrace. When his lips brushed against her neck, a wave of nausea crashed through her belly. She shoved him away and took two giant steps back. This had to be a bad dream.

Nope.

It really was her ex standing in the foyer of her mother's inn. Only looking at him now, Elle wondered what she ever saw in Jeremy. His dark hair appeared a little too perfect with its preponderance of gel. One of his thick eyebrows arched up. Beneath it, his gray eyes were icy within his arrogant expression.

How had she ever thought she could love this man? Everything about Jeremy was cold, hard and dark. Whereas Hayden was warm, easy and caring. The two men might as well have been night and day.

"What are you doing here?" she demanded, not bothering to hide her pique.

"Surprise," he replied, the word coming out as more of a question. His smile looked forced, more like the Big Bad Wolf baring his chemically whitened sharp teeth.

Elle was surprised all right. Just not in the way Jeremy assumed she would be. Not one bit.

A throat cleared behind them. Elle turned to see Livi and Hayden standing at the entry to the parlor.

Perfect. Just perfect.

Hayden had come to clear things up with Livi, and now they were getting an entertaining sideshow courtesy of Elle's ex. The decorator looked between Jeremy and Elle, her eyes wide with curiosity. Hayden's expression was more stoic as he stared Jeremy down. The air in the room practically sizzled when Jeremy shifted his gaze from Elle to Hayden.

"Um, Jeremy . . ." She quickly stepped between the two men. "You remember my friend, Hayden."

The word "friend" felt funny coming out of her mouth. They were so much more than that. But this wasn't the time or place to clarify their relationship status. Especially since they hadn't figured it out themselves.

"Deputy." There was no mistaking Jeremy's condescending tone.

"Keneally." Not surprisingly, Hayden matched it.

Elle rolled her eyes. "And this is Olivia Turner. She is a guest here while she works on a project over on Bald Head Island. Livi, this is Jeremy Keneally. He lives in New York. Which means we can only assume that he has lost his way."

Jeremy aimed his well-honed, enrapturing smile at Livi. "Nice to meet you."

It was the same smile he'd given Elle when they first met during pre-service training for their Peace Corps assignments. The one that made her weak at the knees. The one that made her fall in love with him a little more every time he wielded it at her.

Too bad she hadn't known he was using that very same smile to lure other women into his bed. She knew it now, though. And she needed to let Livi in on the secret.

She glanced over at Livi. If the other woman was falling under

Jeremy's spell, she hid it well. Livi was made of sterner stuff than anyone thought. Elle felt a lick of pride for the other woman's composure.

"Nice to meet you as well, Jeremy," Livi said. "Will you be joining us here at the inn?"

And just like that, Elle felt something else for the woman.

"I am as a matter of fact," he replied.

Elle felt the room start to spin. "What?" She was going to kill her mom for not giving her a heads-up.

"Like I said," Jeremy continued, "I wanted to surprise you. I had my secretary make the reservation under her name."

Behind her, Hayden made a little growling sound. Before he could act on it, however, the speaker microphone clipped to his shoulder chirped with an incoming radio call. The sound made Elle jump.

Hayden cleared his throat. "If you'll excuse me, I have to get back to work." He nodded to Livi, then turned toward the door without meeting Elle's eyes. Or saying goodbye to Jeremy, she noticed.

"I'll walk out with you," Livi called after him. "I'm on my way to the bookstore to pick up a Christmas present. I look forward to seeing you around the inn, Jeremy. Elle, I'll save you a seat at the show tonight."

"There's a show tonight?" Jeremy asked when the door closed behind them.

Elle heaved a sigh. "Not one you'd be interested in seeing. What exactly are you doing here, Jeremy? And cut the bullshit."

He had the audacity to look taken aback by her tone. "We were part of each other's lives for years. Is it so strange that maybe I'd want to see you?"

Her immediate laughter surprised them both. "Oh, Jeremy, it's more than strange. Especially since you came all this way to my 'provincial' hometown to do it when we've both been living in the same city *for the past year.*"

Elle hadn't realized she'd raised her voice until one of the guests popped their head out from the music room. She reached for Jeremy's hand, then thought better of it.

"Come with me," she commanded, turning and marching toward the study. It took everything she had not to slam the door when they were both inside.

Jeremy dragged his fingers along the desk, stopping to touch the papers West had left behind. "Is this the room West is using to finish his book?"

"He works in a variety of places." She snatched the papers off the desk and shoved them in a drawer. "But we are not discussing Mr. West. We are talking about you. And why you are here. Carrying a dozen roses, no less. Surely you didn't think you'd give those to me and all would be forgiven?"

One corner of his mouth kicked up. She used to think it was sexy when he did that. Not anymore.

"You mean flowers won't work?"

"Your dry sense of humor won't work on me, either." She crossed her arms over her chest and waited him out.

With a frustrated sounding sigh, he laid the bundle of roses on the desk. "Look, Elle. You have every right to be angry with me. I know it sounds cliché, but I never meant to hurt you. I loved you. Still do."

Those were not the words she expected him to say. Too bad for him, his confession only stoked her ire. Because he was lying. If he was honest about loving her, he wouldn't have cheated.

"What kind of fool do you take me for, Jeremy? Are you forgetting I caught you banging Cassie? In. Our. Bed." She scoffed. "I should have wondered why you always chose that one bar for drinks. It was a dive that wasn't even close to our place. What I didn't know was that you were enjoying your own private happy hours with the perky blond bartender."

"Elle, honey, I told you it was just one—"

She held up a hand, ashamed to see it was shaking. "Don't you dare lie to me by telling me it was 'one time' because I know for a fact it wasn't. Cassie confessed everything to me when she realized you weren't going to replace me with her after I left."

That little tidbit left him speechless.

"Now that we've got that cleared up, why are you really here?"

One thing she'd learned about her ex—he would never come crawling back to Elle unless he needed something. And that something had to be big.

He leaned a hip on the desk. "My grandmother likes you."

She gave him a shrug that said *tell me something I don't know.*

"I'm throwing my hat in the ring for an open congressional race. She's promised to back me if I present a more"—he swallowed— "settled persona."

Elle's knees nearly buckled. Was he saying what she thought he was saying?

"We were good once," he said softly. "I fully intended for you to be my forever girl. I know I messed up. But I promise it won't happen again. And I'll spend the rest of my life making it up to you."

She really wished Jeremy wasn't standing between her and the bottle of whiskey right now.

"Way to sweep a woman off her feet," she said.

"Elinor." He reached for her hand, but she hid both behind her back. His eyes narrowed. "I just said we were good together. We both know it. People make mistakes. You can't forgive me? Hell, you probably forgave Cassie."

In fact, she had. The bartender may have been complicit, but the man in front of her had duped them both in the end.

"Let me see if I can understand this," Elle said, trying her best to control her disgust. "Your grandmother will only open her purse strings if you keep your pants zipped and settle down. Why come to me?"

"I told you. She likes you. I like you," he added hastily.

"Look me in the eye and tell me this cockamamie proposal has nothing to do with my family connections," she demanded.

He opened his mouth before closing it again a few seconds later.

"That's what I thought." She moved to the door. "Stay here tonight. Don't stay here tonight. I don't care. Just leave me the hell alone. My family is too good for the likes of you."

HAYDEN HOBBLED out of the shower at midnight to find Elle making herself at home in his bed. Beside her, Beula thumped her tail in greeting.

"You didn't show up at the inn," Elle said.

"I was working on one of the pieces Livi commissioned. Time got away from me."

She gnawed on her bottom lip. It was her tell that she didn't believe him. "Are you mad about something?"

Hell yeah. He was furious at that dick Jeremy for showing up out of the blue and putting his hand and lips all over his woman. Not that he was admitting to it.

"I'm confused, that's all. Why is Jeremy in town? What does he want?"

From you.

A crestfallen look settled in her eyes before she shook it off.

"Elle?"

"Promise you won't get mad?"

No!

"Yeah."

She slid to the edge of the bed, the T-shirt of his she wore riding up her thighs when she placed them on either side of him. Reaching up a hand, she traced a path around his navel. His arousal edged against the towel.

"He claimed to still be in love with me," she said right before pressing her tongue to his belly button.

"What the actual fuck, Elle!" he yelled.

Beula shot off the bed and disappeared down the hall.

"You promised not to get mad."

"I lied." He wasn't mad. He was furious. And he was going to get dressed and go tear the asshole from limb to limb. "Is he still at the inn?"

"I have no idea. And I don't care." She reached beneath the towel and wrapped her fingers around him.

"Don't try to distract me, Elinor. That jerk has no right to mess with you the way he has."

"I knew he was lying. He practically admitted it when I confronted him." She reached both hands beneath the towel. "Besides, even if it was true, I don't love him. I realized today that I never loved him." She looked up at him from beneath her lashes. "Because he's not you. And I'm your Belle," she whispered as she pulled the towel from around his hips.

Her declaration didn't do much to calm him down. The blood from his brain rushed to other parts of his body, and he wasn't proud of the way he reacted. Tossing away his crutch, he bent Elle back on the bed and knelt between her legs.

"I'm your Belle," she repeated as he made love to her with his tongue until she was screaming the words, her fingers fisted in his hair.

He didn't bother waiting for her body to settle back down after her orgasm. Instead, he tossed her like a rag doll to the head of the bed. He rolled on a condom and covered her in an instant. Her eyes flew open when he thrust into her fully. They glazed over when he began to move.

Her fingernails dug into his shoulders as he pounded into her. He was behaving like an animal, taking out his anger at her ex on her. Except he couldn't help himself.

"Say it again," he growled next to her ear before sinking his teeth into her collarbone.

"I'm your Belle," she gasped out.

"Again," he ordered until the bedroom was filled with her chants of "I'm your Belle."

He could feel her closing in on her pleasure again. "That's right. You're mine." He wasn't sure if he was talking to her or to Jeremy. But he was sure he should be ashamed of himself for using her this way.

Her back arched when she cried out beneath him. "Yes, Hayden. God, yes!"

He pressed up on his forearms and stared down at her. Her hair was a tangled mess on the pillows. He hadn't even bothered to strip off the T-shirt of his she wore. It was rucked up beneath her armpits. She had every right to hate him for using her to soothe his anger.

Instead, she laughed. He hated that it sounded more manic than happy.

"Can you believe the jerk thought I'd marry him?"

Hayden froze above her. "He *what?*" No wonder she'd seduced him. To keep him from killing Jeremy Keneally.

Her humorless laugh was loud in the room again. "His grand-mother is cutting him off unless he becomes more respectable. Apparently, *I'm* respectable. Not because he loves me though. That was just a lie. It's because I'm a McAlister. A nepo baby with good connections but not deserving of his love and respect."

He winced at the crack in her voice. A tear leaked out from her eye. He bent down to catch it with his lips.

"No, Elle," he murmured against her skin. "He's a jerk, and he's wrong. He doesn't deserve you. Don't you dare let him get to you. You hear me?"

She heard him all right because she pressed her palms to his chest, swiftly reversing their positions until she straddled him.

"Damn right he doesn't deserve me," she panted out as she began to ride him.

He shoved his hands beneath the T-shirt to grip her waist. When she tossed her head back, her hair billowed through the air. She was a vision above him.

"He doesn't know me like you know me, Hayden. And he never will."

Her declaration had his orgasm swiftly surging through him. They both cried out, then she slumped into his arms. Their hearts raced, seeming to beat as one.

Hayden's emotions were all over the place as he stroked her back and breathed in the musky sex smell from her skin. When her breaths began to even out, three things became crystal clear to him. One, she was taking the promotion at *Vantage*. If for no other reason than to prove to that dickweed Jeremy—but mostly to herself—that she was more than just a McAlister. Two, Jeremy Keneally—or any other man, for that matter—wasn't ever going to know Elle the way Hayden did, because three, he was leaving his protective cocoon of Chances Inlet and going to New York with her.

He loved her that much.

THE BEACH in front of the city pier was crowded the following afternoon as observers came out to watch the snowman-in-sand-making contest. Fortunately for Elle, West was happy to let the professionals show off today. Wet sand on a chilly day wasn't exactly her idea of fun.

A huge tent stretched along the shore, beneath which ten sand sculptors set up shop on various spots along the beach. They had eight hours to produce a unique snowman that stood at least three feet tall. Among them were a few amateurs from town who decided to try their luck.

"Isn't this fabulous?" Bernice practically bounced on the toes of her bright red Crocs, the movement lighting up the soles.

The older woman had never met a fashion risk she didn't take. Today was no exception. She was wearing a puffy red jacket over forest green velvet pants to go with her crazy shoes. The elf hat that had become synonymous with her this time of year was perched jauntily on her head. A wrist full of bracelets jingled whenever she moved. Even her glasses had a holiday vibe, sparkling silver whenever the sunshine hit them just right.

Elle panned the crowd with her cell phone camera. "I have to admit, Bernice, this is an out-of-the-box idea that will probably take off. It will get us tons of hits on social media, that's for sure. I think I'll interview some of the sand sculpture artists for a blog we can post on the town's website."

"Don't forget to get some video of the kids building their snowmen." Bernice pointed to an area on the beach where one of the sand artists instructed Emily, Henry, Whitney and a couple dozen other kids on the best techniques for building a snowman out of sand. "Everyone loves an adorable kid playing in the sand."

"Unless they are on the beach towel next to them," Gavin said when he joined them.

"Oh, you are a party pooper," Bernice accused.

"Not today. We just got an offer on the loft, and I'm ready to celebrate," he replied.

"No way! Congratulations. That's great." Elle bumped her brother's shoulder. "Although I'm going to miss that place."

"I'm sure West will let you come visit him there," Gavin said.

Elle rocked back on her heels in surprise. "West bought your loft?"

"Yep. It'll be a bachelor pad once again." It was ridiculous how proud her brother sounded stating that fact.

"Humph." Bernice donned a cat-ate-the-canary grin. "Not for long, if the scuttlebutt around town can be believed."

"Says the purveyor of the town's scuttlebutt," Gavin teased.

Bernice shrugged. "It's about time Kitty got out of her sister's house and started living again."

Gavin shuddered. "Yeah, especially since Claire Lovell was on the warpath this morning."

The older woman's ears perked up. "And you know this how?"

"I just came from the inn. Claire was having a hissy fit that Livi Turner flew the coop early."

Hayden's mom wasn't the only one shocked by that news. Elle was caught off guard when she arrived at the inn for breakfast and learned that Livi and Jeremy had already checked out. Together, it would seem.

According to Elle's mother, Jeremy offered her a ride back to New York on his private plane. Livi's parents were arriving home that evening, and she was anxious to see them, her mom explained. As relieved as Elle was that Jeremy had left, she hated that she didn't get the opportunity to warn Livi about him. She prayed the woman had enough sense not to join the mile-high club on their flight today.

Bernice tsked. "That woman hasn't been right, since—well, since you know when."

Gavin draped an arm around Elle. She leaned her head on his shoulder, grateful, as always, for his silent show of support. At least Claire Lovell was the only one who blamed Elle for the events of ten years ago. They stood that way for a peaceful minute until Tatum wheeled her pastry cart up next to them.

"Yum." Gavin pulled away to check out the holiday treats on Tatum's cart. "How do you always know to show up when I'm hungry?"

"It's not that hard to figure out, Gavin. You're always hungry," Tatum quipped.

Elle laughed while Gavin plucked two snickerdoodle muffins from the cart.

"Keep laughing and I'm not going to share, sister o' mine." He handed the muffins to Elle then pulled out his credit card. "Bernice, what would you like?"

"To be twenty years younger." She reached for a sugar cookie decorated as a reindeer.

"I ought to charge you a surcharge for what your mangy mutt did to my store the other day," Tatum said, holding out her credit card reader for him to tap his card against. "Where is Midas the Menace anyway?"

"He's been banished from town while the sculptors are working," Bernice announced.

Gavin sighed. "Midas is still adjusting to no longer being an only child," he said. "He'll come around. Eventually."

Tatum laughed. "Be sure to take out an ad in West's new newspaper when he does. Inquiring minds will want to know."

Elle spun around to face Tatum. "'West's new newspaper?'"

The other woman nodded. "Isn't it great? It's will only be a weekly, but that's better than nothing. And everyone is excited about it."

"He's renting out the space in the torpedo factory that's on the other side of Tiny Dancers for his office," Gavin confirmed.

So that's what he was doing in the ballet studio with the tape measure. His meetings with the various community groups in town made sense now, too. Elle couldn't help the feeling of pride that trickled through her. After globe-trotting around the world, West was planting roots in Chances Inlet. And he was offering up his talents to boot.

"But that doesn't mean you get to stop helping us with social media." Bernice gave her a mulish look. "West says he knows nothing about all that whoiswhatis involved with that. He assured us that you can easily do it from New York. You promised you would."

Tatum donned a pleading look. "You did promise."

"I did. And I will," Elle insisted. "We'll work it out. This is my home. I'll never stop supporting you."

The kids screamed when an errant wave destroyed several of their snowmen.

"Uh-oh," Tatum said. "Excuse me, y'all. We've got an emergency that can only be helped with free Christmas cookies."

KNOTICAL BUZZED with energy when Hayden entered the workroom located at the back of his mother's store that evening. The veterans from his support group, their families and friends were busy wrapping the Angel Tree presents that would be handed out at the youth center the following day. Simone immediately handed him a box of Legos to wrap.

"You're late," his partner said. "Don't tell me you were home pouting after Livi took off with Elle's ex this morning."

Hayden stared at Simone in disbelief. Was she kidding? *Livi and Jeremy?*

"Who told you that?" he demanded.

Simone hiked her eyebrows at him. "An unimpeachable source."

"Bernice."

"That woman has her finger on the pulse of this town." Simone's chuckle sounded full of appreciation. He wasn't surprised. Both women thrived on minding everyone else's business.

"I take it she didn't give you a goodbye kiss?"

Hayden glared at her.

"Mm." Simone reached for his finger and pressed it down on the silver paper she'd wrapped around a box of Play-Doh. She wrestled with the tape dispenser while he held the paper in place. "Then where were you all day if you weren't mending your broken heart? Elle was in plain sight at the sand sculpting contest. That rules out any hanky-panky."

He peeked over to the other side of the room. Elle and Emily both giggled as they attempted to wrap a basketball. He'd missed her today. Even after a night spent making love to her, he still felt incomplete when she wasn't near.

He'd spent the day up at UNC Wilmington working with the seniors from Chances Inlet's high school cross-country team as they prepared for college tryouts. The process was always bittersweet for him. Even more so today. If things went the way he planned, it would be the last time he'd get a chance to coach the kids. He'd miss it. But he'd miss Elle more if he let her go back to New York alone.

"I have a life outside of this town, Simone."

Except he didn't. Or he hadn't for many years. But that was all going to change. His head swam, and he blew out a long, controlled breath to help hold the anxiety at bay.

Elle is worth it.

Beside him, Simone had gone uncharacteristically quiet. She was staring at him with a concerned look when he turned back to her.

"My God," she whispered. "You're going to leave me."

Shit.

She pushed his hand away and frantically finished wrapping the gift.

"I love her, Simone," he said softly.

"Duh!" She looked up at him, her eyes shiny. "Don't mind me. I'm happy for you. Really. And I have Gabby now. It's been seven years since you saved me. It's about time I learned to stand on my own two feet."

Hayden placed his hand over one of hers. "You'll always have my extra foot to keep you balanced," he told her, repeating a joke they'd shared since meeting at the rehab hospital years before.

It had the desired effect. Simone laughed. "Get away from me before I make a sloppy mess all over these presents."

He patted her on the shoulder, then weaved through the crowd toward Elle. Just as he walked up, Emily scurried away to fetch a new gift to wrap, allowing them a moment of privacy.

"Livi and Jeremy?" he asked quietly while brushing Elle's hand with his fingers.

"I know. Nobody had that one on their bingo card," she murmured. "Imagine my surprise when I arrived at breakfast, and my mom hit me with that bombshell."

"Should we be concerned about her?"

Elle's eyes grew soft as she smiled at him. "Don't worry, Captain America. I spoke with her this afternoon." She chuckled. "It sounds like we ought to be more worried for Jeremy. Livi may give him a run for his money. Literally. She's eager to land a husband. If she doesn't marry before she's thirty, she'll lose the trust her grandfather set up for her."

Hayden didn't know whether to be insulted or relieved he'd dodged that bullet. "Wow. A trust fund match made in heaven."

"Your mom doesn't think so."

"Mm." He laced one of his fingers through one of hers. "She doesn't dictate how I live my life." And if she didn't get onboard with his plans, she was going to miss out on his life.

"I found another ball, Aunt Elle." Emily raced back to their workstation.

Elle groaned. "You're killing me, Em. Why must you pick the hardest things to wrap?"

The little girl giggled.

Hayden glanced around the room. "Is my aunt here?"

"She was earlier, but she was swamped," Elle said. "I wanted to ask her if she knew where I could find West. He's been playing least in sight all day."

"He's probably tired from all the dancing last night," Emily remarked. "We got a standing ovation, you know."

"And it was well-deserved." Hayden leaned down to brush a kiss over Emily's head. "I'm going to look for my aunt. Save me some of the hard presents. We'll wrap them together."

"Yay!" Emily exclaimed.

He found his aunt in the front of the store waiting on the last of the day's customers. When she'd finished, he followed them to the door, locked it after they were outside and turned the open sign to closed.

"That was a helluva long day," Aunt Kitty said. "Christmas Eve is the day after tomorrow, and everyone has decided to knit their last-minute gifts."

"My mom wasn't here helping?"

Aunt Kitty's face told him everything he needed to know. "She wasn't feeling well today."

He swore.

"She loves you, Hayden." His aunt rubbed her forehead. "She hasn't dealt with your life's difficulties as well as you have, that's all. The only way she can think of how to handle things is by overcompensating. Trying to 'fix' everything so your life is perfect."

"Her idea of perfect and my idea are not the same." He loathed the anger in his voice. His mother was the only one he had. And for the most part, she was a good mom. Her contempt of Elle wouldn't be tolerated, however.

"All she wants is for you to be happy," Aunt Kitty said.

"Let's hope so, because odds are she won't like my next act."

Aunt Kitty plopped down on the stool behind the counter. "How so?"

Hayden sighed. "Uncle Theo's brother, the woodworker with the storefront. You mentioned he was looking for an apprentice to take over his business. Do you think you could reach out to him and see if he still has an opening?"

She was quiet for longer than was comfortable. He began to worry that he'd already lost his shot.

"His business is in Connecticut, Hayden. You'd have to relocate."

"I'm already relocating to New York City. I researched it today, and it's an hour train ride from Elle's place to his showroom and workshop."

His aunt pressed her fingers to her lips. He couldn't tell if she was happy or upset. Then she was jumping off the stool and throwing her arms around his neck.

"Oh, Hayden," she cried. "That's wonderful news. I'm so happy for you both."

He patted her on the back. "Elle doesn't know yet, so let's keep this on the down-low for right now. I want to get all my ducks in a row before I share my plans with her."

"Of course." She dropped her arms and wiped her eyes. "You're right. Your mother won't take this well."

He rubbed a hand over the back of his neck. "I know. But I can't change how I feel. There's room for my mom in my heart as long as there is room for Elle in hers."

Aunt Kitty contemplated him. "This shouldn't have to be a choice." She cupped his jaw. "Leave your mother to me. I'll call Theo's brother first thing in the morning and let him know you're interested." A sly smile formed on her lips. "But I'm going to need a favor from you tomorrow. No questions asked."

"Why does this sound like something illegal?"

She laughed. That bright melodic laugh she used to have before tragedy landed in both their laps. He was happy to hear it.

"Nothing nefarious. Just impulsive," she replied, the joy in her voice easing his anxiety about what he was taking on in the name of love.

"Impulsive seems to be the flex move right now. Count me in."

CHAPTER TWENTY-THREE

ELLE FOUND West seated at one of the breakfast tables at the inn the following morning. He was playing a rousing game of Fish with Emily, Whitney and Henry.

"Please tell me you're not teaching these children how to gamble," she said.

Henry laughed. "I play poker with Ryan all the time."

"Got any twos?" Whitney asked no one in particular.

West dropped the two of hearts on the table. "You are becoming a card shark, Whit."

The little girl giggled.

"That right there is my favorite sound in the whole world," Tanner Gillette said as he and Ryan entered the room.

"Who's ready for a round of putt-putt golf?" Ryan asked.

"Me!" the three kids shouted as they tossed their cards into the center of the table and scrambled out of their chairs.

"Do you two want to join us for school vacation daycare?" Ryan looked at Elle, his expression hopeful.

She was about to say "Why not," when West interjected.

"Elinor and I have an appointment this morning," he said. "Perhaps another day."

"We do?" Elle asked.

West got to his feet and adjusted the cuffs of his white dress shirt. How had she not noticed he was wearing a tie? And a suit?

"Yes. We do."

"Have a good one," Tanner said as he and Ryan herded the kids out the door.

West went in the opposite direction, headed for the study.

She hurried after him. "Is this about your newspaper?"

"I was wondering when you were going to ask me about that." He slipped into his suit jacket.

"You were very cryptic the other day when Livi asked."

"Nothing was finalized yet." He used the mirrored glass behind the bar to check his reflection.

Elle looked down at the leather leggings she wore. She'd paired them with the Stella McCartney dupes she'd gifted herself for Christmas and an oversized cashmere sweater with little Christmas trees stitched into the neckline. "Should I go change? This meeting is obviously formal."

"It's an *appointment,* not a meeting. And you are driving me because I'm not familiar with the roads in this area." He dropped his gaze from her head to her toes. "You look fine the way you are. Very festive in fact."

The man was sparing with his compliments. She could work with festive.

"We have a few minutes before we need to leave." He bent down behind the desk and came back up with an awkwardly wrapped package. "This is for you. Merry Christmas."

Elle eyed the gift warily. "But I don't have a gift for you." Guilt clogged her throat. Why hadn't she thought to get him something? "I can't accept it."

He tilted his chin toward the ceiling and mumbled something. "Elinor. The most rewarding gift you can give me is to accept this gift with humility. The only thing I need in return is for you to enjoy it."

She would get him something anyway. Hayden was taking her to the fly-fishing store later to pick out a new rod for Lamar for Christmas. West could be a fly fisherman, couldn't he? He dressed like one half the time.

"Thank you," she said as she took the package from him. "Did you wrap this with your eyes closed?"

He grinned. "I had a little help. Put it up in your suite. You can open it later. I don't want to take a chance you'll get all mushy on me. The note inside explains the gift. I'll meet you out by the garage. Your mother said we could take her car."

Ten minutes later they were turning out of the inn's driveway onto the main road. The GPS instructed her to turn toward the highway.

"You already programmed the GPS?" she asked. "Control freak much?"

"After a month in each other's company, you're surprised by that?"

Elle couldn't help it. She laughed. "Not at all. You're a gamer, West. You'll keep me guessing until we pull up to wherever this place is."

"Nonsense," he said. "We are going to Tifton."

"What's in Tifton?"

"The county courthouse."

Her pulse began to race. "West, why exactly are we going to the county courthouse?"

"To get married."

He reached for the dash when she swerved.

"Dammit, not to you, Gidget. To Kitty."

"Oh my gosh! No way!" she croaked through the emotions unexpectedly clogging her throat.

West and Kitty are getting married!

"You'd better get your emotions under control. Or else you'll be waiting in the car," he warned.

She swallowed the excited chirp that threatened. No way was

she missing this. Out of the corner of her eye, she could see him nervously drumming his fingers on his knees. He wasn't as composed as he appeared. Smirking like a lunatic, she relaxed in the driver's seat and steered the car toward Tifton, where West's future awaited.

———

EVERETT TOYED with the ring on his finger. It had been two years since he'd worn one. The simple platinum band felt heavy against his skin. It also felt right.

He looked across the inn's grand salon at Kitty. *His wife.* She was radiant talking with the judge who had married them earlier in the day. The fifteen-foot Christmas tree behind her paled in comparison. The platinum band she wore on her ring finger was studded with diamonds, causing it to shimmer in the lamplight every time she moved her wrist.

"Oh, Mr. West is my most famous groom, by far," the judge told Kitty and Patricia. "Although I once officiated a marriage that included the guy from those fried chicken commercials you see ten times a day on football Saturdays."

"You hear that, West," Lamar murmured when he walked into the room carrying a tray of champagne glasses. "You're more famous than a fried chicken pitchman."

"I'll be sure to have my agent include that in my bio," Everett joked.

Just then, Claire Lovell charged into the room, her husband in tow. "You got married? Without me?" The woman looked dejected.

Kitty took her sister's hands in hers. "It was a spur-of-the-moment decision. We didn't want to make a big deal out of it. Especially around the holidays." She smiled in Everett's direction. "And we didn't want to wait."

Lamar popped the cork on a bottle of champagne. "A toast doesn't count as a big deal, does it?"

"A toast works for me," Everett said.

"Hear, hear," Tim Lovell chimed in.

When Lamar had filled the glasses, Patricia passed them around.

Claire's eyes were shiny as she accepted hers. "But you're my sister. I should have been there. At least as a witness."

"They had two fine witnesses present," the judge announced.

Everett moved over to stand beside Kitty. He wrapped his arm around her waist, anchoring her to him, knowing that what came next wouldn't sit well with her sister.

"You did? Who?" Claire asked, sounding even more hurt.

"Hayden stood up for me. It was only fair since he wasn't around for my first marriage." Kitty tried to make a joke of it.

Her sister wasn't buying it. "Hayden? And who else?" The lack of color in her face told them all she already had a good idea who the other witness was.

"My assistant, Elinor, stood up for me," Everett said.

Claire's hand began to shake so hard her champagne nearly sloshed over the rim of her glass. Her husband quickly removed it from her grasp.

"Well. Then I guess it was a good thing I wasn't invited if *she* was there."

"Don't be silly, Claire. No one was 'invited,'" Kitty insisted. "And don't you think this grudge you've been holding against Elle has gone on long enough?"

"Grudge?" The woman bristled. Tim lifted his hand to her shoulder to calm her, but Claire shook it off. "Is that what you think this is?"

"Yes," Patricia added tersely. "And you've taken it too far, Claire. It's time you stop persecuting my daughter for something she wasn't responsible for. She didn't coerce Hayden to that party. In fact, she left well before he arrived."

"That doesn't matter. She was always doing something to get him in trouble. It wasn't enough that she already had a boyfriend. She wanted to keep my son on a string, too."

Patricia opened her mouth to protest, but Tim beat her to it.

"That's enough, Claire," he told his wife.

"That girl ruined our son's life!" she cried.

"If it wasn't for 'that girl,' your son would have done time in prison," the judge interjected.

The air in the room seemed to still. The judge sighed heavily. He pulled a folded piece of paper from his suit jacket.

"Since Hayden was a minor at the time, the court documents are sealed. I know because I was the one who signed off on his plea deal. Meeting him today, and seeing the man he's become made me feel justified in my decision not to sentence him to prison. And it's thanks to this letter from his best friend that I changed my mind."

He handed the letter to Tim. He scanned the page. "Elle wrote this."

Her first persuasive piece, Everett thought proudly. He was glad he and Kitty were able to convince the judge to help them help Hayden. Hopefully, it would do the trick. He wanted Elle and Hayden to have what he'd had with Keeley. What he had now with Kitty.

Tim cleared his throat and began to read.

Your honor,

I am writing to you today to tell you about my best friend, Hayden Lovell. It's not a lie to say I have loved him since kindergarten. As you weigh his fate, I would like you to know more about what an incredible human being he is.

I am deeply saddened that a family lost their home and the irreplaceable treasures within it. I know they want justice. But the fire was a result of an accident, not malice. Hayden Lovell wouldn't know how to commit malice if he tried. This is a boy who routinely gives his lunch to a classmate whose family is struggling. The boy who took on a bully in the second grade because he was tormenting another boy who stuttered. A boy who tells his parents his running shoes are worn out long before they are so he can give them to another kid on the team who can't afford decent sneakers. Malice isn't in his DNA.

Hayden went to that party because he thought people he cared about might be in trouble. Namely me. It's a guilt I will live with for the rest of my life. But he didn't go there to start a fight, much less a fire. Hayden made a mistake. My father has a favorite James Joyce quote that he's always reciting to us kids: A man's mistakes are his portals of discovery.

Hayden has so much more to discover in this world. So much more good to do. I humbly ask you to consider that as you weigh his sentence. Hayden Lovell is an irreplaceable treasure to his mother, his father, his sister, his friends, and the people of Chances Inlet. And most of all to me. Please don't bury that treasure away.

Sincerely,
Elinor McAlister

. . .

KITTY DABBED at her eyes when Tim finished reading. Claire slumped down into the nearest chair. Lamar cleared his throat. Patricia kneeled in front of Claire.

"I have five children." She placed her hand on Claire's knee. "I know exactly what it feels like to be helpless when all you want to do is protect your child from the world around them. You know in your heart Elle isn't responsible for what happened to your son. And Hayden's life is far from ruined. But you are hurting your relationship with your son by blaming Elle." Patricia sighed. "Those two are still writing their story. And whichever way it ends, they need our support."

Kitty placed her arm around her sister's shoulders. "Let it go," she said. "It isn't like you to carry around so much hate toward someone. Much less a girl you once thought of as a second daughter."

Claire gulped a sob. "I don't know if I can," she whispered. "It's easier to bear if I have someone to blame."

"I felt the same way when I lost my husband. Always looking for someone to blame for him being taken away from me," Patricia said. "But it gets easier if you accept the fact that life happens. And Hayden is still here. You need to embrace that fact and be happy instead of holding onto the pain of the past."

"I'm so sorry for my behavior, Patricia. I'll—I'll try with Elle. I really will," Claire said between sniffles. "I'm grateful to you for understanding. And to Donald for everything he did for Hayden back then."

"He loved your son like one of his own. Because Elle loves him."

Patricia's words brought on another strangled sob.

"Maybe we could get to that toast," Lamar said when his wife stood. "I think we all need a drink about now."

Tim handed his wife her glass then took her hand in his. He

raised his glass in the air. "To second chances. We are the town for it, after all."

His meaning wasn't lost on anyone as they toasted.

CHAPTER TWENTY-FOUR

Later that night, Elle sat cross-legged on her bed, staring at the clumsily wrapped gift West had given her, wondering what was inside. Their relationship had come a long way in the past month. Probably because West had come a long way since arriving in Chances Inlet. A happy smile twitched on her lips as she recalled the intense way he looked at Kitty while he was vowing to love and cherish her always.

As touching as the simple ceremony was, it was also a painful reminder of what Elle was leaving behind in Chances Inlet. A life with Hayden. Every day—*and night*—they were together, the idea of living separate lives seemed more and more daunting.

Not that he'd offered her any kind of life with him. It was hard for her to be miffed at Hayden for that, though. He, of all people, knew how important this opportunity at *Vantage* was for her. He loved her enough to let her go chase her dream. And she loved him even more for it.

Except that left their relationship up in the air. And Elle was beginning to feel edgy about things between them being so open-ended. They'd put off having "the talk" long enough.

Following the wedding ceremony, she'd suggested to him that

they grab dinner to discuss their future. He'd cried off, however, saying he needed to finish his Christmas shopping. Adding insult to injury, she'd be alone in her bed tonight. Getting some uninterrupted sleep was a priority for him since he and Simone were pulling a twenty-four-hour shift beginning at noon tomorrow through Christmas morning. As the only two deputies without kids at home, they had drawn the short straw, so to speak.

Elle groaned in frustration. Two nights without Hayden would certainly be a test for the months to come. She looked over at the pile of clothes she still kept by her bed. During her first session with Kate's friend, the therapist had reiterated exactly what her sister said when Elle told her about her idiosyncrasy. The therapist reaffirmed that Elle had chosen an excellent coping mechanism. That she had nothing to be ashamed of. Best of all, she told Elle that she would be more concerned about her if she didn't have lingering stress after her ordeal.

Take that, Jeremy. I'm not a baby.

Her post-traumatic stress would ebb and flow over time, the therapist explained. Elle wasn't necessarily worried about the nightmares tonight. She felt safe at the inn and in Chances Inlet. But she would still be lonely.

Hoping for a little distraction, she ripped at the wrapping paper to reveal the leather-bound journals belonging to West's late wife.

"What the hell, West?"

The bundle was tied up with a red and green ribbon. An envelope was tucked beneath the stack, and she pulled it free. Her name was written on the front in West's neat script.

She flipped through the pages of one of the journals. Keeley West's lyrical handwriting flowed haphazardly over the pages. These were the innermost thoughts of a woman Elle had never met. Intimate writings that Elle didn't feel comfortable reading. She slammed the journal shut.

Had the man gone crazy? Why would he give them to her? She tore open the envelope and unfolded the note within.

Elinor,

I'm sure you are asking yourself why I have given you these. Within the pages of these journals is the story of my late wife's life. The words written there are more precious to me than my own breath. I loved Keeley dearly.

Also contained within these books are some hard truths. Truths about life and war and survival. Truths that need to be told.

I'm too close to this to do Keeley's legacy the justice it deserves. I would only sully the dogmatic spirit of her stories with my pragmatism. And my bitterness at her loss.

It will take someone who writes like Keeley to pull a book like this off. Someone who leads with their heart. Who puts others first. Who writes with empathy.

That someone is you, Elinor. I believe that Keeley somehow worked her magic to get these journals to you. She knew you were the right person for the job even before I did.

Helen Keneally never really wanted my memoir. She only signed me because she covets these journals. As Keeley's long-time editor, she's probably worried about what will be revealed within their pages.

However, I am prepared to offer them to her on one condition: that she allow you complete editorial control over the book. My agent will stipulate such in the *contract, as well as additional compensation beyond your salary at Vantage.*

As you have no doubt discovered about your esteemed publisher, Helen does not play fair. By accepting my offer, you will be shielded from any manipulation she might try in the future. The contract will also guarantee that the promotion she promised you will be awarded to you immediately. It is long overdue.

I hope you will give this offer careful consideration. It will be life-changing. You will have your name on the masthead of the magazine as a lifestyles columnist as well as on the cover of a book as an editor. The possibilities beyond that are endless.

It's time the world knows Elinor McAlister.

Merry Christmas,
Everett West

ELLE WIPED her tears with the sleeve of her pajamas. Her heart was racing. What West was proposing was an enormous challenge. One that she'd be a fool to turn down. And he was correct. The possibilities beyond this were endless. Her fingers were already twitching to begin writing.

The most rewarding gift you can give me is to accept this gift with humility. The only thing I need in return is for you to enjoy it.

"Oh, I'm going to enjoy it all right, West. And you've just given me the idea for a perfect gift for you in return."

She'd return the fly-fishing vest after Christmas.

THE CHRISTMAS EVE parade was more crowded than ever. It seemed everyone from the neighboring towns had descended on Chances Inlet this year. Not that Hayden could blame them. The weather was chamber of commerce perfect, and everyone seemed to be in a festive mood. Spectators were three deep along the parade route. Kids raced along the sidewalk carrying popcorn balls and candy canes the local bank was giving out.

Even his mother was feeling the holiday spirit. She'd invited him over for his favorite breakfast of French toast this morning. Apparently, all was forgiven about him not choosing Livi. He had a harder path to hoe regarding his decision to move to New York. Perhaps she wouldn't take it as badly as he thought, though.

His aunt texted him last night, telling him not to worry about his mother any longer. Maybe Christmas miracles did come true. Across the street, his mom waved to him from the steps of Knotical. Hayden and Simone waved back.

"Check it out." He elbowed Simone and pointed toward the television truck parked in front of the diner. "The media showed up."

Simone shook her head. "They're probably hoping for another spectacle like last year. Like it's our shtick to have Santa find his long-lost dog every Christmas during our parade."

"Who knows? Maybe his cat is missing this year."

"You're awfully perky today," Simone grumbled.

"It's Christmas Eve. What's not to be perky about?"

"I take it you've finalized your plans?"

He'd spoken with Uncle Theo's brother Cam this morning. Cam had agreed to allow Hayden to continue with his commissioned work while he was also creating pieces for his store. The profit share he was offering was decent. Living in New York would be tight, but Elle lived rent free in one of Gavin's lofts, which meant a cost savings to start. Hayden didn't feel right about that long-term, though. Once they got on their feet, they'd find another option.

"All systems are go," he told Simone.

"Have you told the sheriff?"

"Not yet. I'll tell him tomorrow. My mom and dad are going to my sister's house in Lumberton tonight. I'm having Christmas dinner with the McAlisters."

Simone snorted. "That's fortuitous. You can delay the inevitable for a few more days. She's not going to take it well."

His palms began to sweat just thinking about that conversation. "My aunt insists my mom will be okay with it."

"Ha! Your aunt is riding high with newlywed bliss, Hayden. I'm not sure I'd trust anything coming out of her mouth these days."

"One step at a time. I need your help tonight, though."

Simone shot him a side-eye. "I am not helping you down Elle McAlister's chimney, Dirty Santa. No way. No how."

"For crying out loud, Simone." Hayden shook his head. "Could you be serious?"

"What am I saying? You're Captain America. You don't need my help," she joked.

The high school marching band played "White Christmas" as they marched by. Hayden and Simone paused to let them pass before crossing the street.

"That's the closest this town is going to get to a white Christmas," she remarked with a laugh. She linked her arm through his as they walked toward the gazebo. "What's the favor you need from me?"

"I'm taking my dinner break at midnight. I'm going to meet Elle here." He gestured to the gazebo. "I want to tell her my plan. It's her Christmas gift from me."

"And you want me to stand guard in case she's really grateful?" She held up her hands when he growled. "Kidding! You want me to keep the area clear in case someone *else* has the same romantic idea?"

"Exactly. Thank you."

"Oh, don't thank me yet. I didn't agree not to listen in."

A little boy lost his grip on his balloon. Simone raced ahead and snagged it for him. She turned toward Hayden and executed a perfect curtsy.

"Admit it. You're going to miss all this fabulousness." She waved her hand from her head to her toes. "They don't make 'em like me in New York."

He *was* going to miss her. "Thank goodness," he quipped.

She nudged his shoulder. "I'm proud of you for listening to your heart. You and Elle are going to be so happy."

Hayden hoped so.

"Hey, you two!" Tatum called from the bakery. "I have some eggnog cake here with your names on it."

"Now I know you'll miss *that* when you go. Because I love you, I'll be sure to mail you some next Christmas," Simone said as she strolled in the direction of the Queen of Hearts Bakery.

"How about you bring me some when you and Gabby visit?"

She smiled up at him. "It's a deal."

***

Elle was running on adrenaline. She'd been up most of the night formulating a plan. Now it was time to execute it. She schlepped the heavy box into the study. With the exception of Kitty and West, the inn's guest suites were occupied by the McAlister family for Christmas Eve. It was a tradition Elle's mom intended to continue until there was no more room at the inn. Given how they kept adding family members, she'd need to build a stable in the backyard to house some of them.

West appeared in the doorway. "You wanted a word?"

"I did. You didn't think you could just gift me your wife's journals and I wouldn't have thoughts, did you?"

He laughed as he closed the door behind him and sat down in

one of the chairs. "Gidget has thoughts?" He pressed his hand to his chest. "Say it isn't so."

"I need to know you are one hundred percent serious with this offer."

West sobered up. "You should know by now that I'm serious about everything I do."

Elle nodded. She nudged the box in his direction.

"What's that?" he asked.

"Your Christmas present."

"I told you—"

"I know what you said," she interrupted. "Just open the box, West."

He gave her a dirty look before he stood and pulled the top off. He stared at its contents for a long moment. "How—how?" He looked bewildered.

She took pity on him and lifted the old typewriter from its box. "It took a lot of hard bargaining with Garth. You might have to dedicate a few editions of your paper to him." She put it down on the desk. "But I thought if you're starting a newspaper, you need a mascot. And what better than the one that hung around the newsroom of Chances Inlet's last newspaper?"

"I don't know what to say."

"Don't say anything. Just accept this gift with humility," she told him, echoing his words to her.

He laughed again. "Thank you, Elinor. I will treasure this. And thank you for accepting my gift. I appreciate you taking on my wife's story."

"Yeah, about that . . ."

West's smile faded.

"I have a counteroffer to propose."

He crossed his arms over his chest. "I'm listening."

CHAPTER TWENTY-FIVE

Chances Inlet was normally quiet at midnight during the winter months. Hayden loved that he was able to run along streets as familiar to him as the veins in his own hand. He wouldn't get that same feeling running the streets of Tribeca. Building a life with Elle would be worth what he was giving up, though, he reminded himself.

The lights of the gazebo twinkled against the clear sky. Somewhere in the distance, he could hear the strains of "Silent Night" being sung by a church congregation. He climbed the steps to find Elle waiting on one of the benches, wearing a Santa hat cockeyed on her head and a half-drunk smile, likely courtesy of the annual McAlister Christmas Eve dinner.

"Right on time," she said. "It's Christmas."

The bells from the nearby church confirmed it.

Elle jumped up and threw her arms around his neck. "Merry Christmas, Hayden," she whispered before pressing her lips to his.

She tasted like peppermint—and joyfulness. And he couldn't seem to get enough of her. He instantly regretted suggesting they meet here. The conference room at the station would have given him more privacy for what he wanted to do to her.

Except this was supposed to be romantic. A declaration of love. A promise of commitment.

Not to mention Simone was somewhere out there watching them.

He pulled his mouth away before he did something foolish. "I want to give you your Christmas present tonight," he told her. "Out here without the craziness of your family."

"But I didn't bring yours," she pouted.

He led her back to the bench. "That's okay because mine will blow anything you got me out of the water."

She laughed. "Cocky much?" She sat down and gave him her undivided attention. "Okay, Lovell, let's have it." She glanced behind him. "Where is it?"

His palms began to sweat. "It's not an actual thing as much as it is a . . . gesture."

Elle tilted her head to the side, making the Santa hat slide off. "A gesture?"

This was a lot harder than when he'd practiced in the mirror of the men's room at the station. He sat down beside her and reached for her hands.

"I love you, Belle. I'm pretty sure I've loved you since you stole my purple crayon in kindergarten. I know I haven't actually said it. But I hope you already know this."

"Oh, Hayden," she whispered. "I do know it. But it's really nice to hear you say it out loud. That's the best Christmas gift you could ever give me."

"No. No." He was screwing this up. "That's not the present. I mean it's the reason behind the present. Just not the actual gift itself."

She gave him one of those adoring looks of hers. The one that said he was a blundering idiot, but she loved him anyway.

He scrubbed his face with his palms. "What I'm trying to say is

I know how important chasing down your goal is. And the job at *Vantage* is your dream."

"Hayden—" she interrupted.

"No, let me finish. I want you to realize that dream. But I want this, too." He waved his hand between them.

Her face lit up. She pressed closer to him. "Oh my gosh, Hayden. I'm so glad you said that. I want us, too."

"Good, because I'm coming to New York with you."

The world seemed to stop spinning. Elle stared at him, a mixture of disbelief and confusion on her face.

"Wh—what?" Her tone was a lot less enthusiastic than he'd envisioned.

"I took a job with Kitty's brother-in-law. He makes custom furniture in Connecticut. It's a little more unitarian than the style of furniture I make, but he's agreed to sell me the business when he retires."

She scrambled to her feet. "Why would you do that?"

Really not the reaction he was expecting. He stood also. "Uh, let's see, because I love you?! Because I don't want to live apart from you? Scratch that. I *can't* live without you."

He was breathing hard now. And he really hoped Simone was kidding about listening in, because, *dammit*. Elle pressed her hands to her face and bent over at the knees. Was she crying?

He placed a hand on her back. "Belle."

She heaved in a breath as she lifted her head. Tears were streaming down her face all right, but she wore a sloppy smile, too. "Just when I think it isn't possible to love you any more than I do, you do something wild and crazy like this."

Then she was kissing him again, their bodies pressed together as they slowly spun around trying to gain better access to each other's mouths. Hayden sank back down onto the bench, pulling her into his lap so she could straddle him. She kissed him more deeply before pulling her lips away to drag in some air.

He brushed the hair off her face. "You had me going there for a minute. I thought you were angry about me coming with you to New York."

"Oh, you're not coming with me to New York."

His fingers froze in her hair. "Come again?"

There was that "bless your heart" smile again. It was starting to annoy him.

"Because *I'm* not going to New York."

"What are you talking about? You've been offered your dream job. You put up with West for the last month to guarantee it." *Wait a minute.* He swore violently. "I'll kill him. Even if he is family now. The man will finish that book and turn it in if I have to hold him at gunpoint. He's not messing up your promotion."

She laughed. "Calm down, Captain America. His memoir is finished. It has been for a while."

He didn't understand. "But you are still here? You didn't go back to New York."

Elle pressed her lips to his neck. "Nope. You see, I can't live without you, either. West and I have been holding the book hostage so we could stay here in Chances Inlet a while longer."

Hayden wrapped his arms more tightly around her, pulling her closer so he could feel her heart beating against his. "You're turning down the job at *Vantage*? You're sure that's what you want to do?"

"Absolutely. And don't worry. I've already got another dream job. It's one where I'll still get my name out there. But I won't have to ever leave the people and town that I love. And neither will you." She kissed his nose.

"What are you talking about?"

"You are looking at the new managing partner of The Chances Inlet Courier. West is starting up a new weekly newspaper."

What had she been drinking at dinner? "But that's not what you wanted. That wasn't the goal."

"Mm. Turns out goals can change. And this is what I want

because it means I get to be with you. But that's not the best part." She bounced up and down on his lap nearly unmanning him. "I'm getting my name on the cover of a book."

"I don't follow." Not that he cared much anymore. Her excitement was enough of a gift for him.

"I'm going to edit West's late wife's journals. The book is going to auction next week." She let out a little squeal. "It could go in the eight figures, and West is splitting it with me!"

"Holy shit."

"Yeah." She touched her nose to his. "We can keep doing the things we enjoy, living in the town we both love. Together."

That ugly sense of eventually being found lacking forced him to speak up. "You won't regret this later?"

"Silly man." She kissed him. "You are my dream, Hayden Lovell. And I could never regret choosing us. I've been searching for who I am supposed to be all this time. What I could contribute to the world as a McAlister. And the answer has been right under my nose. I want to be Elle McAlister *Lovell*, wife, daughter, sister, aunt, publisher, and editor."

He breathed a sigh of relief, the self-doubt vanquished by her words.

"Throw in cat mom, and you've got yourself a deal," he said right before he kissed her.

Neither of them heard Simone's whoop in the distance.

EPILOGUE

Patricia McAlister Hollister stood in the shadows of the hallway, reveling in the beautiful chaos that was Christmas morning at the Tide Me Over Inn. Her family had more than doubled in the past two years. Watching her children, their significant others, her grandchildren and her found family, laugh, and celebrate together was more satisfying than any Christmas gift she could ever receive.

She brushed her thumb over the nutcracker that was a Scottish bagpiper. The one her late husband had gifted to her when her dream of owning a B & B was just that—a dream. But one he'd made come true before he passed away.

"Thank you, Donald," she whispered. "Thank you for bringing them all back home again."

Deep in her heart, she believed her late husband was still looking out for her. And for his family. One by one, he'd guided his children home to Chances Inlet. It was a feat that took some divine guidance since their kids had been determined to leave their small hometown in the dust as soon as they were old enough. Yet here they all were, living their lives and building their families in the coastal hamlet she and Donald had decided to call home when they were still newlyweds.

She swiped away a stray tear of happiness just as two strong arms wrapped around her waist from behind.

"Don't tell me you've had enough of Christmas already?" Lamar asked as he nuzzled her neck. "We haven't even had brunch yet."

Patricia relaxed against his broad chest. "Never. I'm savoring the moment."

She glanced over at Miles, who was rubbing his pregnant wife's belly, seemingly talking to their unborn child. On the floor in front of them, Ryan was helping his soon-to-be stepson, Henry, sort through some Legos. Across the room, Gavin bounced a laughing Hazel on his knee while Midas lay at his feet happily chewing on a Nylabone. Baby Max toddled around the room with his hands in the air for balance, his laughing father trailing him. Kate, Paige and Donella sat close to the huge tree helping Emily and Whitney dress their American Girl dolls.

"Mm," Lamar replied. "I'm still pinching myself to make sure this isn't a dream. I'd given up on knowing my daughter, and now look at Paige. She owns a bookstore in Chances Inlet. And she wants me to walk her down the aisle when she and Tanner marry next month."

Her normally stoic husband had been at a loss for words when he'd opened that gift earlier. Leaning back, she brushed her lips against his. "That was probably the best Christmas present of the morning."

Lamar rested his chin on her shoulder. "Are you sure? Because I don't think I've ever seen your smile as bright as it was when Elle announced she was staying in town and working with West."

She peered over toward the far corner of the salon where Elle stood with West and Kitty. The three of them were laughing at something when Elle's face lit up. Patricia watched as the reason for her daughter's glowing smile slipped into the room from the veranda. Still dressed in his uniform, Hayden hurried over to his best friend and pressed a long kiss to Elle's lips.

Patricia sighed. "Finally. I was beginning to give up hope."

Her husband chuckled. "I never doubted you and Bernice for a moment. The two of you should offer your services to the government. You are both masters at manipulation. Although, I have to admit, firing the town's public relations firm right before the holidays was a risk. I'm glad to see it paid off."

"That was Bernice's idea. She remembered how much help Elle was last year when Santa's dog ended up in town."

"But you're the one who coerced Helen Keneally to send Elle to babysit West in the first place."

"And I'm not apologizing for it. I saw an opportunity to get my daughter home for longer than a twenty-four-hour drive-by. Helen wanted to tie up one of my rooms for weeks on end during one of the busiest times of the year. I leveraged my bargaining power to my advantage." Patricia shrugged. "It all worked out in the end. West finished his book and he's bringing back the town's paper. A real win-win." She smiled at her daughter and Hayden who were now making the rounds within the salon. "And Elle and Hayden got the happily ever after they'd been dancing around for more than a decade."

"And all your chicks have come home to roost."

"Mm-hmm. That they have. All grown up and finally behaved."

"Hey!" Gavin shouted. "We forgot about the pickle ornament. The first one to find it on the tree gets out of cleaning up after brunch!"

The melee that followed nearly brought down the towering Christmas tree. Elle yelled at Gavin for pulling her hair. Kate sucker-punched Miles to gain better access to the back of the tree. Midas raced around the room barking, only to have Kringle and Tessa join in. Hazel let out an ear-piercing scream. Ryan lifted Henry to his shoulders to search the top of the tree while Emily cried about the unfairness of it.

In the end, little Whitney crawled between Gavin's legs with the pickle ornament securely in her hand. She raced over and handed it to Lamar who promptly scooped her up and kissed her on the cheek. The rest of the room groaned in defeat.

"What were you saying about well-behaved?" Lamar asked with a laugh.

Elle should have been dead on her feet after spending much of the night snuggling with Hayden in the conference room of the sheriff's office where they planned their future together. Instead, she felt like she was floating. Her life was finally in focus, and she felt freer than she ever had. Hayden loved her. The career she never knew she wanted was gifted to her with no strings attached. Best of all, she was home, where she belonged. With the best people she knew.

"How soon before we can politely leave?" Hayden whispered to her.

"I already packed us a to-go basket of food," she replied quietly. Not that anyone was paying attention. Her rowdy family was too busy trying to find a glass pickle ornament among the boughs of the giant Christmas tree. "I say we make a break for it now."

Hand-in-hand, they hurried to the kitchen, only to find West and Kitty sharing a hot kiss in front of the Sub-Zero refrigerator.

"Hey," Hayden complained, albeit half-heartedly. "That's my aunt you're manhandling."

"Wife trumps aunt," West quipped. "And where are you two kids sneaking off to?"

"To feed the cat." Hayden looked at Kitty. "I don't suppose you've been over to check on Beula?"

His aunt donned a guilty look.

West gestured to the cooler bag Elle was holding. "That must be one hungry cat."

Elle kissed the older man's cheek. "Merry Christmas, boss."

Kitty gave Hayden a hug. "See you later, you two."

"Don't count on it," Hayden promised as they rushed out the door.

Laughing, they raced for Hayden's cruiser, jumped inside and sped off. Five minutes later, Hayden fumbled with the handle on his kitchen door as he tried to open it without breaking their kiss. Elle let the strap of the insulated bag slip from her shoulder. The bag dropped to the floor when he pressed her against the fridge and his hands began roaming her body. Things were about to get really steamy when Beula decided to let her presence be known.

The cat's wail echoed off the walls of the small kitchen.

"Oh, you poor thing." Elle slipped from his embrace to fill the cat's water bowl. "Daddy is going to feed you."

"And then Mommy and Daddy are taking a nap," Hayden said before he began rummaging through the cabinet.

Elle meandered over to the table where the little Christmas tree sat, it's LED lights blinking red and green. Beneath it was a brightly wrapped package. It was bigger than a shirt box and soft. "It looks like Santa's been here."

She heard the sound of the cat food landing in Beula's ceramic dish before Hayden made his way over to the table. "That wasn't there when I left for my shift yesterday."

He lifted the flap of the gift tag. It was addressed to Hayden and Elle. The handwriting belonged to his mother.

Elle sank her teeth into her bottom lip. Why would Claire give her a gift?

Hayden nudged it toward her. "You should do the honors."

It was some consolation to her that Claire wouldn't put anything inside the present that could harm her precious son.

She gently tore at the paper, revealing a well-loved afghan, crocheted with soft off-white yarn. An envelope fell to the ground when Elle stretched out the beautiful blanket. Hayden picked it up and opened it. He quickly skimmed the page and, with a heavy sigh, handed it to Elle.

"It's a peace offering," he explained. "Aunt Kitty made this for her as a wedding gift. She wants us to have it." He leaned in to kiss her forehead. "My mother is coming around. Aunt Kitty said to leave things to her, but I suspect this is more of a true Christmas miracle."

In the note, Claire asked them to be patient with her while she unraveled the narrative she'd been holding onto for the past decade. She insisted the most important thing was for Hayden and Elle to be happy together. Elle choked up when Claire ended by saying she would love them both even if they decided to make their life outside of Chances Inlet.

"We need to call her right now and tell her we are staying," Elle said.

Hayden wrapped his arms around her more tightly. "We'll tell her in person tomorrow. Right now, I want to unwrap the only Christmas present I ever wanted—you."

Then he kissed her at the same time as he undressed her. His touch had her heart melting and her hands wandering over his hard body. Hayden was absolutely right. Claire could survive one more day, especially since they had a lifetime of days ahead of them.

I hope you enjoyed spending the holidays with Elle, Hayden, their families, and all the quirky residents of Chances Inlet. And how about West and Kitty? Want to know what they are up to in the New Year? Click the QR code for an exclusive bonus chapter featuring the newlyweds and his "fan club."

If you want more day to day details about my books, my crazy writing life, and opportunities to name places and characters in future books, come hang out with my reader group, the X's and O's, on Facebook.

And please, don't forget to tell other readers how much you enjoyed Elle and Hayden's story by leaving a review on the site where you bought it, on Goodreads, and BookBub. It's the best way to show an author some love and I ALWAYS appreciate it!

More Chances Inlet books:
Have you read Gavin and Ginger's story? Click the title to grab your copy of **Back to Before.**
You can read Miles and Lori's story in **All They Ever Wanted.**
And what's this story about Santa's dog, Kringle? Read all about it in Ryan and Jane's story, **Second Chance Christmas**
Are you curious about Lamar Hollister's daughter? Get her story in **It Had to Be You.**

Then check out these fun sports romance books:
Game On – a grumpy hero romance
Foolish Games – a secret baby story
Risky Game – a fake relationship romance
Sleeping with the Enemy – a second chance romance
Gossip Game — a fake relationship novella

Or hang out with the Milwaukee Growlers in:
Just for Kicks – A marriage of convenience romantic comedy
Double Dog Dare – An enemies-to-lovers romantic comedy
Catch and Release — A second chance romance

How about a little suspense with your romance?
Recipe for Disaster – a mistaken identity Secret Service romance
Shot in the Dark – a forced proximity Secret Service romance
Between Love and Honor – a second chance Secret Service romance

ACKNOWLEDGMENTS

My name may be on the cover, but this book would not have been possible without some amazing people propping me up behind the scenes. Mainly, my husband Greg, whose favorite phrase "make the magic happen" is immortalized in the pages of this book. Spoiler: Everett's reaction when he hears it is a lot like mine. Much love to Austin and Meredith for anticipating the need for a sweet text or call when I'm on deadline. Of course, that could be their father's doing but who cares.

Thank you to Melanie, Hope, Catie and Kim for the beta reads. Your insights always make my books better. Thank you to Jenny Sims at Editing for Indies whose careful and thorough reviews make my writing better. And to Samantha Pierce at Radiant Editorial for making sure all the i's were dotted and t's were crossed. Shout out to Jeannie Moon for always answering when I hit the panic button. And, as always, a great big thank you to my assistant, Rachael, who knows what needs to be done even before I do!

One of the things I didn't expect when I embarked on this author career was how large my circle of friends would grow through the shared love of reading. I spent 2024 traveling to a slew of book events across the country where I met so many avid readers and authors. Many of whom have become dear friends. Romancelandia is the best! Thanks to all the bloggers and book-stagrammers who share my books. And to the indie bookstores who support the genre we love.

Finally, thanks again to all of you who take the time to read the crazy stories I write. I'm still pinching myself every time I think about it. Thanks for coming along for the ride.